THE GOLDEN CRUCIBLE

THE GOLDEN CRUCIBLE

Jean Stubbs

STEIN AND DAY/*Publishers*/New York

First published in the United States of America, 1976
Copyright © 1976 by Jean Stubbs
All rights reserved
Printed in the United States of America
Stein and Day/*Publishers*/Scarborough House,
Briarcliff Manor, N.Y. 10510

Library of Congress Cataloging in Publication Data

Stubbs, Jean, 1926-
The golden crucible.

I. Title.

PZ4.S933Go3   [PR6069.T78]   823′.9′14   75-37713
ISBN 0-8128-1903-9

Acknowledgements

Thank you for your help, hospitality, encouragement and friendship in SAN FRANCISCO: Camille Barnes, who showed me the view across the Bay which began the idea of this novel; Gene Arceri and Lyle Letheridge, who squired me round the city; Mike and Sue Harrison who found me a temporary apartment and lent me most things from a saucepan to a typewriter; 'Pat' of the Ross Arms Hotel who not only welcomed me there but says she wants me back. Irish and Snoopy, such great characters that they crept into the book and influenced two of my creations. Clara Kenyon for a long and informative chat on old San Francisco. In LOS ANGELES: Ray and Betty Dwyer for just about everything, that lovely weekend. Harold L. Beard and Russell W. Costin for lending me a treasure-house of a book on 1906 background. Wayne and Ardis Lichtgarn (my bags always come *last* out of the hold). In NEW YORK: my friends and publishers, Sol Stein and Pat Day – thank you for the farewell party, here's to the next meeting.

J.S.

To the Newcomers,
Jo Stannon and the Miller

PROGRAMME

A TEMPLE OF DELIGHT

THE VANISHING LADY

SYMPATHETICAL FIGURES

A MOST WONDERFUL DELUSION

DEFYING THE BULLETS

—— INTERMISSION ——

FANTASMAGORIA

THE CURIOUS SPY GLASSES

GRAND EXPOSURES

TEMPLE OF FIRE!

FAREWELL!

America is God's Crucible, the great Melting-Pot where all the races of Europe are melting and reforming!

The Melting Pot
Israel Zangwill (1864–1926)

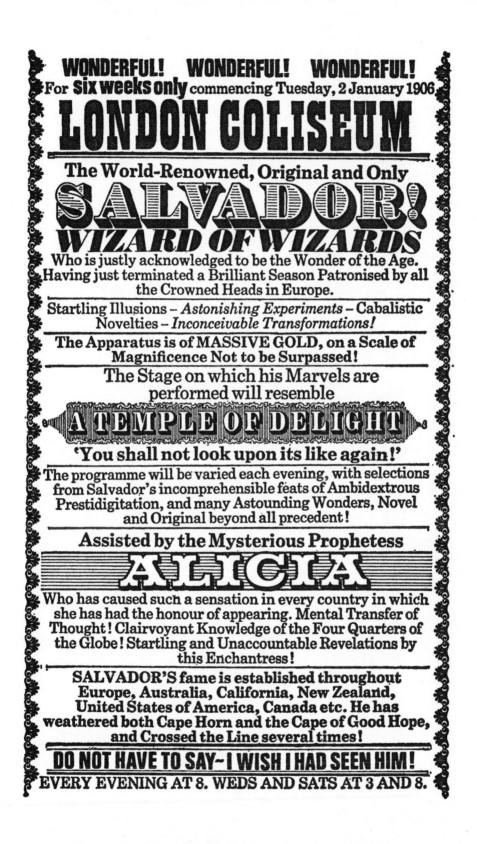

A TEMPLE OF DELIGHT

*'It is not the trick which impresses
the audience, but the magician.'*

Houdini (1874–1926)

ONE

A BUZZ OF EXPECTATION among the children as, in ones and twos, the dry musicians rustled into their chairs and tuned up. A spattering of polite handclaps as the conductor bobbed on to his rostrum. A hush as he tapped once–twice–thrice and the orchestra swung into the overture as though their lives depended on reaching that last bar. Spontaneous applause, partly because they had played with zest and mostly because they had finished. An electrified suspense as the house-lights dimmed. A long ecstatic *aaah!* as the curtains drew back to reveal Eldorado.

A silken tent glowed with caballistic symbols. A golden altar bore sacramental vessels. Spotlights of brazen green, of sulphurous yellow, of passionate crimson, of celestial blue, transformed folds and shadows. The gleaming cavern was at once limited and limitless. A rainbow which vanished as you approached, an iridescent bubble which burst if you touched. Magical, strange, empty.

In the stillness a deep voice cried, 'I invite you to the Temple of Delight!' Cymbals crashed, gold sparks showered. From the centre of sound and colour walked the magician, huge, smiling; splendid in full evening dress, his Mephistophelian mantle swirling scarlet and black. To the outburst of their welcome he strode the stage, arms extended, head uplifted. He gave himself to his audience, yet drew it to him: judging and being judged in these first moments.

Here am I, SALVADOR! I, SALVADOR, the only, the world-renowned entertainer of the crowned heads of Europe. I, SALVADOR, who erase reality with one stroke of my magic wand. I, SALVADOR, master of the visible and the invisible. I, SALVADOR, whom to see is to marvel, whom to miss is to be impoverished. Salvador, Salvador, Salvador, SALVADOR!

He stood at the zenith of their homage and swept off his top hat, bowing low, very low. The noble head almost touched his knees. He was about to enchant them. I, Salvador, Emperor of the Magic Universe!

Casually he skimmed the hat on to a small table, folded his arms across his breast – and started in surprise. He was holding a white rabbit. Shouts of rapture. Such a snowdrift of a rabbit with bright eyes. He set it gently down and they watched it hop into the wings. He switched a handkerchief from his top pocket. No, not one – a dozen handkerchiefs, each more brilliant than the last. His astonishment aroused their hilarity. He balled the string of coloured squares in his hand and they vanished. He patted his pocket hopefully and produced two eggs. Spun them, humming, and was again confounded. They became three, four, five eggs. Spinning skilfully, he invited the children to count. Six eggs. One small boy, standing on his seat in spite of maternal protest, shouted, 'Seven!' A man possessed, Salvador spun an ever-increasing circle of flying objects, which gradually diminished until he held out empty hands. Where were the eggs? Why, *voilà!* Under his shining top hat, on that small table.

'And don't you go trying that dodge at home,' Inspector Lintott warned his two grandsons. 'There's more to it than you might think!'

He saw that his daughter Lizzie was as fascinated as the children, and sat back satisfied. Worth half a sovereign of anyone's money to take her mind off her troubles for an afternoon. He squeezed his wife's arm.

'Enjoying yourself, are you, Bessie?' he whispered.

'Hush!' said Bessie.

Grey head on one side, square hands planted on his knees, Lintott muttered to himself, 'That chap'd make a first-class pickpocket!'

'And now, illustrious ladies and gentlemen and my young friends,' Salvador was saying, 'I should like to introduce ALICIA, the mysterious prophetess!'

But this time there was no fountain of sparks, no noise. A soft light on the golden hangings grew so brilliant that she appeared to be created from it. She stepped lightly to his side, smiling. A vision from the seraglio in her white silk and gauze, in her gold bracelets and anklets. His bow was homage and they echoed it with reverent applause.

'You and I are going to keep secrets from Alicia if we can,' Salvador promised, smiling. 'I shall blindfold her, and ask her to turn her back on us, and then I shall walk among you and borrow articles ... Would this young man on the front row care to come up here and inspect Alicia's blindfold?'

A bashful lad of thirteen, in a Norfolk suit, clambered into view. He stood proudly, arms stiff at his sides, and tried to catch his brother's eye.

'Now tell me the truth, young sir,' Salvador was saying, in his English which was too precise to be his mother-tongue. 'Can you see through this scarf? You cannot? That is good. Now I tie it round the lady's eyes, so. You approve the knots?' The lad nodded vigorously. 'Do you think she is beautiful?' The lad hung his head and frowned. 'You do not wish to tell me? Then do not wear your heart on your sleeve, young sir!' And he plucked a scarlet velvet emblem from the tweed, tossed it in the air, caught it, opened his hands. 'But I most humbly beg your pardon,' he said charmingly, 'this is not a heart at all. It is half a crown, which I think you may keep. Thank you for your assistance, sir!'

He was walking among them, smiling, endearing himself, enquiring. Alone on the stage a small white figure lifted its pale head, blindfolded, back turned, and waited.

'What is in my hand? A watch, you say? That is not good enough for our young friend here. He wishes to know what is written inside the cover. I have not opened it. Is the lady telling the truth, sir? She is? That is good. And now, young miss, what secret have you to keep from Alicia...?'

'It's an eye-opener and no mistake,' Lintott agreed. Besieged by his grandsons, who regarded him as an oracle, he was forced to admit, 'How should *I* know how they do it? System of signals, probably. Look, if I knew what they knew I'd be up there earning a living at it, wouldn't I?'

'And now, my noble friends, the secret which alchemists have tried to discover, but in vain. How to turn common objects into gold! For this you need a magic crucible – and here it is, before your very eyes!'

The magnificent cauldron glowed in the centre of the altar, barbaric in its splendour.

'This golden crucible was unearthed in the region of fabled Babylon, and purchased by Salvador for a King's ransom. Babylon the great is fallen. Babylon, city of gold. Alone of her treasures remains the crucible. I, Salvador, possess the secret of the greatness of Babylon – I transform into gold, gold, GOLD!'

He passed his wand rapidly over the surface and luminous flame leaped into the air. Adults and children sat in hushed silence. Remote, impassive, he held them in thrall a moment longer, then switched to humour.

'Shall we turn the rabbit into gold? I promise you it shall not hurt him. He will be a very grand and important rabbit.'

They were charmed by this prospect.

'Hey – presto!' And out he wriggled in his fine new glittering coat.

'Aaaah!'

'And my pack of magic cards – *voilà*! Our friends the doves – *et voilà*!'

But one dove had forgotten his role in the general exaltation, and flew out into the audience. Uplifted faces marked his soaring progress. He alighted on the back of a seat in the stalls, quivering. Flew again as small fingers reached for his gold feathers. Rested on the ledge of a theatre box. As they turned to watch him, Alicia suddenly crouched in the middle of the stage, hands on each side of her head, staring past the bird into some vision she alone could see. She had been so gentle in tone and movement that her inhuman cry brought them to their feet.

'Fire! Fire! Fire!'

Lintott, using eyes and nose, perceived no cause for alarm, and before they could panic the magician struck a piece of apparatus with his wand.

'Fire!' he cried, smiling.

A tree of sparks distracted the attention of all but the Inspector, who was looking intently at the occupant of the box.

An uncommonly fine lady, she seemed out of place among the unsophisticated crowd of matinée attenders. Above the blonde-lace *jabot* her delicate face mirrored Alicia's terror. Her dark hair crowned her abundantly. She seemed so exotic a specimen of femininity that Lintott expected to see some companion or protector with her. But she had evidently come alone, and was about to depart in haste. Ringed hands gathered up the sable coat lying carelessly on the chair beside her.

'Fire!' Salvador repeated, striding the stage, calling forth flames. Then he held out his wand, reduced to a few inches in length, and the children shouted with merriment at his comical expression.

Lintott observed Alicia, now rising and returning to the performance under cover of her master's foolery. He looked again at the box.

The lady had retreated into the shadows. He saw a waxen complexion, a sable hat trimmed with velvet flowers, the flourish of a sable muff. The door opened sufficiently to allow her exit. She had gone. Salvador whistled up his errant dove: a soft peremptory call. The bird ruffled golden feathers, spread golden wings, sailed home to the magician's shoulder.

For a few moments the performance had been thrown out of joint, become strange and disturbing. Now, smoothly knit together again, it proceeded urbanely.

'Here is a pair of handcuffs such as your English policemen use to keep their criminals safe,' the magician was saying.

17

'They are genuine. I propose to ask a member of the audience to secure them on my wrists. I shall then step inside this curtained booth and remove them in a few moments, without unlocking them.' Raising his hand for silence, 'You think I play a trick upon you?' Sternly, 'Salvador does not play tricks! Have we someone here today who has some knowledge of handcuffs?'

'No, I won't,' Lintott whispered dreadfully, as his grandsons tugged at his arms. 'Making an exhibition of myself!'

'Go on, Father,' Lizzie urged. 'You *are* an expert. Show him!'

'Nothing doing,' Lintott hissed.

'John,' said Bessie, 'just you get up and tell him who you are!'

Slowly Lintott levered himself up, cleared his throat, embarrassed.

'You, sir? Can you give us your name, if you please?'

'Ex-Inspector Lintott of Scotland Yard, sir.'

'Excellent. If you will come up here for a moment, Inspector...'

I wish our seats had been nearer the front, Lintott thought, making his way self-consciously past a row of people and along the endless aisle.

'How are you, Inspector? Very good of you to offer your invaluable assistance. Would you be so kind as to give us your professional opinion of these handcuffs? Loud and clear, if you please, so everyone can hear you, sir.'

Lintott inspected them minutely, turned to the audience, found himself confronted by several hundred interested faces, swallowed, and roared his verdict to the back row of the balcony.

'These here handcuffs are the genuine article, and no mistake.'

Salvador smiled. The spectators cheered.

'Thank you, Inspector. How long were you in the police force, sir?'

'Above forty years.'

'Forty years. You must have captured many dangerous criminals in that time. Did any of them escape from handcuffs like these?'

Lintott forgot his lonely prominence.

'No, they did not, sir. They was handcuffed to *me*, you see, and I wouldn't let 'em!'

The surge of laughter surprised him. He jumped slightly, smiled sheepishly.

'Well done, Inspector!' Salvador cried, delighted. 'Nor could I have removed them were I handcuffed to such an excellent detective.' More laughter and applause. 'Now will you fasten these manacles and keep the key? Perhaps you would like to search me, to make sure I have no other key on my person?'

Lintott was into his pockets and patting his elegant legs.

'That is good,' said Salvador, amused. 'Shall I remove my shoes?'

'Yes, if you please, sir – and leave 'em with me. I'll keep your jacket, too, if you've no objection.'

He ran his hands through Salvador's hair, examined his mouth, his ears, the soles of his feet, opened his palms and looked under the fingernails. Nothing, nothing, nothing. The magician's eyes gleamed gold and green.

'Very well, sir,' said Lintott, standing back and gripping the handcuffs in case they changed into something else.

'Here is my stop-watch, Inspector. I wish you to time my escape. Ah, one moment!' Finger to forehead. 'How long do you give me to release myself?'

Lintott measured the width of the magician's wrists, the length of his bony hands, at a glance. He wouldn't wriggle out of those in a hurry.

'How *long*, sir?' Enjoying himself. He paused to let the remark sink in. 'I'd say *very* long!'

The laughter almost drowned the opening bars of a rousing march by the orchestra. Lintott stood at his ease, watch in one hand, key in the other. Ten seconds, twenty seconds, thirty seconds. Salvador swept aside the curtains of the booth, free. He held out the locked cuffs, bowing. Lintott examined them again, stared at the smiling man in his shirt-sleeves, wagged his head, scratched it – and shook hands.

Salvador held up a commanding arm.

'Ladies and gentlemen, never before have I been searched so thoroughly. Appreciation, if you please, for this gentleman in whose keeping the cause of right and justice has been so admirably placed.'

The theatre rose, cheering him to the garlands in the roof. Lintott, strangely moved, had yet something to say.

'I'd like to see Mr Salvador get out of a pair of handcuffs as wasn't regulation,' he offered, courteous but firm.

'I accept your challenge, sir. You shall be my guest at any performance you choose. Bring them along, please. I thank you once again.'

This time Alicia, too, came on stage and shook hands. She seemed both insignificant and powerful, vulnerable but strong. Lintott felt a rush of – what? Protectiveness? Reverence? Fear for her? All three. He had experienced the same emotion seeing nuns work in the East End. Not for you, he had wanted to say. Not the sort of place you should be in. Not the sort of people you should know. But their faces always silenced him, so that he simply raised his hat and walked away, as he was walking away now. Only this time as a hero of the occasion.

'Leave off, will you?' he grumbled, greatly pleased. 'Making a fuss about nothing!'

For the two boys were begging, 'Grandad, can we come with you when you fetch the other handcuffs?'

Lizzie, transfigured, kissed his cheek. Bessie said tartly, 'You'll be going on the Halls next, John Lintott. And don't expect *me* to come and watch!'

It was her way of saying she loved him, was proud of him.

'What a lark, eh?' he whispered, for Salvador was confounding them with another illusion. 'If that chap set up a school for criminals we'd be in a proper fix, and no mistake.'

'My friends, I am about to alter the law of gravity. Is this possible?'

Anything was possible. Had he told them to fly they would have endeavoured clumsily to skim the magic air. Only his closest observer, Alicia, could have known he was tiring. As he shrugged on his coat she saw that the back of his shirt was wet. Still his hands executed miracles, his voice rang out its heraldry. On the wings of his performance he rode, exhausted but faultless. His creations carried them forward to curtain fall. At the end he took the stage alone, no longer demanding but quiescent beneath the weight of their acclaim. I, Salvador, your humblest of servants.

'Have you got everything?' Lintott asked, in a welter of hats, coats and reticules. 'Billie, is this your catapult? What did you want to bring that for? Here, I'll take it. I don't want any windows put out afore we get home. What have you lost, Bessie? Your hat pin? Jackie, crawl under those seats and see if you can find Grandma's hat pin. It's a regular picnic fetching you out!'

'Father, this gentleman wants a word with you.'

Lintott straightened up, and paused. The man's stillness was disturbing. Perhaps the healed scar running from cheekbone to chin gave him this cold air. Perhaps it was his self-containment. Fair hair, cut closer than was fashionable. Brown eyes which reflected no discernible mood. Well-dressed, but uneasy in his clothes. Something foreign about him.

'And what can I do for you, sir?' Lintott asked, civil but observant.

'Mr Salvador sent me, Inspector.' The syllables were drawled as though he had all the time in the world. His face was expressionless. 'About these special hand-irons. He would like for you to give your name and ad-dress.'

'You're American, aren't you?' Lintott asked, interested.

The man nodded. His eyes never left the Inspector's face.

'I'll write it down for you,' said Lintott, feeling for the note-book that lived in his overcoat pocket. An old habit. He licked his pencil point.

'I thank you, Inspector. I am obliged to you.'

'No trouble. Excuse me a minute. Mr Salvador isn't American, is he?'

'No, sir. He is a cosmopolitan kind of guy. I am his secretary.'

'Ah!' Lintott liked to know these things.

Lizzie stood a little apart, daydreaming as usual in some sorry world of her own, while her mother performed duties she had forgotten.

'Penny for 'em,' said Lintott, good-humoured.

'I was wondering what it must be like to be the Salvadors, father.'

'Living from one day to the next? No home of their own? Roaming the earth like a pair of gipsies? One eye on the box-office and the other on old age? What do *you* think?'

'I think I might like it,' said Lizzie wistfully. 'It'd make a change.'

She was retreating into the dowdy suffering silence that had become her habit, and he could not bear it.

'Count your blessings,' he advised briskly, 'and look to those lads of yours. You leave too much to your mother, and she's brought up four of her own already!'

Lizzie was instantly conscience-stricken, and that hurt him too.

'I'll take Jackie, mother.'

'Oh, no, you won't,' said Bessie, flushed with effort, 'you can't control him. I can.'

She saw Lizzie redden with resentment, and covered her tactlessness by saying, 'Here, Jackie, go to your mamma – and behave yourself, mind!'

'Oh, come along, all of you,' said Lintott, annoyed and saddened.

As they walked out into the raw reality of a January day, a uniformed attendant caught up with the Inspector.

'Excuse me, sir. If Mr Salvador could have your full name and address he'd be much obliged. He'll be getting in touch with you about those handcuffs.'

'He must be sending a mort of folk running after me,' said Lintott, quietly full of his new importance. 'Here you are again, then!'

They stood in front of the London Coliseum, waiting for the rain to stop before venturing forth to find an omnibus.

'Well, that was nice,' said Bessie, with the satisfaction of a woman who has enjoyed a pleasant afternoon and looks forward to a pleasant evening.

Lintott mused on the prospect of strong tea and hot buttered muffins. The two boys pulled faces at each other covertly from the shelter of female skirts. Lizzie stared ahead of her, saying nothing.

TWO

'MR BELA BARAK of San Francisco. That's a foreign sort of name!' said Bessie, wiping her hands on her apron before receiving the embossed card. 'Who might he be, John? Oh, giving a reception tonight and wishes to see you beforehand on private business. What business might that be, John? Do you suppose he wants you to watch the jewellery? How was he to know you could come at such short notice? And how does he suppose you'll get home afterwards in the early hours of the morning? Why don't he give you a minute to make up your mind? You're not running round after him, I hope, are you?'

'Which question would you like me to answer first, my love?' Lintott enquired drily.

'Surely you're not thinking of walking from Mayfair to Richmond at your time of life?' Bessie persisted, bridling. 'Just for some jumped-up foreigner as has more money than sense!'

Lintott waited until she ran out of breath.

'When you've done, my love,' he said patiently. 'We don't know what the gentleman wants, so I'd best go and find out. And we ain't rich, Bess, and the money would come in handy.' His tone altered perceptibly. 'And since I've always made up my own mind I'd thank you to brew us a pot o' tea, my love, and stop telling me what to do!'

Mr Bela Barak of San Francisco understood a great deal

24

about money and almost nothing about his wife Francesca. This was not due to lack of effort on his part, but he equated love with expenditure, and was consequently disturbed when his investments in her did not pay off. He was accustomed to buying people and things in order to use them for particular purposes. Apart from the minor disappointments which will pinprick any successful career she was his only failure.

Now he fastened a collar of diamonds about her throat and instructed her on the evening ahead. Her French maid Genevieve stood by, lips pursed in disapproval.

'Honey, there is no such thing as over-dressing. When I give a reception in your honour I spare no expense. This is going to cost a hundred dollars a head. So all these rich aristocratic Britishers expect to see a very special person. I want them to get an eyeful of diamonds that will make them blink. I want them to know that this dress was designed by Mr Worth. Understand me?'

There was spirit in Francesca Barak's face, in the wing of her dark eyebrows and the curve of her mouth, in the brightness and swiftness of her changing expressions. But this spirit was carefully controlled in her husband's presence, as though she had learned the folly of setting it free. Therefore the waxen reflection gleamed passively, the dark blue eyes answered him softly.

'And you, Genevieve,' he continued with deliberate geniality, 'I should hate for you to think you can't dress your mistress's hair just as good as any English hairdresser. But the gentleman I brought in for tonight dresses the Court ladies' hair. Know what I mean?'

Genevieve bowed her head. She was middle-aged, long-nosed, spare of figure. She despised and feared her master, but had been with her old mistress in the old days in Virginia. She knew her place, and her lack of power.

'So that's okay then,' said Barak, surveying both women.

His pride in her touched Francesca Barak for an instant. She held out her hand to be kissed. She smiled under the weight of his exacting devotion, from which only business freed her.

'Where were you on Wednesday afternoon, honey?' he asked suddenly, in a tone which sounded gentle and held menace.

He felt the lie escape into the faintest movement of her fingers, now withdrawn from his grasp. Still she smiled at him.

'I went for an extra fitting, for my new riding habit, Bel.'

'Why didn't you take Genevieve with you, honey?'

So someone had informed on her, as soon as he had returned.

'Oh!' Francesca shrugged and smiled. 'She has to have *some* time off!'

'I don't like my wife going out alone.'

'Then I'll just have to take you with me, next time!' she replied gaily. 'And don't you dare refuse me, Bel!'

She could never interpret his reactions, so continued to use her smile as a shield, while his imperturbability shielded him. A powerful man, close to fifty, he carried himself well. His black hair was turning silver now, over the close-set ears, across the broad forehead, but grew as thickly as in his youth. Increasing age became him. He was more handsome, more distinguished, than in his greedy and relentless younger years.

A knock on the door released her from his attention.

'Excuse me, honey,' said Barak, 'but I have to go. Where is he?' to the servant outside.

'I put him in the library, Mr Barak, sir.'

In the relief of his absence Francesca said to her maid, 'Tell me honestly, Genevieve, what do you think of this *toilette*?'

'Madame is grievously over-dressed!'

Lintott had survived the cold civility of the butler, the grandeur of the house in Mayfair, and the vulgarity of the reception. He had acted as an eye on society's jewellery in this sort of mansion before. Thirty rooms on three floors, staircases back and front, stables attached. A gilded warren on a vast scale. Still, a sovereign at the end of the evening, and the glimpse of another world. So he stood comfortably in the book-lined masculine retreat and waited for his employer.

'Well, hello there again!'

A familiar voice, soft and toneless. A familiar face, cold and expressionless. An outstretched hand that was only a token of welcome. The scarred man, Salvador's secretary, said, 'I guess you remember me, Inspector?'

'Mr Barak?' asked Lintott, puzzled and suspicious.

'I have not the honour of being Mr Barak, Inspector. And I guess I owe you an apology. I am not Mr Salvador's secretary. But I had to have your ad-dress and that was the only way I could get it at the time. My name is Hank Fleischer.'

'Sir,' said Lintott, with a reserved nod. He disliked tricks.

'Can I offer you a drink, Inspector? Scotch or Bourbon? Do sit down.'

'I don't drink on duty, sir.'

'Not even now you are retired?' asked Fleischer lightly, but a sting lay beneath his tone.

'Not even now, sir,' Lintott answered.

'Mr Barak will be here presently,' said Fleischer.

They did not speak again until the library door opened, letting in light from the incandescent hall. Silhouetted against it was a huge man, immaculately tailored. From his gold cuff-links to his hand-made shoes he was a valet's dream of perfection.

Fleischer said softly, 'Stand up, Inspector. This is Mr Barak!'

Years ago, a small stout lady had ridden sedately by in her open carriage, and someone had said with the same note of reverence, 'That's Queen Victoria!'

Barak trod the carpet soundlessly and took up a stance by the open fire. He waved Lintott back into his seat, and accepted a glass of Bourbon and ice from the scarred man. He chose a cigar from the box held deferentially open. He accepted a light. Not until he was quite ready did he turn to the Inspector, smiling genially. The smile was intended to cover or soften his survey of Lintott, who stared civilly but steadfastly back. Apparently satisfied, Barak said, 'Go ahead, Hank! Go ahead!' sipped his Bourbon, and drew on his Havana.

Fleischer said, friendly and casual, 'I happened to mention your challenge to Mr Barak after I got back from the Coliseum the other afternoon, and he was kind of interested in having a bet with a magician. Mr Barak is a great better.' He slid a pair of handcuffs across the broad desk to Lintott. 'He wondered, how would you like to win your bet against Mr Salvador with these?'

Lintott donned his spectacles and looked at them curiously.

'Very interesting, sir,' he said courteously to Barak. 'I'm by way of being a bit of an expert on locks. The man who made these knew a thing or two. They aren't British, neither, by the look of them.'

'That doesn't matter,' said Fleischer tonelessly.

'No, it don't. Not when they're as good as this.'

The two men looked at each other and smiled.

'Great!' said Fleischer, satisfied. 'And you get one hundred dollars for using them. What do you know about that?'

Lintott, who had so far been simply mystified, became alert.

'What do I know about it?' he repeated slowly, using the expression in his own way. 'Why, not half enough, sir, that's my opinion. You should be asking *me* to pay for them, not the other way about. They beat anything as I can offer. Why not take them yourself, sir, as you enjoy a bet?'

Displeased, impatient, Fleischer replied, 'You're a cop, aren't you? With some kind of a past reputation at Scotland Yard. That way it looks more official. Unless the money bothers you some?'

Lintott said gravely, 'It *is* the offer of money that bothers me, sir.'

The scarred man looked to his master, who nodded again.

'Two hundred dollars, then. No? How much do you want? This is a greedy cop!' he added, and Barak's stance altered and his smile vanished.

'Just a minute, sir,' said Lintott. 'I'd like a little light on this matter. Excuse me, if you please.'

He took a magnifying glass from his pocket and scrutinised the handcuffs under a lamp which shone on the desk. The silence was heavy, affronted.

'They're riveted!' said Lintott in disgust, and tossed them back.

Barak raised one hand as Fleischer moved forward.

'Let's not have any misunderstandings, Hank. This is a very smart English detective!' He smiled on the Inspector. 'Sure, they're riveted. We intended to win that bet. Now how much do you want? Five hundred dollars?'

'You need five hundred dollars,' said Fleischer, smiling.

'How do you know what I need?' Lintott replied, very quiet, very cold.

Fleischer waved a little dossier in the air, saying, 'We know an awful lot about you, the way things are with you, Inspector John Joseph Lintott. You would go for a buck just as fast as your hands and knees would carry you.'

Lintott said, 'You and I don't seem to understand one another. I may not be rich but as poor as I am I can't be bought.'

He would have liked the comfort of his bowler hat between his hands, but his boots made their way sturdily to the library door.

'Inspector Lintott,' said Barak lazily, 'just one moment!'

His voice was as composed as his big body within the elegant suit, but he had lowered his head as though about to charge. His black eyes were contemplative.

'I have all the information I need on you,' said Barak, 'and I don't mind how expensive you come, but I mind like hell when you cross me.'

Fleischer was listening, waiting, scarred face rapt and intent.

'I'm sorry for that,' Lintott replied with chill sarcasm, 'but you'll have to find somebody else to play your dirty tricks for you, sir.'

Fleischer's hand moved swiftly to his breast-pocket, and as swiftly Barak said, 'No!' and again contemplated the Inspector.

'You say you can't be bought?' he mused. 'Let me tell you this. Anybody can be bought. Anybody. Because everybody has some price. I could find yours.'

He turned his back and warmed his hands at the flames.

'Take him out by the side-door, Hank.'

The hall was brilliant with light. Liveried footmen flanked the walls. Waiters held silver trays of champagne glasses. The scent of transported hot-house flowers cloyed the nostrils. Orchids and asparagus ferns entwined the pillars. A vista of long rooms showed glimpses of an orchestra tuning up, of white damasked buffet tables resplendent with food, of spindly gilt chairs and waxed parquet floors. On a lilied trough floated three drugged swans.

And down the staircase, disregarding all but her own beauty, trailed the lady who had fled from the Coliseum theatre box. The chandeliers shone on thousands of pounds' worth of diamonds. They shimmered on her arms and neck and bosom, glittered on fingers, sparkled in hair and ear-lobes. Their icy perfection set off a delicate perfection of her own.

'Who's that?' Lintott asked involuntarily.

The under-footman who had been sent for his hat and coat gave a superior smile. *Ignorant fellow*, he seemed to be thinking.

'That lady is Mrs Barak, of course!'

Barak was coming to meet her. She greeted his compliments with a parting of lips, a raising of eyebrows. The first guests were arriving, and she did not wish to spoil the effect of her entrance.

'I'll manage!' said Lintott angrily, as the under-footman made a pretence of helping him with his coat.

He observed how Barak stood at her side, and how he could take no ease in his possession of her. He heard the pride in the man's voice as he introduced her, and saw the uncertainty in his glances at both guest and wife.

'This way, if you please,' said the under-footman, losing patience.

Fleischer had disappeared to fulfil some unobtrusive task. Lintott guessed that the scarred man belonged to the less respectable side of Bela Barak's entourage, and would be little in evidence at such a function as this.

'*Would* there be anything else?' demanded the under-footman.

Lintott clapped his bowler hat smartly upon his head.

'Yes, there would,' he replied. 'Get me out of this here Belshazzar's Feast!'

The night was cold and wet. Still, this was his city. These pavements were old friends, old enemies, old haunts beneath his boots. He cut down a short dark alley, knowing why he took this deliberate risk. He had to disprove the sense of helplessness which Barak and Fleischer had aroused. Ears keen, eyes alert, he strode on, watching and listening. The attack came as an anti-climax.

'Oh, you would, would you?' cried Lintott, catching the man's arm as it struck, locking it behind his back, holding him like a reluctant shield in case he had accomplices. 'Come along with me and let's take a look at you.'

He stooped rapidly and picked up the blackjack. Thrust the man ahead of him into the blessed gaslight of a lamp-post.

'Haven't you had enough of the cockchafer, Charlie?' he asked, grinning.

'Mr Lintott,' Charlie gasped. 'Oh, my Gawd! I didn't know it was you.'

'What's that got to do with it?'

'Cross me heart and hope to die, Mr Lintott, I'd never lay a finger on you.'

'Oh, I know that,' unimpressed, sarcastic. 'You've gone up in the world, Charlie, tackling grown men in dark alleys. It used to be babbies and old ladies on street corners! Stand there and don't move or I'll fetch you a tap with this!'

'It's me wife, Mr Lintott, as drove me to it.'

'Don't give me that, Charlie. Your wife's a better woman than you deserve. An honest woman, poor creature.'

'She's dying, Mr Lintott.'

'What? Your Lillie?'

Charlie nodded. A few minutes ago he had been a terror of the night. Now, under-sized, under-nourished, he flattened himself against the brick wall: a victim of circumstance.

'What's amiss then?' Lintott asked more kindly.

'She's got a growth inside of her, Mr Lintott. She suffers

somethink cruel. I hadn't a mag to bless meself with. I been begging, Mr Lintott.'

'With this?' Lintott asked drily, flourishing the blackjack.

Charlie shook his head.

'On the streets, Mr Lintott, since this morning. Begging. I begged. Nobody don't want to know, Mr Lintott. Nobody don't care. I got bleeding nothink.'

'You've got grown children, haven't you? Poor sort of a father, but their mother was one of the best. Can't they help her out?'

Charlie spread his arms, crucified, and let them fall.

'All gone, or else up to their necks in trouble, eh?'

Charlie nodded. Lintott's face was a battleground of anger and pity.

'Is Lillie in hospital?'

'She's feared to go, Mr Lintott. You know what it's like.'

'Aye, Charlie. A rough choice for poor folks. What are you doing for her, then?'

'Kath and Jenny look in. They live near.'

'Changed their beat since my time! Still turning a trick, are they? Nice sort of company for a decent woman like Lillie, I must say. What were you going to buy with what you nicked, Charlie?'

'Brandy, Mr Lintott. It keeps her under, a spoonful at a time, given regular. Gin makes her sick. Kath says that if we get enough brandy down her she'll go off in her sleep, peaceful-like.'

Lintott reached into his pocket.

'Hold your hands out,' he commanded, and emptied all his loose change into them. 'Buy Lillie some brandy, and remember me to her, for old times' sake. And if one drop goes down your thieving throat, Charlie, I'll have your liver and lights! Savvy? No, don't thank me. I'm not doing it for you, God knows. Now scarper!'

He watched the man scuttle along the lighted wall and disappear into the darkness beyond. He slipped the blackjack inside his coat. He started on the long walk to Richmond.

THREE

Wednesday, 10 January 1906

LINTOTT HAD ALWAYS FEARED hospitals. He knew he should look upon them as havens of healing, but his contacts were usually with the moribund and this predisposed him to link them with death. His boots creaked fearfully down the long ward full of iron beds, and by his side the nursing Sister's starched apron creaked in company as she led him to Bessie. He stood, holding his hat to his chest with such sorrowful awkwardness that the Sister said, 'She's going to get well, Mr Lintott, but it'll take time. Just a few minutes now. She's feeling sick with the chloroform.'

Only childbirth had invalided Bessie so far. Apart from the occasional cold or influenza, both she and he had taken their good health for granted. Lintott sat down as quietly as possible and watched his wife doze. One round cheek rested on her hand, a faint frown drew her brows together. The other hand lay on the coverlet, wearing the wedding ring he had placed on her finger forty years ago. She had never taken it off.

Her eyes opened, blue and bewildered and minus their spark of domestic authority. Her lips formed his name soundlessly.

'Here I am, my lass,' said Lintott. 'I came as soon as I could, but you were in the operating room. I've been a-waiting.'

For hours, on the hard bench, afraid.

He laid his blunt hand on her cheek for an instant, and nodded cheerfully. She stared at him: a child needing re-assurance

'You were knocked down by an omnibus in Oxford Street, Bess. Do you remember?'

'My – legs?'

'Right as rain and plastered up nicely. A few cuts and bruises and a bit of a shake-up, otherwise. It'll take time,' said Lintott, repeating the Sister's words, 'but you'll be all right, Bess.'

Tentatively, her fingers touched the plastered limbs beneath the covers. She digested his information without replying. Her mind picked hazily, haphazardly, among scraps of recollection. She hooked one up.

'What about – your supper, John?'

'I'll cook myself a couple of mutton chops. I ain't a babby, you know.'

She contemplated his shirt front.

'And Lizzie'll do my washing,' he said, interpreting the look. 'We'll manage, right as ninepence. Just you get yourself better, my lass.'

She traced the plaster again with her fingertips, forehead puckered.

'What about – the sheets?'

'Lizzie'll wash them. Never fear.'

Fretful, insistent. 'The sheets – as I bought – in the Sales!'

A tear trickled down her plump cheek.

'Oh, those!' said Lintott, knowing nothing about them. 'Safe and sound!'

He leaned forward and whisked the tear away with his handkerchief.

'They were – well-wrapped – in brown paper,' she persisted.

'Not a mark on 'em. Very good value. Cheer up, my lass.'

'But it – isn't – *right*.'

To have harmed no one, and to be brought to this. Tracking down bargains, rubbed purse in hand. Rummaging in the linen treasure-houses to replace sheets which had been mended and sewn sides to middle until they would give no more service. To have modesty outraged and dignity overthrown beneath an Oxford Street omnibus. Folks must have seen her stockings and garters, perhaps her drawers and petticoats. The red flannel petticoat was shabby. She had tried to pull down her skirts as they fetched her out.

Sounds returned. Grinding wheels, the driver's shout, horses whinnying, bystanders screaming. She saw above her, as she clutched her parcel of sheets, the iron shields of horses rear to heaven. She saw the whites of eyes.

She began to cry, and every sob hurt her. She wept for the supper she could not cook, the shirts she could not wash, for the humiliation of her betrayed body. She rejected the comfort of her husband's handkerchief.

'Now, now, now, my love,' Lintott murmured, riven. 'Hush a bit, Bessie.'

He remembered the violets, stowed carefully in the breast of his overcoat, and brought them out, a little crushed – but fragrant. He laid them on the pillow and waited. After a minute or so she dried her face, acknowledged the flowers, and smiled at him woefully.

'That's better, my love. Ah, here's Sister!' Relieved.

'I think Mrs Lintott must have an admirer!' cried Sister, noting the tear-stains. 'Just look what the messenger has brought.'

The whole ward was reviving in this marvel of a bouquet, whose cost would have kept any of their families for a month. Bessie stared at its perfection.

'And all fancy!' she whispered of the wrappings and ribbons.

She would keep the ribbons when the flowers had died. She would keep the card, decorated with paper lace, its satin centre embroidered with tulips. She would remember the four lines of verse wishing her well, saying that the sunshine had departed until she walked in its rays again. She would...

'Read the – message, John – will you?'

Puzzled, good-natured, Lintott donned his spectacles and drew the thick sheet of paper from its envelope.

Dear Madam,

Forgive a stranger presuming to write to you, but Inspector Lintott and I discussed a business matter the other evening, so you are not unknown to me. I heard, by chance, of your unhappy experience this morning, and hasten to send these flowers, with sincere wishes for your good recovery.

Your humble servant, dear Madam,

Bela Barak

Lintott saw Barak's lowered head, his contemplative black eyes. He heard the gravelly voice drawling its brief sentences.

Everybody has some price. I could find yours.

He said, slowly and carefully, because he was shocked and afraid and did not want to frighten her, 'Bessie, how exactly did you come to get knocked down?'

She recognised the controlled tone and presumed he was blaming her.

'Not my fault – the crowds – somebody jostled – and I went...'

Tumbling in the mud. Hooves, wheels, open mouths, up-flung arms, shouts.

'Who jostled you, Bessie?' Holding his voice steady. 'Did you see?'

She could feel the shape of every bone and muscle. Her legs were weights. Chloroform had burned her mouth and made her sick. Now something had made him angry and he was hiding it.

'Don't – know – how should – accident – not my – fault...'

She wept bitterly. The material of the hospital nightgown was harsh. She could not imagine what she had done wrong.

'Questioning – me ...,' Bessie accused pitifully, and sobbed again.

'Inspector Lintott,' said Sister quietly, 'I think you had better leave now. Your wife is upsetting herself, and that will not help matters.'

Take him out by the side-door, Hank.

'I beg your pardon, Sister,' he said, humble.

He patted Bessie's shoulder. A plump hand sought his, and squeezed it.

36

'Now I'm not leaving you like this,' said Lintott, 'so you'd best give me a smile and a kiss, and then you'll be rid of me!'

He winked at Sister, who was waiting with relentless patience. He overcame his horror of the bouquet for Bessie's sake.

'Rich gentlemen sending you flowers!' he chided lovingly.

She lifted her head, the tears drying on her cheeks as children's tears do, as though they had never been. A faintly coquettish air was evident in her reply.

'Yes,' she said, 'however – did he – hear about me?'

I have all the information I need on you.

'Ah, well. He's got business connections all over London. Somebody might have been – passing by – when you ... you never know!' he finished roundly.

I guess you remember me, Inspector? My name is Hank Fleischer.

'Well, I think – it was – very kind!'

Anybody can be bought. Anybody.

'Why didn't – you take – his job?'

'He needed somebody different from me. That's all. Go to sleep now, Bess.'

'She'll be brighter in a day or so, Inspector Lintott,' said Sister, leading him away. 'You mustn't worry. But it will take some time...'

'John! John!' And as he hurried back she made everything right with him in her own mind. 'It's just that – I wanted to say – I don't like his – flowers better – than yours!'

'That's good then!' he said heartily. 'Thought I'd lost you, for a while.'

FOUR

DUTY CALLS YOU TO THE POLL! *It is the plain duty of every citizen to vote.* Balfour and the Conservatives had gone to the country, upholding privilege and tradition. Lloyd George and the Liberals were fighting on social issues. Not new issues, never new. The poor had always suffered. But Liberals were demanding a new responsibility towards old issues. Rescue deprived children! Fill empty cupboards! Warm fireless hearths! Ease hard times!

Lintott was all for that, but – this Lloyd George chap. Something of a rabble-rouser, a charmer, a womaniser. Not reliable. Young Winston Churchill had turned his Party coat, too, standing as Liberal candidate for Manchester. Another weathercock sort of fellow, plenty of spirit and precious little stability. Interesting to see how he would come out, though. Brilliant failure like his father, probably. Well, well.

He knew when he opened his front door that the house was occupied. No voice greeted him. No homely sound betrayed a presence. He stood in his small lobby, face dappled with many colours by courtesy of the stained-glass fanlight, listening. He called, 'Lizzie?'

The pause told him she was in trouble, then she answered, 'I'm in the parlour, Father.'

Apprehensive, Lintott entered and found her sitting neat and upright by the fire.

'I'll brew some tea,' she said lifelessly. 'I dare say you need it. Tramping miles and endways. As usual.'

These were Bessie's phrases, but delivered without Bessie's vigour. He did not gainsay her. He had suffered enough the last few days. Lizzie could burden him with her explanations later.

In silence, she set the kettle on the trivet. Brooding, she toasted bread. He ate and drank, sat back, filled his pipe, looked at her. Her mouth was set in sorrow. Pride held her erect.

'What's to do, my girl?' Lintott asked, and could not bear to hear.

'Eddie's turned me out.'

The officer of the law came uppermost.

'He can't do that,' said Lintott. 'He took you for better or worse. He's responsible for you.'

'I'll put it another way, then. I don't mind leaving, and I'm not going back.'

'And what about those two little lads of his? Are you leaving them, too?'

Lizzie shrugged, though that decision had cost her more than simple dismissal.

'Since his mother moved in to look after them, while I was ...' she interpreted Lintott's frown, and did not say *in prison*, '... while I was away, well, she won't move out. She says I'm a bad influence on them.'

Lintott removed the comfort of his pipe stem, incensed.

'Interfering old faggot! Never liked her. What else?'

'Oh, too many reasons. All of them seemingly good. Oh, what's the use?' she cried, accusing him, 'of hanging on to something that was dead before it began? You couldn't prove my marriage right, Father, if you argued for a hundred years!'

Bessie was not there to check her daughter and soothe her husband. They were free to battle.

'Right? Right? You gave your sacred promise, my girl, six years since. You took on Eddie and a couple of stepsons, and nobody forced you. You made your own mind up!'

39

He knew that she had probably made up her mind on this matter, also, and it enraged him.

'Wilful and obstinate!' He flung the words at her. 'Never satisfied. Ah, that's your trouble and always has been. Reaching for the moon and crying when you fall flat on your face. Upsetting everybody as cares for you.'

He saw that his tirade was strengthening her resolve, and changed tactics.

'Lizzie, Lizzie,' he said gently. 'Think on, my lass. Eddie's never ill-treated you as I know of. Has he?'

'He never blacked my eyes, if that's what you mean, but there's worse than that!' And as his policeman's mind docketed marital offences, 'Oh no! He's done nothing that *you'd* call wrong!'

She was impatient of legalities.

'Well, then?' said Lintott, mollified, 'what are you complaining about? He runs a steady business. He's decent and honest and sober. He liked you well enough at one time – maybe more than you liked him!' Shrewdly. 'What do you want?'

'A bit of understanding.'

He huffed uneasily.

'What reason does *he* give for turning you out?'

'Women's Suffrage. He says I'm the talk of the neighbourhood and his customers don't like it. He says I make a fool of him.'

'I've thought as much myself, only milder. I told you years ago, Lizzie,' shaking his pipe at her colourless face, 'that no good would come of it. Handcuffed to railings. Sticking up posters. Making an exhibition of yourself.'

'I never *harmed* anybody. They harmed *me!*'

Violations in the name of the law.

'They put you in prison because you were a public nuisance. Prison!' he repeated in disbelief. 'My daughter treated like a common felon. Pulled about by doctors and wardresses!' He put the vision firmly from him. 'You should have stayed at home and looked after your family. Done your duty.'

'I left their food ready,' she cried, near to tears. 'I did what

40

I had to before I went. It was *my* time I spent. Afternoons.'

'And some of theirs, too, while you waited to get out of jail again. Your mother fretted herself to death, trying to keep two homes a-going. Selfishness.'

The mention of Bessie, who had understood nothing and done her best, hushed them temporarily.

'How was mother today?' Lizzie asked, subdued.

'I'm glad you remembered her,' said Lintott, sarcastic. 'She's coming along. Coming along.'

Lizzie's reproof was quick and direct.

'Being different from her doesn't mean I don't love her, Father – it'd be easier if I didn't.'

'Well, well.' Silenced. He pondered over her marriage. 'Perhaps it'd be better if you talked to your mother. Women see things as men can't fathom. Sleep on it, Lizzie. When couples quarrel they say things as they don't mean.'

He patted her shoulder, but it stayed rigid beneath his fingers.

'Oh, no, Father. They say what they do mean, and then pretend after. I'm done with pretending.'

'Let me go round and have a friendly word with Eddie.'

'What about? If there was more to say I'd say it myself.'

Furious, helpless, withdrawing from her, Lintott cried, 'He was your choice, my girl!'

Her thin face seemed all sad mouth and eyes. Her voice was soft and final.

'I never had much choice, father. You know that. I could never do anything I really wanted, and marriage seemed the next best thing. We've both paid for that mistake, Eddie and me. Poor Eddie. He'd have been comfortable with somebody else.'

Lintott lifted the iron tongs and placed three lumps of coal on the fire.

'So you've come to me, then?' he observed quietly. 'What can *I* do, my lass?'

She shed her pride, laid aside her defensiveness, appealing to him.

'Let me stay with you while I sort myself out, Father. I can look after you. It'll be company for us both. We had a good time together when Mother went nursing Grandma. Do you remember?' Suddenly younger, eager. 'We were by ourselves for above a month. Ten years ago. I felt important, looking after you all by myself. I used to keep your stew warm for you when you were out late, and you'd tell me your news while you ate it. Do you remember?'

She was the youngest of their four children: the most intelligent, the most troublesome, and to him the most dear. The other three had made steady progress from infancy to maturity, accepting life with good-humoured phlegm. From birth Lizzie had been his deepest source of concern. He loved her, feared for her, stood between her and Bessie – who could make neither head nor tail of the child. He had had two sons to provide for, on a policeman's wage, and expected his daughters to employ themselves usefully and respectably until they married. John was doing well in the Force, at Brighton. Joseph was an army sergeant. Mary, image of her mother, had never been known to complain of more than the price of children's shoes. But Lizzie had wanted to go to university.

'Take no notice!' Bessie had counselled, after an explosion of tears and reproaches one evening. 'It's another of her high-flown ideas, and comes of too much reading. She's wanted to be just about everything, ever since she could talk. A missionary in China. An explorer in Africa. An opera singer. Mark my words, she'll have read some nonsense about these new-fangled lady doctors – *lady*, indeed. She's the moody age. She'll settle down.'

Lizzie's outbursts were short-lived, he had to say that. Her silences were never sulky. She needed affection so badly that she would always make amends, come round to their point of view. But from each frustrated hope sprang fresh endeavour and each enterprise seemed wilder than the last. She had tried to educate herself, and coaxed tuppence from her father in order to buy a second-hand French primer. She had read voraciously, without direction or discrimination, starved for she did not know what. Her lack of focus had been Bessie's chief weapon.

'Just what *do* you want?' Bessie would say. 'Tell me one thing as you've stuck at!'

Lizzie could not, since she had tried so many. Office work had answered for a while, bolstered by the joy of earning wages, until she had discovered she could go no further than typewriting and taking down dictation. Then she had met Eddie Peck, a widower with two young sons and his own grocery store. She was young and he was flattered. She was the product of a respectable home with sound values. She was ladylike in her humble fashion, with pretensions to education. She was sufficiently attractive to be a source of husbandly pride, without being so attractive that he need ever worry about her.

'I advised you to wait,' Lintott cautioned. 'You wouldn't listen to me.'

The firelight was kind to her face and clothes. Released by confession, warmed by her father's presence, she seemed less shabby.

'I was nineteen,' Lizzie remembered, lifting her head. 'I saw what I wanted to see. I'm not saying I wasn't responsible, but I hadn't the experience to judge.'

Eddie had appeared to be a safe harbour, until she foundered on the rocks of his limitations.

'He ain't exactly one of the imaginative sort,' Lintott admitted, unconsciously on her wavelength, 'but that's not harmful.'

She smiled and stretched her hands to the flames.

'It was harmful for me.'

He protested, 'But we thought you'd settled down nicely, at one time.'

'Kept down, more likely,' said Lizzie, sombre.

'Eddie's on the opinionated side, certainly,' Lintott pondered, trying to be fair, 'but a man's got a right to his own opinions.'

Lizzie looked up quickly.

'Yes, if he's thought about them. So long as they're not just prejudices.'

'You've got some pretty strong opinions of your own, my lass.'

Reading Eddie's newspaper, questioning, explaining, airing her views, asking for response. Until he, beleaguered, turned from admiration to perplexity and finally to putting her in her place.

'I never understood,' she mused, 'why he got so vexed.'

Lintott chuckled.

'I do,' he said. 'I've got vexed with you myself afore now!'

'Not in the same way, Father,' she replied, chin on hand. 'When you're vexed you stand your ground and argue. Eddie got vexed because he'd no ground to stand on. Then he'd tell me to shut up.'

'You think too much,' said Lintott, knocking out his pipe, rising, yawning.

'He was mean!' she cried suddenly. 'Mean in heart and mind and body and soul. Mean.'

'Here, here,' Lintott chided, 'that's coming it a bit strong, Lizzie.'

She paused and reflected.

'My lass, he did what he could, according to his lights. None of us can do more, now can we?'

'It wasn't enough for me, you see,' said Lizzie in apology.

Lintott knew when he could get no further. Besides, he was hungry.

'Nigh on eight o'clock,' he said briskly. 'A hot cutlet and mashed potato wouldn't come amiss to either of us. I'm not keeping a woman in the house and cooking for myself. So, stir about, my girl!'

She had inherited his resilience in the face of disaster, and would live one day at a time. Her step was quicker, her face brighter, as she set the pan of potatoes on the hob.

'By the way,' she said, 'who did you vote for, Father?'

'We've had enough talk about votes!' he parried.

The intelligence in her eyes disturbed him.

'I voted for what I thought was right,' he prevaricated. 'That's sufficient.'

He had always done his duty as a good citizen. He had never questioned the right of the inheritors to rule. Balfour was a gentleman. Queen Victoria, God bless her, had been a great lady. And yet, and yet, and yet ... Lillie sleeping herself out of the claws of pain, of life, with teaspoons of brandy. Barak's extravagance of flowers in a ward full of patients too poor to afford one of them. Something wrong somewhere. Something that ought to be altered. On an impulse, astonished at himself, he had chalked his cross against the name of the Liberal candidate for the first time in his life. His hands had shaken slightly as he folded the paper and thrust it into the ballot box. Almost he had expected Lintott to arrest Lintott for changing his mind. But most of the country, unknown to him, was thinking and doing exactly the same thing for the same reasons.

Lizzie was smiling at him maternally, sensing the truth. Too delicate to pursue him, she was yet exultant in her perception. He exercised masculine cunning against feminine intuition.

'You know, Lizzie, you're what I'd call handsome when you're not fretting!'

Pleasurably vanquished, she shaved dripping into the frying pan. Lintott wondered whether Eddie might have sweetened matters with the aid of the right compliment at the right time.

'Yes,' he mused, thoroughly pleased with himself, admiring Lizzie's smiling face, her reflective grey eyes, her brown hair swept into a shining knot, 'I'd say – downright handsome!'

Hands on hips, Lizzie surveyed him, leaned forward and planted a kiss on each muttonchop whisker.

'I'm glad you voted for what you thought was right, Father,' she said mischievously.

She smiled again, nodded twice in self-congratulation, and whisked out to fetch the cutlets.

THE VANISHING LADY

'There was certainly no trap in the floor, the chair was of the ordinary kind, and the trick was done in a strong light. The lady, in fact, disappeared before the eyes of the audience: but so quickly was the trick done that no one present saw her escape.'

Paris correspondent of the London *Daily Telegraph*, 29 April 1886, reporting on Buatier de Kolta's first major illusion success.

FIVE

Friday, 19 January 1906

Lintott settled back as the house-lights dimmed. He felt a
traitor to Bessie and Lizzie, but relieved. He could do with an
evening of magic in the Temple of Delight, that he could!
His womenfolk had cost him blood during the last nine days.
And, Lord above, the Liberals were in! He considered himself
to be personally responsible. Well, they must show their mettle
now or he wouldn't vote for them again. No, certainly not.
He'd given them a chance and they must make the most of it.

A concussion of cymbals, a volcano of sparks, and Salvador
in his splendour. Fine figure of a man. Wonderful sense of
theatre. Marvellous dexterity. Aha! No eggs, no rabbit, no
handkerchiefs – that must have been for the children's matinée.

'Noble ladies, my compliments!'

He was producing nosegays from his fingertips and tossing
them into the audience. The lady next to Lintott caught one
and held it to her nose, enraptured.

I wonder, Lintott thought, how long it will be afore I can
smell flowers without sickening at the stomach?

'Shall we toast these beautiful ladies, gentlemen?'

Salvador clapped his hands and two page boys appeared,
carrying trays of glasses. He picked up a tin kettle from the
table.

'This I have bought from your famous Selfridge's. Is any
gentleman willing to join me in drinking to the health of the

49

fair sex? Champagne, hock, claret, sherry. All from this little tin kettle which I now fill with water.'

Young bloods were rising from their seats, ready for a lark. The magician poured and poured. The kettle's volume and variety of liquid roused laughter.

'I say, old chap,' cried one joker, 'this ain't *vintage* hock, you know!'

'Not vintage? I shall complain to Selfridge's!'

His command of the situation was absolute. He ushered his guests from the stage and produced his golden crucible. Illusion upon illusion. Lintott stared, open-mouthed, and detected nothing but the impossible.

'Hey presto!' Salvador had produced Alicia from nowhere and was presenting her reverently to the audience, and as reverently kissing her fingers.

The blindfold was adjusted and the magician descended into the audience. The impact of his personality as he passed Lintott's seat caused the Inspector to hit upon an explanation for miracles. Perhaps if someone like Salvador were a spiritual or temporal leader, exercising this quality of power, you could believe anything? Alicia was another unknown quantity, Lintott reflected. She gave the impression of having wandered on stage by accident. He wanted to put her in a cab and send her home to her parents, warning them that this was no sort of profession for a young lady. Yet her soft voice reached the gallery, her shy head accomplished mental feats beyond his comprehension. She was there on purpose, already naming the contents of a lady's reticule.

'...and a small silver phial, finely engraved, containing a perfume which I think is – *Jicky*!' Respectful applause as even this final detail was confirmed. 'Sorrow and joy in that phial,' she continued in a different tone, 'a memory of a summer evening, a meeting and a parting. I see Lausanne...'

She's gone off the track, Lintott thought. The magician's voice echoed him. Salvador was bringing her back with that ring of benevolent authority.

'The lady holds her memories sacred, Alicia, and we shall

not intrude upon them. I thank you, madame.'

The girl had stopped the instant he spoke, and waited passively.

'Am I standing next to a lady or a gentleman now?' the magician asked.

She lifted her head obediently.

'A gentleman. A military gentleman. He is not wearing his uniform, but he wears medals. Six medals. He has a dark moustache...'

Lintott craned round with the rest of his neighbours, but the military gentleman was invisible in the rear stalls.

'Please describe the medals for us, Alicia.'

She spoke as though she held them in her hand, turning them over to decipher metal, ribbon colours, letters, figures. Then past and present merged.

'You did not expect to be here this evening, sir. You intended to dine alone at your club, but you met the old friend who is sitting next to you. You have not seen each other for some years. He was once of great service to you. I see plumes and spears ... horns ... someone draws horns in the dust to describe ... a movement? No, a formation. It is a formation of war. It is war...'

Salvador had not checked her in this flight, and now smiled at the astonished man.

'Does she speak the truth, honourable sir?'

'By Jove! By Jove! Now that really is incredible,' cried a voice accustomed to giving orders on the parade ground. He stood up to address the audience and Alicia. 'That battle was Rorke's Drift, madam. And this is Bob Fletcher sitting next to me, who saved my life. And I *haven't* seen him for donkey's years. And I *was* going to dine at my club!' The theatre sat hushed, watching and listening. 'You mentioned horns, madam, and rightly connected them with a formation of war. Of *war*, you said. To be absolutely precise, if you will forgive me, it is a *battle* formation. The Zulus form a battle line which is the shape of a buffalo's horns. By Jove! You are incredibly right, madam.'

He laughed, reddened, shook his head and sat down again. Salvador was too good a showman to miss this sort of exit line. Indicating that Alicia merited all the admiration they could summon, he returned to the stage. They applauded with hands, feet and voices.

'Alicia will now prove herself lighter than air,' Salvador remarked, and humorously hitched up his sleeves.

The small silk-and-gauze figure lay obediently on the floor, and rose obediently to the orchestration of his hands. As an afterthought he raised one or two pieces of stage furniture as well. What the devil would the chap do next?

Apparently refreshed, Salvador ran through a few minor amusements: lighting a chandelier full of candles with his pistol, passing a borrowed brooch into a goose egg, and converting wet paper into dry confetti. His appearance was an illusion. His lean figure concealed a marketful of products. His top hat possessed its own repertoire. His hands were a thousand deceptions. Even his smile, except when he smiled in triumph, was a glorious lie, calculated to keep their minds lulled while he further beguiled them.

Fascinated, both personally and professionally, Lintott observed – and learned nothing.

'And now a very old trick indeed. I am almost ashamed to bore you with it, ladies and gentlemen. Also, you may be angry with me because I am going to make Alicia disappear before your eyes!'

Shaking his head ruefully, he spread two copies of *The Times* on the boards, apologetically asked a gentleman to inspect them and the chair in which Alicia would sit. He was, at once, thorough enough to command their respect and amusing enough to hold their interest.

'There is nowhere to which Alicia can vanish, sir? You are sure?'

'I am quite sure, sir.'

'You would be inclined to disbelieve me if I told you I could transport her into the audience, and bring her back on stage in a few seconds?'

The spectators chuckled as the man shook his head. He smiled, embarrassed.

'Thank you for your assistance, sir!'

He was making a pack of cards do extraordinary things, building up tension, waiting for the gentleman to take his seat, holding them ready. The moment had come. Courteously, he asked Alicia to sit in the chair. Smiling, he covered her with a silk sheet. He whisked the sheet off. Aah! they breathed, staring at the empty chair, and as they stared he turned and walked to the footlights, sheet in hand, smiling.

There were a few seconds between the smile and the deep bow, but they registered with Lintott like minutes. Salvador had been expecting something to happen which had not occurred, and decided to cut short the illusion.

'You liked that?' the magician asked. 'Good! Please to take these things away!' he ordered the stage-hand. 'Now I shall do something more!' rubbing his hands.

A cage full of canaries was brought on. He made them vanish. He brought them back again. They had changed into parrots. The evening continued as that matinée had continued, with a question-mark in its midst which Salvador had covered with quick thinking. Lintott was drawn into the entertainment, special handcuffs well to the fore, and despatched in a comfortable seventy-five seconds: chastened but unsurprised. The tricks became more elaborate, as though the magician piled mystery upon mystery in order that they should forget the real mystery which had occupied those few seconds.

The camaraderie of Salvador and audience culminated in a pinnacle of applause. He took the curtain alone, bowing until his head almost touched his knees: a solitary giant.

Well, well, well. A good evening out, and a good evening over. God Save the King and home to trouble! Wait a minute. Better say something about those riveted handcuffs, about Barak, about – no, not about Bessie.

Lintott wrote a brief message, handed it to an attendant, and waited by the stage door. Another attendant was turning away the magician's admirers.

'Not tonight, ladies and gentlemen, if you please. Mr Salvador begs to be excused. Yes, very tired, madam. Quite so. If you will leave your card...'

'Would you come this way, please, Inspector Lintott?'

They tramped down uncarpeted passages which smelled of dust, greasepaint and gas. This was no temple of delight, backstage. More like the compressed and shabby workshop from which all magic emerged fully-dressed. The illusions were over. Salvador turned his head, and Lintott saw a man in his middle thirties who had found life was not easy.

The beauty of his face lay in its bonework. His strength must have been prodigious. And yet? Wouldn't hurt a fly, Lintott decided.

'I was about to send for you, Inspector. Then your message came. I have an interesting conundrum for you!'

He attempted to speak lightly, handing over a letter. He hummed as he shrugged his tail-coat to the floor, where it would presumably lie until someone else picked it up.

'Is this writing in English, sir?' Lintott asked, turning the paper round and round in case the hand deluded him.

The magician paused in the act of shedding his silk shirt.

'I beg your pardon. I did not think. We write and speak to each other in German. I will translate.'

My dear one, I shall be absent for a few days. Do not worry about me. I shall explain when I return. My love to you, always. Alicia.

'When did the young lady write this, sir?'

Salvador said, rubbing his arms and chest thoughtfully, 'When she truly vanished, Inspector.'

Lintott had a mental vision of the magician walking to the footlights. His pause.

Salvador said, 'Alicia should have come out of the audience, and walked down the aisle. I passed a message backstage, thinking she was ill. They could tell me nothing. This letter was waiting for me when I came off.'

He began to cream the make-up from his face, emerging still paler and deeply concerned.

'I don't know anything about you or the young lady, you see, sir,' said Lintott, feeling his way. 'Is she your wife or your fiancée or just an assistant?'

'She is my sister, Inspector.'

So it was not a case of a lovers' quarrel, then.

'Your sister, sir. Is neither of you married? No? Nor has been, nor just going to be? No?' He stared again at the letter, recalling its contents. 'Have you relatives or friends here that might be taken suddenly ill, or anything of that sort? No? What nationality might you be, sir?'

For the first time since his performance that evening the magician smiled suddenly, radiantly, amused by the routine questions.

'We are, quite by chance, of different nationalities. We were born in the circus. Alicia in Vienna, I in Berlin. It could have been anywhere else, almost!'

'No fixed address, sir!' said Lintott slyly, and grinned to himself. 'So without any reason that you know of, and in the middle of a performance more or less, Miss Alicia disappears – leaving you a note that don't make sense?'

Salvador nodded, wiped his face, and dropped the soiled towel to the floor.

'Well, sir, I'd be inclined to think that there was a gentleman in the case, and she's hopped it for the time being.'

'No,' said Salvador emphatically.

'It must have been pretty important to take her off like this, sir,' said Lintott persuasively. 'Can you give me an idea of how close you were, how you worked together, whether there were any differences of opinion and so on?'

Salvador put his hands together gently.

'We were as close as that, Inspector. We quarrelled no more than these fingers quarrel. We had worked together since Alicia left school six years ago.'

'So the young lady is in her twenties, sir?' Lintott enquired delicately. 'She's bound to settle down sometime, then, ain't she? A man chooses whether he marries or he don't, but if a woman don't marry what else can she do?'

Salvador said, shivering, 'Where is my dressing-gown?'

'On a hook behind the door, sir. Shall I get it for you?'

Salvador cried, 'Fredo!'

A diminutive man popped his head round the *papier mâché* screen in one corner of the dressing-room. He bowed low to Lintott, who lifted his hat in acknowledgement. He swathed the magician in his cashmere gown, picked up the coat, shirt and towel, and left the room.

Salvador said, 'Fredo has been with us some few years. He is retired now. He was a clown, like our father. His wife Esmerelda is also with us. We take care of each other. Esmerelda was an equestrienne, like our mother. Then she told fortunes. She has the sight.'

Lintott's sense of humour came uppermost. He hadn't been far out in his remark to Lizzie. Gipsies!

'Well, then, sir, you're ahead of me!' Ironical. 'Your Mrs Esmerelda might see more in the crystal ball than I could in a heap of facts!'

Salvador said, 'You mock us, my friend. A vanishing lady is no mystery to me. A lady who truly vanishes is a great mystery to me – but not to you. When I speak of the sight I speak of another kind of truth.'

Sorrow and joy in that phial. By Jove, madam, you are absolutely and incredibly right!

'I understand you, sir,' said Lintott in a different tone, 'only it's out of my line, you see. I deal in the truth I know, not the other. But no offence meant and none given, I hope?' He consulted the letter, written in a foreign hand in a foreign language. 'Is this her writing? Yes. Might I see the young lady's dressing-room, please, sir?'

Dressed in decent black, the uniform of aged Latin women, Esmerelda was mounting guard, hands folded in her lap. Lintott nodded politely and looked round. An empty mirror, empty costumes, an empty hiss of gas in the globes.

'You've been here all evening, have you, ma'am? Yes. Did Miss Alicia come back at any time? No. Did you hear anybody in the corridor? Sounds of a struggle, anything of that sort?

56

No. Did she take any clothes with her that you know of? Have you noticed her carrying an overnight bag, a carpet bag, at any time recently?'

'Signor, I keep the wardrobe. I see everything. I know everything. All the time. If she leave this place she leave it in her stage clothes. Look!'

She indicated the green velvet dress on its hanger, a *directoire* coat of chinchilla with matching muff, a green velvet hat crowned with plumes.

'What about the clothes at the hotel, though,' Lintott pursued. 'She could have taken them without you knowing, couldn't she?'

'No and no, signor. Tonight at hotel I help her dress. I check everything, because of thiefs. I lock up. Here is key!'

'You're trying to tell me that the young lady mizzled on a raw January night in that flimsy Eastern outfit?' Lintott asked, amazed. They nodded. 'She must have had a cab waiting, sir. She could hardly walk about London in that rig. Either she organised that vanishing act of hers, or somebody else did. Has she ever run away before, sir?'

They were as indignant as though he had suggested she were insane. They spoke together, gesticulating: Esmerelda in Spanish, Salvador in German. They talked to each other, and at Lintott.

'One minute *if* you please!' he cried, raising his hands for silence. 'I'm only asking for facts. Does she do this sort of thing now and again?'

Cool and courteous once more, Salvador said, 'Alicia is a very unusual and delicate person. She is like a shadow. She is like my shadow. Without me she is nothing, she is lost. As my assistant she shows great talent of her own. You would agree? Of course. As a woman she fears men, except for me. I shelter her from life, always. Esmerelda and Fredo shelter her. With us she is herself, she is happy. Outside...?' He shrugged and spread out his hands, let them fall. 'Apart from these considerations she is loyal, she is professional. Yes?' Esmerelda nodded vigorously. 'She would never leave me in the middle of an engagement, of a performance. That is unthinkable.'

'I see,' said Lintott, musing. 'That puts a different complexion on the matter, certainly. And what about you, sir? Don't you have any interest in the fair sex? Have you never thought of getting married and so forth?'

'Why are we standing up?' asked the magician. He produced two bentwood chairs and made himself as comfortable as he could. 'I know what you suspect. You think I have fallen in love with a beautiful woman, that Alicia is jealous or afraid, that she runs away from this situation. Not true. I am a realist. I am also an artist. I do not endanger my work, my personal life, my freedom. I do not wish little children round my knee – I prefer them in the stalls, at a matinée!' Smiling at his own joke. 'No, no, no, Inspector. What has happened to my sister I cannot imagine. But I tell you this. She has been taken away, suddenly, even forcibly. I wish you to find out the rest. I will pay. I will pay well.'

'She feared evil,' Esmerelda murmured. 'She foresee great evil.'

Lintott said sharply, 'You're talking of abduction, sir, is that right?'

Salvador nodded, and his nod was repeated by the old woman.

'This note don't give that impression, sir. It implies, reading between the lines, as she wants you to leave well alone.'

'But I know better,' cried Salvador, 'and I leave nothing alone!'

'Then call in the police,' Lintott advised, cool and factual. 'If she's been abducted they'll endeavour to find her, and charge whoever took her with that crime. If she's run off with a young man – which is what I think – then they'll find the pair of them and fetch them back. The police, sir, will help you.'

Salvador said, 'But you are a policeman, and of a great office, Inspector.'

'I was,' Lintott replied. 'Now I'm in a private capacity. That

58

don't make me official, you see, sir. Hand this over to the Yard, that's my advice.'

The magician cried, 'No!' Then, more gently, 'No, my friend. Alicia's life and mine are private, our work is very public. I will not have either of them violated by an official police force. When I sent for you I sent quickly, but I sent most surely, because I trust you, because I know inside myself that you can help us.'

'I still think it's a storm in a teapot, sir,' said Lintott kindly, 'but I'll do what I can. Now what I must know, if you'll explain it nice and straightforward, is how that Vanishing Act works.'

The magician's face changed yet again.

'My friend, it would be unethical to disclose the secrets of my profession, as no doubt you will understand. Your own profession will have its secrets.'

Lintott rubbed his head and then his chin.

'Well, sir,' he began, 'in that case you must do as I do and give me a bit of a hint here and there. Number one question is – where was Miss Alicia when you started that trick?'

The magician raised a long hand.

'My friend, I repeat. Alicia should have appeared from the audience immediately after I vanished her.'

'I see,' said Lintott. 'Can you tell me how long she had been off-stage, then?'

'Yes,' said Salvador, delighted to oblige. 'She has a rest of almost twenty minutes, after her personal performance. She is tired. She needs to gain strength. For twenty minutes I work alone. Then – the Vanishing Lady!'

'Where does she go during that interval, sir?'

'She come here,' Esmerelda cried.

'Then you *did* see her, ma'am, during the evening?'

'Not then. She must be alone then. For that time, until I dress her, I sit with Fredo, with my husband. I do not see her then.'

Lintott surveyed her grimly. He did like witnesses who dealt with facts instead of personal truths. He contented himself with one brief observation.

'So you weren't here *all* the evening, like you said, ma'am?'

Her feminine logic confounded him.

'I am in theatre all evening. I am here when I am here.'

Lintott left it at that, knowing when he was beaten. He returned to facts.

'So the young lady comes here, to be *alone*,' with a stern glance for Esmerelda, 'and *is* alone for twenty minutes, or near enough. That's sufficient time, sir, for composing a note – where was it found? On her dressing-table! Exactly! Perhaps the young man had a cloak, or a change of warm clothes, with him. He had a cab waiting somewhere. He got her out somehow, wrapped up in something no one would recognise. It stands to reason,' said Lintott, nodding at the velvet and chinchilla coat, 'that a garment like that would be seen a mile off! They wanted to keep things quiet and keep them dark. Then – they mizzle!'

'I do not know your young man,' said Salvador coldly. 'Her abductor, can he take her away without a struggle, without noise? Can he make her write me this note which is supposed to keep me silent?'

'It's possible, sir,' Lintott replied. 'If you've got a knife at your throat you do a number of things as you wouldn't normally consider!'

His tone was dry, suggesting that the magician was unduly fanciful. Then one wild notion married with another in his mind.

'Wait a minute,' cried Lintott, 'I'll be forgetting my own name next! I wanted a word with you, sir, about another matter. Do you know a man called Bela Barak? Big man, dark, clean-shaven. Very rich. Rich as Croesus! American. No?' He shook his head from side to side, baffled. 'Well, he's got it in for you, sir. What about San Francisco? That's where he comes from. Does San Francisco ring a bell, sir? You've been there, a-touring, but that's all? Oh!' Deflated. He brightened. 'Do you know of a man called Hank Fleischer. Scarred face, the scar looks like a knife-fight. American, like his master. Nasty piece of work. Carries a gun. 'Yes,' remembering his sudden coldness as Fleischer's hand flicked into the breast of his jacket, 'carries a gun and don't mind using it!'

Salvador said, 'I know neither of them, Inspector, but I have casual enemies – those envious of me. For the moment, I wish you to find my sister.'

'Sir,' said Lintott deliberately, for the idea was stirring a number of speculations, 'do you recollect Miss Alicia having one of her – sights – that first matinée I was at? There was a wealthy lady sitting in the box, and she scarpered as soon as your sister hollered out about Fire!'

Esmerelda commented rapidly in her own tongue. Salvador translated.

'Alicia foresaw great evil. The flight of the dove disturbed her. Not the lady, whoever she was. Alicia saw flames leaping.'

'But that lady was Mrs Barak, and she mizzled as fast as she could. And that Fleischer was in the theatre, keeping an eye on Mrs B. I dare say.'

'But we do not know them,' said Salvador, patiently, finally.

Lintott pondered, smote his knees with his bowler hat thoughtfully, and prepared to take his leave.

'Sir,' he said, 'would it be all right by you if I made a few enquiries on my own account, as well as yours? I've got a hunch as might be worth following through, with regard to your sister.'

'Do as you think best, Inspector, of course.'

They had had enough time to realise that she was gone, and sat in silence together, forgetting Lintott. He nodded once or twice in sympathy, and got up.

Suddenly there seemed to be another person in the room. A gold and silver costume, stirred by the night wind, filled and moved as though it clothed someone.

'I should shut that window at the top!' said Lintott loudly. 'You can catch a cold, sitting in a draught.' No answer. 'I'll be off then, sir and ma'am.'

They showed no sign of hearing him. A pale gown on the

back of the door swayed towards him like a living thing. Lintott stood in the corridor, collecting himself, heart thumping. Then he walked quickly between the pools of gaslight.

Silence in the vacant passages. Silence on the vacant stage. Silence in the vacant auditorium. Silence.

He turned a corner. Shouting, running footsteps, white wings beating in his face. He cried out, and covered his eyes.

'Sorry, sir,' said a breathless voice. 'It's that ruddy dove of Mr Salvador's again. The lid of its basket must be loose. I'd wring its blasted neck for two pins! Come back here, you little bleeder! Ah, now I've got you, ain't I?' The boy was friendly, confiding. 'Flew right in your face, he did. Sorry, sir. It must have give you a start.'

'No harm done,' Lintott replied, watching the white feathers imprisoned.

'*You* give me a start, too,' said the boy. 'I was on you afore I saw you.'

'Ah! Creepy places ... theatres ... at night.'

SIX

LINTOTT'S QUESTIONING OF theatre staff and cabbies had been almost perfunctory. He trusted his hunches, and had sniffed and padded round the house in Charles Street, Mayfair, until he discovered that it no longer housed Bela Barak and his entourage. Now, unobtrusive and benevolent, he made his way to the back door and knocked.

'A very good morning to you, my dear,' he said to the pretty housemaid, and doffed his hat. 'I ain't a tradesman nor a bailiff!' Smiling broadly. 'My business is on the delicate side, concerning a matter I was looking into for Mr Barak afore he sailed. Inspector Lintott is the name, late of Scotland Yard.'

'Please to come in, sir. Mrs Post, it's a police inspector.'

'And would Mrs Post be that talented lady as produced that royal banquet here a couple of weeks or so ago?' Lintott enquired, beaming. He knew perfectly well that she could not have been responsible for that scale of catering, but pursued his own line of flattery. 'I only have to smell a kitchen, ma'am, to recognise an artist in the culinary line!'

A skeleton staff if ever I saw one, he thought.

The cook bridled with pleasure and indignation.

'You'd best send your compliments to them French chefs, then!' she observed tartly. 'I wasn't considered fancy enough, though nothing but good food ever left my hands, I can tell you. Mr Smailes'll say the same.'

63

'I haven't had the honour of your acquaintance, sir,' said Lintott, shaking hands with a very old butler. 'Another gentleman let me in last time.'

Mrs Post pursed her lips and shook her head, to indicate that this should hardly be mentioned but they would take it very kindly if the Inspector remarked upon it.

'You don't mean...?' said Lintott, horrified.

'Hired their own staff!' cried the cook. 'And Mr Smailes, as has always opened that front door – *his* front door I might almost say – sat in this kitchen like a blessèd dummy! We was treated like deaf monkeys!'

Mr Smailes had a natural tremble of the head anyway. His efforts to convey assent reminded Lintott of a rocking-horse in motion.

'Dear, dear, dear, dear!' he said, and tutted disbelief.

'They *had* to hire footmen and that,' said the housemaid. She had liked one of the footmen. 'But to fetch folks over the heads of Mrs Post and Mr Smailes...'

'Hardly bears thinking about,' said Lintott.

He was in. Sitting at the kitchen table, smiling sympathetically round the circle of injured faces. He had chosen his time well. The house was between rentals, and they had only themselves to look after.

'Now I know a bit about French chefs,' said Lintott. 'Thankee, I will have a cup of tea. Are these biscuits made by your own fair hands, ma'am? Then I can't resist 'em! Yes, ma'am, I have wined and dined in Paris. And the best place I went to was about half the size of this here kitchen, and run by a fine figure of a woman like yourself, Mrs Post.' Delectable proofs of her talent lay in a handsome steak and kidney pie on the dresser, a lordly chocolate cake, and the persistent tap of a steamed pudding against the bottom of a saucepan. 'Honest food, well-cooked, ma'am. Nothing beats it. But, Lord love you, these rich folks can't eat a morsel unless it's covered in aspic jelly and paper frills! They can't help it, ma'am – more to be pitied than blamed. Thankee, I will have another cup – and another biscuit. Melt in your mouth, they do. Am I hindering you, ma'am? I shouldn't like to do that.'

'No, no,' she assured him. 'We take a quarter-hour this time of day.'

'More than enough for what I've got to say, ma'am. You'll excuse me mentioning as this is confidential? Quite so! Well, to cut a long story in quarters, Mr Barak engaged me in a private matter. Like you, ma'am, I give nobody less than my best, and most people consider it good enough...' The cook leaned forward and sugared his tea lavishly. 'I wouldn't say this if I didn't know you had an understanding nature,' said Lintott heavily, 'but Mr Barak, though a liberal gentleman, treated me the same way he treated you – he fetched somebody else in to finish my job for me!'

Mrs Post nodded at her staff, vindicated.

'What did I say to you girls? Didn't I use them very words myself?'

They chorused assent, smoothing their aprons, touching neat hair under frilled caps.

'While the Honourable Mr Fawcett lived here,' said the cook, flushed with outrage, 'he relied on me, sir, absolute. But being obliged to live quiet, along of a heart condition, he don't come up from the country now. So he rents this house out. And the *noovy rich* rag, tag and bobtail as we've all had to put up with is past belief!'

'Now I don't like to name names,' Lintott continued, after a respectful pause, 'so I'll put it as delicate as I can. My enquiry was concerning a young woman in her twenties, fair hair, dark eyes, small and quiet, a bit on the unusual side. If I've said too much, ma'am,' said Lintott, taking up his hat, 'I'll leave this minute, and beg your pardon for troubling you.'

'Why, that's Mrs Fleischer,' said Nellie, the housemaid. 'They found her, sir, on the Friday night afore they sailed on the Saturday.'

'You was looking for her, too, was you, sir?' the cook asked, curious.

Lintott nodded. 'A sad case, ma'am, but then you don't need telling...'

The cook tapped her forehead, eyebrows raised. Lintott inclined his head.

'How did they get her here?' he asked.

Mr Smailes cleared his throat, and everyone turned to look at him.

'Mr Fleischer went out alone with the carriage at a half after seven, sir. Mr and Mrs Barak was at the theatre, and he said he would be back afore ten, and I was to have Billie with me when I answered the door to him.

'That's me,' said the boot-boy, tapping his chest.

Mr Smailes trembled so much at this interruption that Lintott feared he would never recover his speech.

'Thankee, sir. Very precise. Perhaps Billie'll tell me the next part?'

The boot-boy stood to attention and addressed the copper saucepans on the far wall.

'Mr Fleischer was in the carriage, with his arm round the young woman you mentioned, sir. He said she was his wife, and she warn't to be seen because she had strange fancies about folk looking at her. He said to help him bring her in, and fetch Nellie, and make sure as the coast was clear.'

'Very good, my lad. Now, Nellie, what happened?'

'She was a-sitting on a chair in the hall, with her head down – so,' and Nellie imitated the droop. 'I spoke very soft to her, and Mr Fleischer took one arm and I took the other, and we helped her upstairs.'

'Did she seem sleepy? On the faint side?'

'No, sir. She just seemed to be like froze up.'

'And what was she wearing, my love?'

'Like a fancy costume. A fancy Eastern costume. *He* said I was to burn it, and he wanted me to find clothes as she could travel in. I was much her height and build. I brought out my best, and he paid me handsome, sir.'

'Did the lady say anything to you at any time?'

'Not a syllable, sir. Mr Fleischer said as she'd given him the slip when they arrived from America, and he'd been looking for her ever since.'

Lintott accepted another biscuit, and broke it thoughtfully.

'Who looked after her during the night, my dear?'

'I suppose he did. She was his wife. She was put in a guest room, and I was sent off. I didn't see her again until he asked me to help her to dress, early the next morning. They left afore Mr and Mrs Barak – though they must have been catching the same boat.'

Lintott took out his notebook and pencil, pondering.

'How did she seem the next morning, my love?'

'Just the same. It was like dressing a wooden doll.'

'Let me see, now,' tapping his teeth with the pencil, 'Mr Barak was here from ... where did I write that date?'

'Mr Barak come just afore Christmas, but Mr Fleischer was here in November,' said Billie quickly, anxious to impress.

'*He* gives me the creeps,' said Nellie involuntarily.

There was an embarrassed, frightened silence, which Lintott broke.

'It's the scar, my dear,' said Lintott comfortably, 'but that ain't his fault, you know. So he was here by himself, and then Mr and Mrs Barak came?'

'Mrs Barak come later still,' cried Billie, braving Mrs Post's dreadful stare. 'I went in the carriage to fetch her and that French maid and the luggage.'

'Where from?' asked Lintott, alert.

'Claridge's, sir. And she'd been there a good while, too. Mr Fleischer was settling the bill while I picked their bags and trunks up. She'd been there since October.'

'Mr Barak thought a lot about her,' said Lintott, fishing.

'She didn't think as much about him,' quavered Mr Smailes, 'for all her smiling. And though they made up some story about her coming over for the autumn shopping, I didn't take no notice of that! No, no, sir. They'd had a regular old dust-up, I think, and she'd flounced off without him. That was why he sent that other – that – after her, and then followed her himself as soon as he could!' He sucked his teeth, reflecting. 'Yes, sir. Folks don't pay this sort of a rent at short notice unless they're in a hurry for a good address. He wanted it to

67

look right. That was why he give her that reception. Vulgar! I never in all my born days see – such – trash – under this roof.' He was garrulous now, his head trembling, one hand pointing heavenwards. 'And what I say, sir, summing up, is – *noovy rich*, sir. *Noovy rich!*'

'Sharp as a needle, Mr Smailes,' said Lintott, head on one side, admiring him. 'So you think they didn't get on, then? He seemed very lovey-dovey with her, the few minutes I saw him.'

'Ah, but why?' Mrs Post chimed in. 'For why? That's what I say. Men can be lovey-dovey for more reasons than one. He was more worried than he was fond, I can tell you. That scarred tom-cat was a-following her when Mr Barak was away and she went out alone. Shudder! Didn't I shudder, Mr Smailes? Then that poor little wet cat of a Mrs Fleischer turning up. I had my own ideas about her, I can tell you. Oh, yes. If she was mental then he drove her to it, I'll swear. And *secretive*. There was something more to that sitivation than any of us knows!' And she nodded many times.

'Well, well, well,' said Lintott, smiling, reaching for his hat, 'here I am wasting everybody's time and enjoying myself into the bargain. I must be off!'

They were genuinely sorry to see him go.

'Oh, there's just one thing,' said Lintott, pausing at the back door, 'it would be best for all concerned if you forgot I'd been here this morning!' He nodded gravely, and set his bowler portentously on his head. 'I'll just tell you this much – as we've been so friendly and comfortable together – it's an International Matter!' He gave them time to digest this vague threat. 'Now we don't want the Honourable Mr Fawcett dragged into this by the Foreign Office, do we? Poor gentleman, it might be the death of him! And then where would *you* all be? If I was to advise you as a friend, I'd say – don't even talk of this among yourselves!'

They nodded their heads in unison, completely bewildered by this sudden change of circumstances.

'That's all right then,' said Lintott. 'I'll say good-day to you all!'

They did not speak for fully five minutes after he had left. The women were very pale, Mr Smailes seemed stricken by a palsy, and the scullery maid was found crying in the pantry.

SEVEN

AT THE CAPTAIN'S TABLE talk of nothing ebbed and flowed idly, pleasantly. Attention focused on the white shoulders of Francesca Barak, who ate little but very prettily, and seemed unconscious of the effect of her beauty. Her husband was conscious of this impermanent asset, and garnered the compliments paid to her as so much paper money: worth its value if the market held, otherwise nothing.

The Captain, who prided himself on looking like a twin brother of King Teddy, smoothed his beard and moustaches and bent towards Francesca gallantly. He trusted she was comfortable in her state rooms, aboard his ship? Oh, surely, she said. He hoped, being a democratic man, that the Baraks' personal entourage was also comfortable, in a lesser degree and on a lower deck though they were. Why, surely, she said. He smiled in desperation, drank his soup, and enquired as to her interests. His own wife, he added deprecatingly, was extremely fond of needlework and water-colour painting.

'I just love horse-riding,' said Francesca, and became animated in a moment. 'I am simply crazy about horses. When we get back to San Francisco my husband has promised to buy me the most beautiful horse in the world.'

'That is kind of an exaggerated statement,' said Bela Barak, not displeased by it, 'but she shall have what she wants, whatever it costs.'

Murmurs of envy, of appreciation, from the other guests, soothed him. Francesca smiled and smiled: ravishing, passive. The Captain bent towards the millionaire now, in his role as courteous host. Often he did not listen to what he was saying, so busy was he with matters of importance, but this tediousness at his table was a necessity.

'Your – secretary, is it? Mr Fleischer. I hope his wife is recovering? I asked Mrs Macey, one of our most obliging ladies, to attend to Mrs Fleischer personally. Of course, in a private suite she will be entirely free from any intrusion. Mrs Macey is a very tactful and understanding person. As a senior stewardess, of course....'

'Thank you, sir, I believe that has been attended to. You are most kind!'

The manner of his reply silenced further conversation in that direction. Francesca filled in the chasm by, metaphorically, leaping it.

'I hope to buy a Palomino,' she said, in that soft honeyed drawl which bespoke her Virginian origins. 'I believe they are surely the most beautiful horses in the world.'

'The Arab, though...' hazarded the Captain, who knew nothing about horses but wished to amuse or provoke.

'I would not question your judgement, sir,' she replied, though her next words belied that statement, 'but I was referring to the *colour* of the Palomino, and of course you are talking of a *breed* of horse.'

'Of course, madam,' he said hastily. 'Certainly.'

He was saved by another guest who held forth on the merits of the Hanoverian horses. Francesca listened attentively, answered intelligently, ceded to him enchantingly.

'But you are a gen'l'man, sir, and I think of the Hanoverian as a gen'l'man's horse. I like a showy mare, myself, with kind of a feminine temper.'

Her husband listened, darkly delighted by her command of the situation, jealous of the masculine eyes and admiration. An English lady, daughter of a Duke so it was rumoured, joined in with passionate praise of the thoroughbreds.

'...all descended from three Arabian sires. So you have your Arab qualities there, Captain!' He was flattered. 'And your Hanoverians benefited from a shot of English thoroughbred, early in the last century, sir!' The gentleman bowed. 'But the Palomino I know little about!' she concluded.

'They are very popular in California,' said Francesca, with that deceptive sweetness of tone. 'I understand they are descended from Spanish horses, that is of Moorish or Saracen stock. But my father bred Irish horses, and he preferred...'

Barak did not regard the evening meal as worthy of all his wife's diamonds, so this evening she shone most simply in a few of them. The restraint she imposed on herself was evident in the difference between her tone and her expression. An observant person would have seen that she considered the Captain's table a dull place, but she spoke appreciation of it. She was immensely kind to the English lady, who was plain; and demurely aware of the German gentleman's superior knowledge. Now and again the spirit flared forth, to be quenched.

'Can you imagine,' she was crying, 'the movement and colour? Oh, I shall have a chestnut horse with a silver mane and tail, and we shall ride!'

'Honey,' Barak chided, 'there are other interests in life besides a Palomino!'

'Oh, surely,' she replied, and reverted to silent beauty.

She was thinking about Mr Fleischer's wife, who had been removed from the conversation also. She knew better than to ask her husband the identity of this unknown woman on board ship.

Alicia crouched at the cabin door and listened at the keyhole. The feminine voice which was whispering questions had a French accent. Alicia spoke then in French, and the voice warmed, but curiosity rather than compassion ruled the conversation.

'Who are you, madame?'

'I am forbidden to give my name. I am forbidden to speak to anyone. Please go away. You cannot help me.'

72

'Are you his wife? This Fleischer's wife?'

'Bad things happen to my brother if I say anything. Please go away.'

'But if this Fleischer is harming you I can tell madame, Madame Barak. She will tell her husband to make him behave.'

'He is not harming me, except by taking me with him. I must go with him and say nothing to anybody. I must not ask for help. Please.'

Alicia heard the voice on the other side of the door ask itself rapidly whether this Fleischer was capable of passion, a hidden passion. Then it applied itself again to the keyhole.

'You speak French like a native, madame. Are you French?'

'I belong nowhere in particular, madame. French is one of the five languages I speak. Leave me, madame. Forget me, please.'

'But I would help you!'

Alicia said, 'No one can help me. I shall go with him and say nothing. I shall do as he says. Then my brother is safe from him. Goodbye, madame.'

The pause held pity in its silence. Then there were sounds of a rustling dress, a sigh, a creaking of taffeta petticoat.

'Goodbye, madame. I appoint myself your friend. I shall try to speak with you again. If he ill-treats you I shall tell Madame Barak. She has influence.'

'I beg you, say nothing. I am not ill-treated – except that he takes me with him. Madame, where are we going?'

'First to New York. Then by railroad to San Francisco.'

The voice of Alicia changed, and Genevieve stooped to hear the whispers.

'What a long time ago. How can he remember so well? Of course I must pay. That is right. So he can be free. Say nothing. Say nothing...'

'Madame!' sharply, in a thin whistle through the keyhole, 'are you well?'

'Please go away!' said Alicia in her normal tone.

This time her request was answered.

*　　*　　*

'For heaven's sakes, Genevieve,' cried Francesca, 'this is awful! I shall speak to my husband about this.'

'But how will you speak without telling him of me? Think, madame!'

'Now don't you fret, Genevieve. I can be real cunning when I try!'

'Madame, we have already erred in his eyes, you and I. I beg you to be cautious. He is...' and she attempted to describe the power and terror of Barak, '...a proud man.'

'Genevieve, there have been misunderstandings between us recently, and that I surely admit. But look how he treats me now, like a queen. I only have to ask, that's what he said the other night. Ask me for anything, he said, and I'll reach out for it, whatever it costs!'

'You said I could ask you anything, Bel! Well, now I'm asking, honey.'

He brooded over his lighted cigar, while she stood as though posing for a portrait of domestic bliss: one small hand on his shoulder, pretty head held on one side, her gown flowering from her waist.

'Honey,' he said, encircling that waist, 'it began a long time ago, and Hank Fleischer is not a guy who forgets easily. Sure, I knew he was bringing her with him. I know when Hank draws breath! But I can promise you this, honey – no harm is coming to that girl. She has to go through with it, that's all, and she was unable to do that where she was. Circumstances. Influences. You know? What I want to say to you is that this is Hank's business, and therefore my business in a way, and it's all been taken care of. Okay, honey?'

She said, only partially satisfied, 'I never thought of Hank Fleischer as a romantic sort of person, Bel.'

'It's deeper than romance,' said Barak, 'one hell of a lot deeper – pardon me. That's why I repeat, no harm is intended. She just has to go through with this, and then it will be settled one way or the other. Right?'

'Well – right!' she drawled softly, and smiled like payment.

'And then, come here a minute, honey – then I'll tell you all about it, shall I?'

She said, disturbed by the smiling darkness of his face, 'Shall I like it?'

'Oh, you'll just love it, honey. Like I did!'

He enfolded the jewels and fine fashion he had paid for in an embrace that was more desperate than loving. She was passive, even kind. It was like holding mist: the arms closing on nothing.

'Honey,' he cried, 'tell me anything in the world you want. I'll buy it for you, honey!'

EIGHT

Monday evening, 22 January 1906

THE MAGICIAN HAD BEEN about to put on his evening face when
Lintott announced his news. Now he sat very still, and laid the
stick of greasepaint down. Behind him in the glass stood the
grey and stocky messenger of bad tidings, waiting for comments or orders.

'Please to sit down, sir,' said Esmerelda, and Fredo brought
forward a chair as though it had been a throne, and Lintott were
king.

Finally Salvador said to himself, 'Fleischer? Fleischer? I
know nothing of him, nothing of such a man. I do not know
this Bela Barak!' Then he shouted, 'I know nothing of anyone.
I know nothing. Nothing!' And with one blow of his great
hand he swept the rickety dressing-table clear of its contents.
He said to the shocked magician in the mirror, 'I do not understand.'

Fredo ventured to say quietly, '*Illustrissimo*, the performance
begins in half an hour. You must grieve later.'

For another minute or so Salvador sat motionless, then he
nodded. Lintott gave him an answering nod of encouragement. Fredo began to collect the pots and boxes and re-arrange
them on the table. Esmerelda brushed the magician's velvet
coat, shook out his silk shirt.

'Where is that fool Celeste?' Salvador asked, very calm and
cold.

'She is sitting in the lady's dressing-room, wearing the lady's costume, *Illustrissimo*,' answered the little man.

He lifted his chin, patted his hair, minced forward a few paces, stretched out his arms and simpered at an invisible audience.

'Ah, yes. Thank you for reminding me of that supreme impertinence,' said Salvador. 'Tell her that no one is to blame for lack of talent, but a pretty face and a pretty smile are not art. Therefore she will remain in the background, will impede me no more than necessary, and will *not* presume to take the curtain with me.'

Fredo bowed, delighted.

'If she attempts to argue, dismiss her!'

The ex-clown came amazingly to life. He mimed Salvador's message, a broken Celeste stumbling out into a cruel world, and the magician left without a stage assistant. Lintott could not help himself, and chuckled roundly. Fredo bowed, hand on breast, wrinkled face alight. Salvador drew a long quiet breath, and smiled wryly. He leaned forward and found Salvador, resplendent in the glass. He turned to his audience of three for approval. Master of the occasion once more, he adjusted his cuffs, set his top hat on his head and flourished his cane.

'My friend,' he said to Lintott, 'I shall speak with you later, if you please! Esmerelda, tonight I shall be brilliant! Fredo, tell that creature who has made an art of incompetence that I am ready!'

They lingered over their brandy, while the sleepy waiter yawned.

'Villains are my profession like magic is yours, sir,' Lintott was saying. 'Now I dare say that you could walk into a theatre and judge the quality of another magician, or his assistant, couldn't you? You might never have seen them afore, nor ever meet them again, but you could give a fair summary, shall we say?' His weariness, the excellent dinner, the warmth of brandy, had loosened his tongue and set free his thoughts.

'Well, I'm the same about the wrong 'uns, sir. I know a criminal when I meet one, whether he wears a dinner-suit or not, whether he's done time or not. I've met Bela Barak and Hank Fleischer. All the money in the world won't hide Barak from my judgement. And all the guns in the world don't alter my opinion of Hank Fleischer. Villains, sir. Criminals.

'Criminals! They work against society, outside of it, but they're folk like ourselves. Rich, middling and poor. Clever and stupid. Good-natured and ill-tempered. Some of 'em have a code of honour. You'll find craftsmen among them, taking as much pride in picking a lock as an honest locksmith takes in making it. You find gentlemen and artists as have a style of their own. All sorts, just like us. And now and again they'll produce a genius, and he's the worst of the lot. He puts up a posh façade, as you can't fault, and runs his show behind it. You might know what he is but you can't prove it. You can catch a few of his naughty lads, but they daren't squeal. You can spoil a brew as he's cooking up, but he's got many a pot on the boil. He'll be rich, but money don't matter. Most criminals are motivated by greed. He's motivated by power.

'He's the Devil, if you like, playing God Almighty, and since none of us is supposed to fly that high he's dangerous in consequence. Dangerous and a bit cracked. There's no law but his law. If you do what he wants then he thinks that's right, and he pays you. If you don't then that's wrong, and he punishes you.

'I saw Bela Barak for a matter of minutes, and most of the time that scarred Fleischer was speaking for him. But I don't miss much, sir. Not a gesture, not a word, not a change of countenance. Oh, Fleischer is Barak's finger, and he moves when Barak says *move*. But the real villain is Barak, and I don't care if he's a millionaire thirty times over, sir, he *is* a villain. I know. I've met him.'

A brief silence ensued.

'You are unusually eloquent, my friend,' said Salvador gravely.

'Words find themselves, sometimes,' Lintott replied, embarrassed. He cleared his throat. 'Anyway, sir, this Fleischer took a fancy to your sister, whether she fancies him or not – and, excuse me saying so, a delicate-minded young woman like Miss Alicia might find him rather a dashing proposition! Now Barak helped him over this matter, because he had me to the house in Charles Street to offer me a bribe of five hundred dollars – whatever that might be...'

'One hundred pounds, my friend.'

'Thankee. Offered me that sum in order to challenge you with a pair of handcuffs that was riveted!'

'He was a fool!'

'He was indeed, sir. I don't take bribes, nor play dirty tricks.'

'He was a fool because I should have discovered they were riveted, and publicly denounced you as a fraud, Inspector. The newspapers would have been very glad of that little scandal, and I should have used the publicity.'

'Damn me!' said Lintott, temporarily thrown off course. 'I was thinking of you struggling for hours, not me in the Sunday papers!'

'Aha!' said Salvador, eyes gleaming.

Lintott remembered that gleam: green and gold, knowing just a little more than the person at whom it was so amicably directed. Then he took up his point again doggedly.

'But, excuse me, sir, it would have taken you some time to find out.'

'Oh, yes, indeed. A few minutes.'

'And is Miss Alicia on-stage at the time?'

'No. She is off-stage until the next illusion, when she assists me.'

'So, plenty of opportunity, sir, to whisk her away while you're struggling with a pair of riveted handcuffs?'

There was a pause, then Salvador said finally, 'To vanish the lady truly was a clever feat. Timing, speed, unobtrusive planning. He must have watched us.'

Lintott hesitated only for a moment.

'Sir, now you mention that, could it have been done without Miss Alicia's co-operation?'

'You are seriously thinking that she went with this creature of her own accord? That she abetted him in this monstrous abduction?'

The magician's gleam was now hostile, but Lintott had borne hostility towards himself and his profession many times. And, as he frequently said, any fool could be popular. So he continued to arouse Salvador's anger, and draw conclusions, and remain bland of tone and expression.

'I'm asking you, sir. You're the expert. Could he have done it alone?'

'It is possible. In any case I know that she did not betray me and her professional commitment.'

'Excuse me, sir, but nobody can know anything at this stage. We can only speculate. The young lady may have been put in a position where she couldn't help but let you and herself down, whatever she felt.'

'In what way, Inspector Lintott? Waiter! Coffee, if you please. More coffee! In what way do you mean?'

'Where did you say she was at school, sir? Switzerland! You saw her in the holidays then, I dare say? No? You were travelling about. I understand. When did she leave school? At the age of eighteen. Yes. You knew little enough about her then, until what – five or six years ago?'

'I know her as I know myself!' cried Salvador.

'How well *do* you know yourself, sir? Excuse me, but I'm trying to find the truth, you see.' And as Salvador stayed silent, contemplating the end of his cigar, Lintott said, 'She may well have had some kind of courtship, or a girlish love affair, even a girlish elopement or a few days of clandestine marriage. She wouldn't tell you. She'd try to put it behind her, to forget it. I'm only speculating, sir, no need to take it so personal! But he could have come back, couldn't he? Perhaps he even loves her in his way. I wouldn't care for him myself except locked up in a good cell with a long sentence afore him, but women are different. They even love the worst of us, find reasons. Don't they? You have a high opinion of Miss Alicia, haven't you, sir? Yes. I dare say she treasures that opinion, and don't want to lose it. Suppose this Fleischer turns up and lays claim to her? Suppose he says he'll tell you about it if she don't come along with him?' He shed his persuasiveness and asked suddenly, 'Under conditions like that, sir, what would she do?'

Salvador said, as though the words were drawn from him like teeth, 'She might well go, without taking leave of me. That is possible.' Then he said, 'I do not care what she has done. I wish her only to come back. I wish to employ you, Inspector, to bring her back for me. I will pay.'

I don't mind how expensive you come, but I mind like hell when you cross me.

'You're up against two of them, you see, sir,' said Lintott. 'Master and man. Besides, they ain't hopped it to Brighton, nor even to Scotland. They're over the other side of the ocean. Pay? That's the least of it!'

He found his pipe and filled it, unaware of the drowsy waiter's frown. Troubled, he mused aloud, eyes narrowing as he pursued his thoughts.

'Ah! Barak's fly, sir, very fly. He can make a fool of you to your face. Worse, he hits where it hurts most and lets you know he did it. Only the clue leads to a blind alley, and the evidence is circumstantial, and the verdict is not proven. That's what you're up against.'

Salvador's eyes, gold and green, did not leave the Inspector's face as he puffed vigorously at his pipe.

'How did he punish you for disobeying him, my friend?' he asked gently.

'There now,' said Lintott in astonishment, 'if I ain't broke bowl from stem on my old pipe!' He looked at the two pieces and laid them absently on a plate. He said quietly, 'What did he do? He had my Bessie, my wife, pushed in front of an omnibus. I did what was right, so he wronged me and her. He wronged us. And I shan't forget until they close my eyes and put a penny on each of 'em.'

Then he was silent, the warmth of the brandy gone.

'Has he no weaknesses?' asked Salvador. 'This Barak, is he invulnerable?'

Lintott folded his square hands one on top of the other, and pondered them.

'His strength is his weakness, sir,' he said at last. 'He runs two lives, you see. One looks very nice and the other is very nasty, but they both cost a mint of money which he has to make. I saw that reception of his. They had cigarettes as was rolled up in bank notes. Now you have to spread yourself out very far and dig yourself in very deep to spend on that scale. So there's plenty of territory to go at, and somewhere in that territory is a fault. Men like Bela Barak have a mort of enemies to bring them to justice, in the end.'

Salvador smiled and observed and pursued.

'What is your definition of justice, my friend?'

Lintott ruminated, sighed, rubbed his eyes and head.

'Justice is more than the law, sir, though the law administers justice. There are strange ways of bringing it about, and sometimes it happens in a way you couldn't have planned. It's personal, too, sir. Each man carries his own justice with him. I've done a few things in my time, I don't mind admitting, which ain't exactly the letter of the law. But they were always a form of justice, sir.' He looked up, slightly embarrassed. 'I'd best be going!'

'You must take a cab home, my friend,' said the magician, producing a sovereign from Lintott's lapel, 'but come back to see me when you have made up your mind. I am perfectly serious. I wish you to sail with me on the seventeenth of February for New York. I wish you to find Alicia, to discover why she left with this Fleischer, to bring her back if possible. I know, though I cannot prove it, that she wants to return to me.'

'Sir, I am a family man. I have my poor Bessie in hospital, and my younger daughter at home that's quarrelled with her husband. I've enough worry and responsibility of my own without trailing across the world to find more. I'm sorry, sir, but there it is, plain and straight like me.'

The magician lifted his hand as Lintott began to rise from his chair.

'Please, my friend. Listen to me a few more moments. If I could wave my magic wand over your domestic problems would you come with me? Think. You are now free of worry, I am taking care of expenses.'

Lintott shook his head.

'Then what has become of that justice you represent, of that personal justice you carry with you?' Salvador asked, very pale. 'My sister has been wronged, perhaps because she was young and foolish as you say. I would have been wronged in public, if they had had their way. Your innocent wife is wronged, and you are wronged through her. I offer you the chance to see justice done, but you are not interested. You are eloquent, Inspector Lintott, but you are a magician only in words – your programme is empty and lacking in enterprise!'

Lintott said gravely, 'You won't jounce me into action that road, sir. Though I see your point of view.' They sat in silence for a few moments, then Lintott continued, 'I'd like to see justice done, but I'm on my own nowadays. I used to have Scotland Yard behind me, and the government behind them. That's the measure of power you'd need to bring somebody like Bela Barak and his bully-boy to justice. America is a big country, by all accounts, and I'd be a stranger there – which don't help, neither. But, supposing I was free of worry, free to go, I could probably turn up a few facts about Miss Alicia. I might even trace her and do some sort of deal for you with Fleischer. I promise nothing, sir, except trouble! And it'll be dangerous, too, my Lord yes! If he can get away with near-murder in broad daylight in the streets of London, what can he do over there? That's my opinion of the situation, sir.'

They were both silent for a few moments.

Then Lintott said, 'You'd be best advised to fetch in the official authorities, sir. I can't make you, Lord knows, but they've got the connections and the power as I haven't.'

'I have told you, my friend, that I will not allow a public intrusion on our private lives. I require your justice, not theirs.'

'We'll see about that!' said Lintott to himself.

Salvador smiled, offered him a cigar, more brandy, more coffee. Lintott refused, saying, 'Let's get on with the facts, sir!' rather firmly, for he had been hurt.

'Very well, my friend. First, I accept your opinion. Second, I am content if you only give Alicia a chance to make up her own mind. Now let us see what we can do to ease your difficulties. How long will your wife be in hospital?'

'They just say *some weeks*, sir, and she'll be convalescing after that. She ain't as young as she was,' said Lintott, 'so it takes longer for the shock to wear off. But I'd been thinking about that, owing to Lizzie being at home with me. She and her mother don't exactly hit it off, and Bessie'll need a bit of peace and quiet. It'd be best if she went to Mary, my other daughter, until she's on her feet again.'

'I should be honoured to allow Miss Mary expenses on your wife's behalf. Good. Now for Miss Lizzie. Is her quarrel temporary or permanent, my friend?'

'Who can tell, with all that's involved – including a couple of stepsons? But she won't be making it up for quite a bit, sir. This one's gone deep.'

'What did she do before she was married?'

'She was in an office, sir. She's good at figures, and type-writing and Pitman's shorthand, and filing. She's a clever lass,' said Lintott with pride, 'she picks up learning like – like I don't know what!'

'I was afraid you were going to tell me she stayed at home, my friend, in which case I should have been puzzled how to help. Now I see that she can help *me*. I have not only lost my dearest companion, Inspector, I have also lost a secretary and an accountant. Miss Lizzie seems admirably equipped to travel with us and earn a salary at the same time! What do you think of that?'

Lintott pursed his lips, picked up his broken pipe and laid it down again.

'I shall have to square matters up with Eddie – her husband – though.'

'He will be wax in your hands, my friend. But do you not also have to consult Miss Lizzie?' Gently ironic.

'I'll ask her, and know the answer afore she gives it!' said Lintott grimly. 'She'll jump at it, sir. She's a bit of a goose-chaser, given half a chance.'

Salvador laughed aloud, delighted. Lintott smiled ruefully.

'But I ain't accepting the case, yet!' he warned.

The magician shook his head from side to side in amiable mockery.

'My friend, you are already on board that liner. Already you cogitate how to solve the problem. And though you are modest in your estimation you hope for more than you say. I think, perhaps, you hope that in setting this small personal wheel of justice in motion greater wheels will turn. I think you are possibly more of a philosopher than a policeman!'

But Lintott, looking round for his greatcoat and bowler hat, would not engage in such fanciful nonsense. Even when the magician produced sovereigns from his ears and shirt front, and pressed them upon him for past expenses, he only said in return, 'Let's not lose our heads, sir. We've a long road to walk yet, and a rough one by all accounts, and we don't know how it'll end, now do we?'

SYMPATHETICAL FIGURES

Whereby the great force and power of sympathy is displayed by an operation with two boxes, containing an equal number of figures, which are capable of being varied 24 different ways ...

From a handbill advertising Mr Lane, 1780

NINE

Saturday, 27 January 1906

LINTOTT CONFIDED IN BESSIE finally, while minimising the risks he would be running. Her reactions were predictable: astonishment at the wickedness of the world, indignation that he should be involved in it once again, acceptance of the entire situation.

'Only *I* don't want revenging, John!' she pleaded, holding his hand.

'It ain't vengeance,' he said. 'It's justice.'

Now he ruminated over his next problem, who was sitting with an averted face so he should not see she was crying.

'You'd best wipe your eyes and look at me direct, Lizzie,' he said, 'because I've got something important to ask you, and whimpering don't help!' And as his briskness had the desired effect of making her indignant, he smiled to himself. 'That's better,' he said. 'Have you made your mind up about Eddie?'

'I'm not going back, Father, not if I have to beg in the streets!'

'Don't talk rubbish. Right, then, we'll go round to the shop and collect the rest of your things as you're stopping with me!' She sat perfectly still. 'What's wrong now?' he asked, knowing.

'Couldn't you go for me, Father?'

'I could but I'm not going to. What you do you do yourself, and take responsibility for. I don't mind carrying your luggage, but I'm not breaking up your marriage for you. So put your coat on and look sharp about it!'

Peck's Family Grocery had opened shortly after seven that morning, and would not close until eleven that evening. Eddie was measuring sugar into a blue paper bag when they walked in. He looked up smiling, and looked away frowning. Then he confronted the Inspector with some spirit.

'And what can I do for you, Mr Lintott?'

Lintott switched his tactics, and smiled frankly.

'Well, Eddie, Lizzie's been with me for the last fortnight. I know her side of the story, but I've neither seen you nor heard from you so I don't know yours. I've come here to get a straight tale, if that's all right with you.'

Eddie glanced quickly at his wife's unrelenting face, and said, 'I'll ask Mother to take over the shop for me. Come into the parlour, will you? Mother!'

A mountain of sprigged cotton overall eased itself round the door, caught sight of Lizzie and brought forth a torrent.

'So you've come crawling home again, have you? I thought as much. I told Eddie. Give her enough rope, I said, and she'll hang herself. Well, this time things'll be different, I'm telling you ... oh! Good evening, Mr Lintott.'

'Evening, ma'am. Keeping well, are you? You *sound* well,' he said affably.

The mountain heaved a cough in protest.

'It's me bronichals,' whispered Mrs Peck, placating.

'Just come and sit in the shop for me, will you, Mother?' Eddie asked.

The mountain breathed sentiment over Lintott.

'Come to smooth things over, have you, dearie? That's right. Her place is by his side!' She comforted her own side as she spoke. 'It's me stitch!' she explained.

'You ought to take better care of yourself, ma'am,' Lintott purred. 'Helping everybody with their private lives. Sharing their troubles. You ought to be enjoying yourself in your own home, you should!' He smiled dreadfully. 'After you, Lizzie!'

Ushering his daughter into the parlour, which was small and hot and cluttered.

'Are the boys in bed yet?' Lizzie asked over her shoulder, removing her gloves.

Her movements were always neat and precise, but now she exaggerated them.

'No, they're not,' Eddie replied, goaded by her tone. 'They're out playing.'

'They should be in bed by nine o'clock,' eyebrows raised, tone clipped. 'Not roaming the streets. Has she bathed them at all since I left?'

Eddie blundered, a tormented bull, round the little parlour.

'It's none of your business!' he shouted, finding no adequate reply.

Lizzie inspected the cushion on the rocking chair, and seated herself fastidiously. She gave the impression of visiting the undeserving poor.

'I used to keep them clean, you see,' said Lizzie coldly, 'with regular hours.' Suddenly she faced him. 'But *she* likes muddling through, doesn't she?'

'You can put your claws back, my girl,' Lintott commanded, brooking no nonsense. 'I'm not conducting a hen-fight. Now, Eddie, let's hear you, lad.'

Lizzie's husband had no words with which to sear her as she could sear him. He knew before he spoke that she could cut his arguments to ribbons.

So he said roughly to her, 'Have you come back or haven't you?'

'You turned me out, didn't you?' she flared. 'Don't talk as if it was the other way round!'

'Well, then,' puzzled, sheepish, 'what *have* you come for?'

'To fetch the rest of my clothes,' she answered proudly, though they were poor enough for an apology.

Lintott watched, weighed, listened.

Eddie turned a signet ring thoughtfully on his little finger, then polished it thoughtfully on his apron.

'I didn't exactly turn you out, Liz,' he mumbled. 'What I said was – either you mended your ways or you left. That's fair, ain't it, Mr Lintott?'

'You tell me, Eddie.'

'She goes on about my old mother, but she can't have it both ways. Either she's here to help in the shop and look after us, or Mother does it instead. Now don't that sound fair enough to you, Mr Lintott?'

'Fair enough, lad, fair enough. What do you say, Lizzie?'

'I say she's had her foot in our door since we got married. I can't abide her. I give one order and she gives another. Eddie won't stand up to her, and the boys are running wild between the three of us.'

'Your turn, lad,' said Lintott amiably. 'Let's have it all out.'

Eddie rummaged disconsolately among his injuries.

'Mother's a widow woman. She took care of my lads when Mollie died. It was hard on her to give up altogether. And Lizzie was only a young lass, and needed advice.'

'I didn't need advice at all. I needed room to breathe. I had advice forced down my throat!' And she touched her throat, remembering a different violation. 'I was choked up with advice that was just muddle and prejudice.'

'Go on, lad,' said Lintott, missing nothing.

'Well, Liz had her own notions and she and Mother didn't see eye to eye on anythink. Then Liz took up this Woman's Rubbish and Mother stepped in. Now she don't want to step out, and I don't blame her! How are we to manage with Liz rampaging in and out of prison? Ain't I got a home and a business to be run?'

'I've only been in prison *once*,' she interrupted, furious.

Lintott surveyed his daughter with ironic affection. 'Just a first offender – not a hard case!' he observed.

The irony was lost on Eddie, who grumbled, 'It come as a shock to Mother and me, not to mention the customers. Downright disgrace, I call it.'

Lizzie's eyes, very fine and clear and grey, mused on his bowed shoulders.

'I wasn't disgraced,' she said objectively. 'Humbled and ill-treated, yes. But not disgraced. The disgrace was theirs, not mine.'

Eddie found a retort.

'You wasn't humbled at all,' he answered, 'or you'd know your duty!'

'Humiliated then!' she shot at him.

He looked trustingly at Lintott for support, or advice, or both.

'So you don't want her back until she gives up this suffrage business?' the Inspector said. 'Now *if* she did, would that good-hearted old lady of yours stop interfering?'

'Mother was only trying to help,' said Eddie.

'Would she stop trying to help, then?'

Eddie looked uncertain.

'No, she wouldn't,' said Lizzie. 'I can give you my word and hers!'

'I don't know where I am between the pair of 'em,' said Eddie, in truth.

Lintott, feeling sympathy and amusement, quenched a smile.

'This is a proper crossword puzzle, ain't it?' he remarked. 'All you want is a quiet life, and all Lizzie wants is a bit of excitement . . .'

'I want consideration and understanding!' she cried, enraged.

'That sounds grander, but amounts to the same thing. Lizzie, if you interrupt me once more, old as you are I'll fetch you a couple across my knee!'

She subsided, but alert and rebellious nonetheless.

'Now if the pair of you can't reach some agreement, Eddie, you'll be neither married nor unmarried. Neither fish, flesh, nor good red herring, in a manner of speaking. You'll live here with a mother instead of a wife, and Lizzie will have to support herself somewhere else without a husband. Supposing you were both to take a good breather and think it over? I've got a new case,' he added, as though he had just recollected that little matter, 'as'll take me out o' London for three or four months. Would you let Lizzie come with me?'

Eddie was not sure, not sure at all, not sure of anything.

'She won't be roaming round, suffragetting,' Lintott assured him, 'because she'll have work to do for me, and I'll keep an eye on her. How about that?'

Lizzie looked from one man to the other. Lintott saw her leap over his dry scrap of information, light on a temporary solution, and accept it. Bemused, Eddie clasped and unclasped his hands, seeing nothing but what was set before him, and taking that simply at face value.

'You want to part us, do you, Mr Lintott?'

'Not a bit of it, Eddie. I want to give you both time to think matters over. Time and distance,' said Lintott weightily, 'are great healers, my lad.' He warned Lizzie with a lift of his eyebrows as her mouth opened. 'What's a few months of separation when you're thinking of the rest of your lives?' he asked. Eddie hesitated, perplexed. 'It takes a broad-minded man, a far-sighted man,' Lintott persuaded, 'to deal with a situation like this, Eddie. But you're patient, like me. You won't be hurried and you won't be pushed. You take the long view. That shows character,' said Lintott, watching him, 'and strength of mind. It ain't easy. Sometimes it involves a sacrifice. But a man o' purpose takes these here obstacles in his stride, don't he?'

Eddie surveyed this new image of himself with considerable respect. His mother made him feel a victim. Lizzie made him feel a fool.

'So what do you say, Eddie?' Lintott asked, with some compassion.

'I'll leave her with you while we think things over, Mr Lintott.'

The Inspector said to Lizzie, without looking at her, 'Get your things!'

His tone conveyed, but only to her, that this was a shoddy victory. She knew that too, passing from exultance in her temporary freedom to shame at the ease of Eddie's deception.

But who wants a simpleton for a husband? Smoothing one knob of the brass bedstead. *I wish I loved him.* She struck

94

the knob with her fist and turned away. *Father said he was my choice. He wasn't a choice, he was a poor way out.* She slipped her grey merino wedding costume and mantle from the wooden hanger. *That wasn't my choice, either. Mother said it'd be serviceable.* The velveteen toque lay in its cardboard box on top of the wardrobe. She dragged forward a rush-bottomed chair, lifted her skirts, reached for the box. *The only blessed thing I chose was the pink feather!* Her buttoned boots were scuffed, her shoes down at heel, her underwear mended. She needed new stays, new drawers, new stockings. *Still, I kept my sateen petticoat for best.* She slipped a small bottle of lavender water into the carpet-bag. *This hairbrush is nearly bald.* She looked round the room without affection, hands on hips. *I'm not coming back. I'll earn my own living somehow. I'll go to evening classes and improve myself.* She touched the empty shelf over the fireplace, puzzled. She lifted the bed flounce and peered into the dusty twilight beneath. She mounted the chair again and ran her fingers along the top of the wardrobe. A nail scored her palm. She sucked at the scratch, scrambling down again.

'Eddie! Eddie! Where are my books?'

He stumped up the dark staircase for an unwilling confrontation. He advanced towards her, in his guilt, afraid of spoiling the little truce Lintott had forged. He did not know how to explain.

'What have you done with my books?' she asked.

'I was vexed,' he said, stretching out a hand in apology.

Her breathing became difficult. She retreated, waving him away, hysterical.

'Something come over me,' said Eddie, halting, helpless.

Lizzie's world became a narrow tube between herself and eternity. She screamed for breath, eyes frantic, beating him off as he tried to soothe her.

'Mother! Mr Lintott! Mother!'

Thunder in her head and in her breast as she drew on air that diminished.

'She's having one of her turns,' cried Eddie, thumping

Lizzie's back as though she had swallowed a plum-stone.

'Here, help her on to the bed,' Lintott ordered. 'Prop her up with the bolster. Don't hit her as if she was a navvy, man!'

'Nothing but trouble,' bawled Mrs Peck from below. 'Is she stopping or is she not? Tell me that.'

'No, she's not!' shouted Lintott.

'Then good riddance to bad rubbidge!'

'Get some boiling water, will you?' cried Lintott, furious. 'And put a spoon o' wintergreen in it, or something sharp-smelling as'll clear her passages. And fetch a towel – and tell that old besom to hold her tongue!'

'Sickly, that's what she is. Sickly!' Mrs Peck declared, as Eddie squeezed past her. 'I never could abide a sickly woman. She's got the hystericals.'

'It's her asthma, you old heathen!' roared Lintott.

'It's nothing but spoiling and bad temper, and my poor son's had enough o' both. The sooner she goes the better for all of us!'

The world widened a fraction, gradually opened, finally quietened to a steady heartbeat.

'It happens when she's crossed,' Eddie explained. 'She won't be crossed.'

'Reg'lar tyrant she is with it!' yelled Mrs Peck. 'He ought to fetch a strap to her, worriting him to death with her non-sense. Reg'lar tyrant.'

The tyrant, round-shouldered and red-eyed, accepted Lintott's arm. Eddie picked up her carpet-bag, silenced, and stumbled down the stairs after them.

'I'm sorry about your books, Liz,' he said awkwardly at the shop door. She shook her head to indicate that this no longer mattered. 'Only you don't want to get yourself in a state like that over a few books,' he said, vindicating himself. 'That's silly, that is.'

'Fetch us a cab from somewhere, will you, Eddie?' Lintott asked patiently.

Glad to be useful, Eddie hurried down the High Street in his apron.

'Put your coat on, love,' Mrs Peck shouted after him. 'She's not worth catching the peumony for. He should never have married her. I said so at first, and I say it again. Never should have married her.'

'Been worrying you with this recently, has she?' asked Lintott, unfriendly.

'Ever since she come out o' jail. Jail! That my son should marry a felon!'

'Is this one of the ladies as you're trying to earn the vote for, Lizzie?' And as the beginning of a smile dawned on Lizzie's mouth, he added, 'Because I'd say you were wasting your time. She don't need a vote, she needs a gag!' Raising his voice. 'She's nagged one husband into his grave, and the rest have too much common sense to be bothered with her – except poor Eddie.'

'Libel!' cried Mrs Peck, searching her person for a hand-kerchief, to cover the lack of tears.

'No, ma'am – slander!' replied Lintott blandly. 'Slander, and not a witness to prove it.' Then, quick and kind, 'Are you feeling better, my lass?'

Lizzie nodded. The mountain retreated, rumbling discontent.

'A smart lass like you,' Lintott went on, smiling, 'and never asks where we're going to on this here case?'

Her eyes questioned him.

'How does America sound?' he asked. 'How does New York sound? What about San Francisco, then? And St Louis, and Chicago, and Lord knows where else, eh?'

A laggard tear rolled down Lizzie's cheek. She nodded vigorously, and wept.

'Anywhere but here, eh?' said Lintott, comprehending. 'And the further the better.' He squeezed the hand that clung to his arm. 'All right, my lass.'

'I've found a cab,' called Eddie, running up, 'but it'll cost you sixpence, Mr Lintott. Ain't she well enough to walk if you take her slow?'

'Just ask the cabby to drive up here, will you, Eddie?' said Lintott, grimly amused. He smoothed his whiskers. 'You were right, Lizzie,' he murmured, for her ears alone. 'He *is* mean!'

TEN

LIZZIE, FOLLOWING HER FATHER into the hushed world of a great hotel, discovered that her wedding finery was no longer fine, merely neat and respectable. She minded this, but Lintott cared not a fig for the effect of his stout boots and cheap linen, and called the supercilious page-boy 'my lad'.

The magician, refreshed, was finishing a late breakfast and communing with his livestock. The doves perched on his shoulders. The rabbit relished a carrot. He sprang up as Lizzie entered, casting his napkin to the carpet, and kissed her hand. His shimmering green brocade robe made her feel even drabber.

'Welcome, madame. Please to be seated.'

He rang the bell and ordered more toast and coffee. Then, noting his attire, he begged to be excused while he dressed.

'My very good colleagues will entertain you!' he observed, indicating the rabbit and doves who ignored this introduction.

Lintott and Lizzie exchanged glances of amusement.

'I shouldn't think he's one of the practical sort,' said Lintott in a low voice, 'so I daresay you'll find a regular pickle of letters and bills. Still, you'll enjoy that, won't you?'

She had been holding her bottle of smelling salts ready all the way from Richmond. Now she pushed it into her reticule, too interested to worry about her asthma. She knelt on the carpet, making overtures to the snowy rabbit, until Salvador returned in full regalia and startled her to her feet.

'A nosegay for madame!' Smiling, he produced violets from his fingertips. 'Pray, have you eaten breakfast?' Lizzie shook her head, captivated and flustered. 'Please allow your magnificent hat to boil an egg for you, so. *Ach!* It is hot. *Pardon!* I see you put butter balls in your pocket. How strange! You keep toast under your gloves? My goodness. I pour your coffee. *Bon appétit!*'

He sat down laughing, accepting their pleased protests as thanks enough. The size of the audience did not, in the long run, matter. Any audience was important, was worthy of his perfection.

A further diversion was provided by Mam'selle Celeste, who opened the adjoining doors and enquired whether Salvador wanted anythink more.

'We have a matinée at three,' the magician replied, somewhat disturbed by this apparition. 'Go to the theatre, if you please, mam'selle. Practise!'

Lintott fingered his whiskers. Lizzie sipped her coffee. Mam'selle Celeste's eyes were malicious, taking in the respectability of the magician's visitors.

'What I want to know,' she said, bent on petty revenge, nursing injury, 'is whether you've made up your mind, after what happened, to take me with you? There's managers all over London wanting me,' and she indicated a superfluity of employment with one empty gesture. 'I can't just 'ang about, dear, waiting on your pleasure – now can I?'

And she yawned loudly, and scratched her satin backside, grinning.

'I shall speak of this another time, mam'selle,' said Salvador, already distressed, becoming annoyed. 'Please to retire.'

'That's all very well for the likes of you, dear,' she said unpleasantly, testing her temporary power, 'but us poor working girls can't pass good jobs up.'

'Then take your magnificent offer, mam'selle, and please go!'

'You mean – go right now? For good? That'll cost you, dear!'

He strode towards her, furious, and she cringed theatrically, with one arm across her face. The lace in her *négligée* sleeve was torn.

'Out! Out! Out! You do not come with me to New York. Never!'

'And who are you going to find when you open there, I'd like to know?'

He was perplexed.

'Is your precious sister waiting on the dock for you, with her fancy gentleman? Don't you raise your hand to me, or I'll have you up for assault. I got witnesses, I have.'

'If you mean to include me among 'em, my dear,' said Lintott softly, 'you'd best make sure that I won't be witnessing against you. I've met your sort afore!'

He was hampered by Lizzie's presence, so wagged his head from side to side in a jocular fashion, to indicate that he knew a thing or two. Oh yes!

'Mam'selle Celeste, my eye,' said Lintott unkindly. 'Naughty Betty Watkins of Cheapside, more like. Now you be off and behave yourself!' She hesitated. 'Mizzle!' Lintott ordered sharply. She mizzled.

Lizzie smiled into her coffee, and wiped her lips. The magician stood, head bowed, in ruined dignity.

Lintott said, 'I think my daughter had best start on her duties, sir.'

'But of course,' brightening, 'if you are ready, madame?'

She removed her hat and donned a pair of steel-rimmed spectacles. Salvador was saddened. He flung open a roll-top desk, pulled out drawers, brought forward a bulging portmanteau.

'All is here, my noble lady,' he announced.

His noble lady surveyed chaos.

'Well, this should keep me busy, Mr Salvador,' she said, plain and matter-of-fact as Lintott. 'I'll be a long time, Father,' she said over her shoulder. 'I'd best make my own way home. I can take a cab.'

Salvador divined the Inspector's reluctance.

'And I shall go to the theatre, my friend.'

Lizzie fixed him with her spectacles.

'I shall need you to explain a few things, Mr Salvador. I've never done secretarial work for a magician before.' Briskly, 'It's all right, Father.'

Lintott hesitated. Oh, well, no help for it. Lizzie was hardly the magician's cup of tea. At least, he could remove one impropriety.

'I'll take that Miss Celeste to the theatre, sir,' he said firmly. 'Will your Mr Fredo keep her in her place there?'

'Ah! You solve all problems for me. Fredo will be there already. Celeste?' She poked a sullen face round the door. 'You will accompany the great Inspector!'

'Where to?' she enquired, apprehensive.

'The theatre – as yet,' said Lintott, 'and be quick about it.'

She disappeared as quickly as he could have wished. Salvador shook both his hands, and surveyed him with increased respect.

'Father,' Lizzie said absently, 'can you buy the chops, as I'm busy?'

Enraged, he opened his mouth. Realising she would be too late to buy them herself, he shut it again.

'I suppose you'd like me to fry them as well?' Sarcastically.

Abstracted, Lizzie said, 'That'd be nice, if it's not too much trouble.'

'I might even try my hand at a steamed pudding!' Very sarcastically.

'Oh, I shouldn't do that, Father, it's more difficult than you might think.' His silence broke her concentration. She turned round, taking off her spectacles, and looked at him lovingly. 'If I'm working for you one way, Father, I can't work in another, now can I?'

Partly mollified, he nodded. Mam'selle Celeste appeared, clad in her street attire. He summed up her character, background and prospects in one shrewd glance.

'You come along with me, my dear,' he said, 'and behave yourself!'

Salvador wandered the room, intrigued by Lizzie's composure.

'I regret the lady's behaviour, madame,' he offered.

'It's not my business, Mr Salvador,' calmly. 'Now are these American bookings to be confirmed, or are they already fixed?'

She hardly glanced at him, sorting papers, clipping them together.

'The muddle is mine, madame,' said Salvador. 'I look for one paper and confuse them all. You will find that Alicia has done everything correctly.'

'I understand. Now if you can explain certain matters to me I can work for you until Father finds her. I'm considered very quick,' said Lizzie, pushing her spectacles back on her nose, 'and I soon pick things up. Do I contact the American printers, or do the theatre managers take care of that side?'

He drew up a chair and sat near her, hands folded between his knees. She glanced round to find him observing her minutely.

'Your distinguished father is right, as always,' said the magician. 'You are most intelligent. You are also very sad, and possibly a shade too serious-minded, but that is a good fault.'

Lizzie could not think of an apt reply, so asked another question.

'I believe you will find that in the address book,' he answered, and then said, 'Were you in the theatre when this man Fleischer first spoke to your father? Tell me, not sparing my feelings out of mistaken kindness, what you thought of him. Consider!' warning her with a signpost finger. 'I want spontaneous impressions!'

Lizzie took off her spectacles and thought back. The soft voice drawling behind her, the scar moving as he smiled, the smile that was merely social, the self-containment.

'He seemed a person who kept himself to himself, as we say. He wasn't ugly, in spite of his scarred face. He would have been quite handsome if he had shown a bit of human feeling. But he held himself back, if you know what I mean, as if he was afraid you might brush against him.' She added, embarrassed, 'Father would say I was being fanciful!'

Salvador inclined his head in thanks.

'Would you think him attractive to women, madame?'

Again she bent her head in thought, and in spite of his trouble the magician smiled to himself. She was touching in her honesty, her desire to help.

'Oh, yes, he could be, though he worried me. But then, gentlemen always worry me when they look as if they're going to walk all over me. I'm not the sort,' Lizzie explained, 'that likes being mesmerised. Do you know what I mean, sir?'

'Why do you use the word *mesmerised?*' he asked, disturbed.

'Mr Fleischer had a way with him. I can't explain. Even those few minutes I was watching. I always watch people when they're talking to other people. You learn such a lot about them. I know that if he told me to do something I should be afraid to disobey. Ruthless,' said Lizzie. 'You couldn't appeal to him. He can't be reached like ordinary people.'

Salvador stood up and walked the hotel room, hands in pockets.

'Madame Lizzie, your impressions are magnificent. I see this Fleischer. So she could have gone with him because he had a power over her, or because she was afraid of him, or a little of both? Strange, for I know her and would have said she was content with our life. She feared something, but Alicia sees more than we do. She saw flames, she saw fire. We took double precautions in case it was some theatre at which we performed. How could we know that this fear was bound up in *him*? Why did she not tell me?'

'He might have threatened you if she did,' Lizzie suggested.

'True. We were very close,' he said, turning and smiling at her. 'We were as close as fingers on one hand, Alicia and I. I cannot think that she was close to Fleischer. She was so gentle, almost child-like. She lived within our little circle like a child in a magic ring. She was afraid of the dark, as a child is. She kept her toys, as a child does. Come, I show you.'

With a sigh for the tumble of papers, Lizzie followed him obediently. He unlocked the adjoining door and there, imperceptibly, intangibly, was Alicia.

A tall plain figure in her decent grey dress, Lizzie moved forward. She watched wistfully as he opened cupboards and drawers, displaying luxuries that Lizzie had only glimpsed in Ladies' Fashion Plates. It was the little things which captured her fancy: a belt ornamented with bead and bugle work, a green satin parasol trimmed with chenille fringe, black kid slippers with ribbon bows, spun silk gloves. Then her attention was caught by the row of small dolls on the mantelpiece. They were barely five inches tall. Their clothes were as elaborate and elegant as those of their owner.

'Please!' said Salvador, seeing Lizzie's fascination. 'Please do pick them up. They are dear friends of Alicia, not models.'

Yet they were models, wearing a curiously life-like expression of complacency. Their hair was real, their features delicate. Lizzie stroked a waxen cheek whose bloom pretended vitality. Miniature shoes, miniature jewels, ruched bonnets, coats inset with lace. Exquisite eyes staring.

'Oh, how curious,' she said, chilled, and set the dolls carefully back on their shelf.

'They are Montanari dolls,' said Salvador. 'Alicia never had more than a clothes peg with a scrap of material wrapped round it when she was a girl. I bought them for her when I was rich. I bought back her childhood for her.'

The chill had remained with Lizzie, creeping along her arms and round her back insidiously. It was worse than the chill aroused by Fleischer, sinister though he was.

'You mustn't mind me asking,' she said, 'but is Miss Alicia a highly-strung young lady?'

'She is open to any influence,' Salvador replied. 'That is why I fear for her. She must always be sheltered. If I thought he would take care of her I should not worry, though I should miss her. Instead, I uproot your good father and your excellent self so we can be sure she is safe.'

Sitting again at the wildly strewn desk, Lizzie said, 'Oh, you needn't worry about uprooting *me*, Mr Salvador. I haven't any roots to speak of. I always seem to live in other people's lives.'

He replied earnestly, 'Then from today you must learn to

live in your own, Miss Lizzie! And I shall watch to see you do not stray from that path!'

He had spoken to her as he would speak to a sister, and this both delighted and saddened her. When she was alone in the suite she unlocked the adjoining door again and peeped in.

The Montanari dolls stood in their beauty on the mantelpiece, and smiled and smiled.

A MOST WONDERFUL DELUSION

*An illusionist should never tell the public
what he is going to do. If people know what is
coming they will not be surprised. If they are
not surprised, there is no effect. The illusion
is worth nothing – it is nothing.*

Buatier de Kolta
(1847–1903)

ELEVEN

'I'M COMING ON MY own conditions, sir,' Lintott had said, 'so I'll tell you what they are. Number one – I don't know you, except as a public figure. Number two – Lizzie is not my daughter, and I don't know her either. She's a widow, and must find herself another name. I shall be travelling as Frank Teale, a retired locksmith. Number three – at no time do we communicate directly on board ship.

'When we arrive in New York you will be starting a three-month tour of various cities, ending up at San Francisco by the middle of April. But I might as well go there straightaway and look about me. The post can only be a hit-and-miss method with you moving around, sir. Therefore, if we have to contact each other we must use the telegraph – remembering assumed names! You had best give me a list of theatres, and the dates on which you'll be there.

'As soon as you reach the Palace Hotel, San Francisco, you will find a letter from me, and I'll arrange a meeting. I hope by then that I'll have some news of Miss Alicia. Is that all understood, sir?'

'Perfectly, my friend. But why not travel first-class with us? You have no need even to raise your hat when we encounter each other, and you will be much more comfortable!'

'No thankee, sir. As a retired locksmith I'm lucky to travel at all, let alone in the first-class. Besides, when you see somebody as you know your eyes show it, though it might be no more than a flicker.'

Lizzie was wearing one of her mother's expressions: incredulous and ironic. 'I'm taking no chances!' said Lintott brusquely. 'When you walk into a den of lions – quiet and easy does it, and keep your eye on them. No sense in rattling the bars to let them know you're coming! No, no.'

The excitement of departure was enhanced by Salvador's showmanship. Many were sailing for New York on that cool grey day, but one would have thought only Salvador sailed. He managed to produce more luggage, give more orders, possess more distinction, than any other passenger. His vast leather brass-bound trunks, each stamped with a sinuous S, teetered and swung over the ship's side, mimed into safety by Fredo (who caused a minor stir on his own account). Esmerelda, a black pool of solitude, attracted attention by seeking to avoid it. Only Lizzie approached normality, composedly checking through the lists. Even she was observed, if only in contrast to the magician.

Several yards apart, a stocky figure in a grey overcoat remained unnoticed, which was what he wanted.

To some, this voyage to the new world was one of discovery or rediscovery. Those who were returning home were recognisable by their exuberance. Their clothes were more dashing, their voices louder, their geniality insistent. The English took their pleasures in sombre good taste and dressed accordingly. Heavy with history, schooled in the art of withdrawal, they observed these euphoric children with amusement or distaste. The Americans would sometimes give offence without intention. The English could make an offence of politeness.

The photographer who took pictures of the state-rooms on board ship must have been highly ingenious. He must have lain on the floor at the far end of the alleyway to produce such spacious vistas. He must have owned the cleverest camera in existence, for it lied exceedingly.

Lizzie, preparing to sweep into her cabin, was brought up against the porthole almost immediately, but nothing could destroy her intense happiness. The magician, knocking at her door later in the afternoon to enquire after her welfare, found her sitting on the edge of her bunk, smiling at nothing.

'Miss Lizzie!' he cried, as though he raised a theatre curtain for her command performance. 'The voyage has begun! Time is suspended. Reality is no more. The ocean becomes our universe. Try, if you please, not to succumb to the *mal de mer*. Endeavour to eat heartily four times a day, and to enjoy yourself. Little else is required of you, except that you dine with me in the evening. Allow me to explain my habits. May I come in for a moment?'

'Please!' Lizzie answered, with a gracious gesture of the hand which she observed in some astonishment.

Salvador smiled. He filled, illuminated the little cabin. He was too much for this cramped space: the sun in a back yard. She looked up at him, dazzled.

'First of all, on both our behalfs, I have courteously refused seats at the Captain's dining-table. I find that my professional achievements are a subject of such popularity that I am unable to eat my dinner. Instead, knife in hand, I must explain how to saw a lady in half!' Lizzie laughed in delight. 'So, I say no, thank you, honourable Captain. I tell him I require to discuss future plans with my private secretary, and for this purpose I desire a small table in a secluded corner. Which means, dear Miss Lizzie, that I shall undoubtedly have to entertain the waiter, but this will be after our coffee and liqueurs. Thus, Salvador eats! Later, if you are willing, we may give our fellow travellers a brief performance?'

Lizzie placed one hand on her throat, and stared at him, afraid.

'I have no assistant,' the magician explained gently. 'You are very quick at picking things up, as you told me. You could not be expected to contribute as Alicia did, in a specialised way. You would be ten thousand times better than Mam'selle Celeste, than all the Mam'selle Celestes who have hampered my past work. We could practise together, and offer our services on the last evening. A mere trifle, a routine, a *bagatelle*! They will not be a difficult audience. They are grateful to be amused!' He dismissed the problem with a snap of his fingers. 'But, if you say no, Miss Lizzie – then I say no, too.'

She thought of the nightly dinner at the private table, of having all this wit and brilliance to herself, and knew she could not refuse him.

'Except,' said Lizzie tentatively, 'that I shouldn't be dressed right.'

'That is of no consequence. I do not expect you to wear a costume. The more natural you are the better. I wish to give an informal entertainment. So?' He picked up her hand and kissed it, replaced it in her lap. 'You will honour me by dining tonight, if you please?'

'Thank you, Mr Salvador. I accept. I do accept.'

He turned and said idly, 'How strange! They must have a silk rose-tree on board ship. Permit me!' He plucked the flower from her porthole and presented it with a bow. 'Please to wear this for dinner, Miss Lizzie. And now I must enquire whether my old friends are comfortable in their quarters. Like your distinguished father, they insist on travelling second-class when I would prefer them to join me – to join *us*.'

He smiled radiantly and bowed his way out, leaving her standing tall and thin and awkward: the *fantasie* in her hand, a flush in her cheeks.

'Whatever would Father say?' she asked herself, and thanked God he was in a different part of the liner. His chastening tongue would have checked this friendship.

In the wilderness of night and water, the ship glittered like a toy lantern, travelling towards the new world. Behind her lay the old world, already half-forgotten. As the velvet dark approached, the ladies donned their finery, prepared to waltz round and round the elaborate ballroom, to smile over spread fans beneath garlands of fairy lights.

Into this august assembly came Lizzie's best Sunday gown of

violet plush, enhanced by a home-made fichu of Indian muslin copied from a fashion plate. She had, after loyal hesitation, laid aside her mother's wedding gift of the family hair-brooch. Instead she pinned Salvador's black silk rose in the folds of muslin, and relied upon its natural *chic* to see her through.

Men and women turned their heads as the magician entered the dining-room with Lizzie on his arm. His presence demanded their notice, held their attention. They stared then at his companion, and wondered whom she might be that he treated her so considerately. Lizzie's colour was higher than usual, but she had faced policemen and judges and prison officials in a different type of ordeal, so she carried herself with dignity and hoped for a good end to all this public life.

He had chosen their small table with tact and perception. From here they could observe the rest of the diners, almost unseen. Starched white napery and shining silver, the spray of bright flowers in a little vase, were reflected in the mirror-wall. They took their places in this picture-frame, and began their first evening *à deux*.

Salvador, master of illusion, felt much at home in a floating world. His relationships with the majority of people were transient, performed to the highest standard under the most propitious conditions. In this dining alcove sat an intelligent woman, wide of mouth and brow, direct and candid of gaze, who was a prisoner of circumstance. He had an affection, a liking, for her. He meant, with the kindest of intentions, to transform her into her real self.

Lizzie, whose passions had been frittered away in life's basement, now looked on a man at whom she could only marvel. A humble realist, she asked nothing more than the opportunity to experience the moment. In return, as thanks, she prepared to adopt whatever role seemed appropriate to his mood: professional assistant, secretary, accountant, companion, quasi-sister. She meant to love him and let him be, without demands. But because she was a woman, and could not help desiring him for herself, she sought to discover what pleased him in other women. Her own self stood drily and sadly apart: imperilled.

In spite of his earlier protests Salvador had voluntarily entertained their corner of the saloon. It was as though he must reassure himself by frequent applause. Now, relaxed again, he talked to her as the waiter replenished their coffee cups. The room was emptying. Glances and smiles, laughter and comments, were vanishing with the guests. A few inclined their heads in tribute, in courtesy. He acknowledged them, with grave good manners, on behalf of the man named Salvador.

'We were born in the circus, in different countries,' he continued. 'Our mother was Mademoiselle Adeline, a famous equestrienne. Our father was Zak, a famous clown. Ah! that was a strange love affair, that one. Beauty and pathos. Alicia was two years old when our parents died, the one soon after the other, of a purulent fever. I was a lad of thirteen. We were orphaned, dear Miss Lizzie, and yet not entirely for we had parents of another sort. We had Esmerelda and Fredo. Beyond them were the great arms of the circus: our home, our work, our family, our universe.'

Lizzie's plush gown wore a sheen under the lamplight. She touched the *fantasie* at the base of her throat, content.

'They had thought I would be a clown, like Zak. The supreme circus artist. Juggler, mime, tightrope-walker, trapeze performer, acrobat ... he must know everything, and add to these accomplishments the unique gift of himself. But I was fascinated by wonders and illusions. I used to creep from my bed, late at night, to watch the Great Marcus. The magician. I became his apprentice, his pupil. Alas! The Great Marcus drank. Terrible for the hands. Also the brain is not so keen, the eyes not so alert. First I learned, then I assisted, finally I took his place when he was too drunk to perform. The experience was terrifying, invaluable. I discovered how to mask mistakes and disasters at an early age. *Eh bien!* He died. God rest him.'

Lizzie said, afraid of her evening being over, 'When did you leave the circus, Mr Salvador?'

114

He replied, 'If I am to bore you with my early history, Miss Lizzie, I shall require a Benedictine. If I have one then I ask you to join me, so that I do not drink alone.'

'Thank you,' said Lizzie, 'you are very kind.'

'I think you are a present day Scheherezade, madame. You encourage me to talk. You listen attentively. How can I resist?'

Her mood was green and gold, the eyes of the magician, the colour of the liqueur. She sipped. Life softened, merged with his tales. She became Alicia.

She had been in exile long enough, obeying rules, observing, and holding her tongue. Now she dared write to him, instead of going home to the circus.

My dear one, May I join you for a while? I shall be no trouble. I can perhaps help you in some small way. If this displeases you I can return to Esmerelda and Fredo. Your loving sister, Alicia.

The letter had come to him at a bad time. She read reluctance in the consent, as though he preferred to be alone but could find no humane excuse. Her need was greater than his withholding, and she packed with gentle ruthlessness, wiring the time of her arrival in Paris. The journey was all steam, noise, people, luggage, sweat. Strangers jostled her as she tried to find a porter.

She stood under the station clock, with her valise and small trunk by her side. The clock ticked *too late, too late, too late.* She found his address in her reticule and tucked it inside her glove. She counted her francs. Outside some protective circle she was lost, forsaken. She was afraid someone would notice her solitary stance and accost her. The porter who had brought her to this appointed place came back. Perhaps she had not tipped him enough? She opened her purse.

'Mam'selle has not found her friends? Mam'selle wishes me to make an enquiry? Is Mam'selle feeling unwell?'

She could only say, trembling, 'My brother will come soon. He will be with me very soon.'

'Mam'selle may wait in the Ladies' Waiting Room. Allow me...'

She hurried after him, protesting, weeping. He took no notice, knowing what was best for her, as they all had known—and not known. He stood in front of her firmly, until she found another tip. Then, his duty done, he left her alone in the safety of this strange place. Tears dried, she sat patient and numb.

The door was flung open and Salvador stood there, radiant as the late sun he had brought in with him.

'I forgot. I shall forget my head. I am a *dummkopf*! Forgive me.'

'But you must *not* forget me. You must *never* forget me!' she was crying.

'Not you, *liebchen*, not you. The time of the train.'

They held each other at arm's length, laughing. They had been parted, that was all. Now they were together again.

In Salvador's temporary lodgings she unpinned her hat and removed her travelling cloak. She poured water from the flowered jug into its flowered basin. She rolled up her sleeves, unbuttoned the tight collar, washed her face and hands. She peered into the speckled glass on the wall and combed her grey-blonde fringe.

'I was afraid you didn't want me, Felix.' Utterly content.

'Drink your coffee,' he counselled. 'Later we must eat and see Paris.'

She placed an ornate card proudly before him.

'I am now qualified for life,' she announced.

LAROCHE SEMINARY

Be it known that Alicia Adeline Salvador has with commendable diligence and proficiency completed the course of study in the Seminary, and by her attainments and correct deportment is entitled to her diploma. Given at Lucerne, Switzerland, 10 July 1900

She interpreted his smile.

'It is not, after all, important,' she said, stricken.

'How old are you now?' he asked kindly. 'Eighteen? So much? What am I to do with you? Do you wish to marry some handsome gentleman? I can provide a dowry of sorts. If you will wait a year or so I can provide a dowry as handsome as the gentleman. I did well in London last autumn.'

Half-mocking, half-serious, he questioned her. The responses, both child-like and vehement, surprised him. She had come a long way. She had waited a long time. She begged him not to send her back.

He had suffered both loss and triumph in the past months and was weary of solitude. They could set up a home in each other, travel together.

'Very well,' said the magician. 'We shall be complete. You may assist me. At least you can be no worse than the ladies who have assisted me so far, and practice will improve performance. On my part, you may be assured that I have no desire to marry.'

'Nor I, nor I!' she cried. 'I stay with you, always. With you I am safe.'

Salvador passed one hand across his face. The dining saloon was empty. Opposite him sat Lizzie, eyes bright with fatigue and excitement. He smiled at her with the immense kindness that was so much a part of his character.

'I had forgotten how she said that,' he remarked to himself. 'I should have known then that something troubled her deeply. But Alicia had always so much of the child in her, and a little of the recluse. She hung back, as I do not, from contact with strangers. I accepted her vehemence without question, and built upon it. I had thought love, as such, was over for me. This strangely gentle affection became ourselves, so that we preferred our company to all others. Oh, I sought others. I sought other women.'

'Did she not mind?' Lizzie cried.

He leaned back in his chair, contemplating her.

'Miss Lizzie, you must answer that question for yourself – and perhaps for her, too. Come, the evening is over. We are both tired. Tomorrow we must practise together. I have promised the illustrious Captain that we shall give a magnificent show for the passengers in first-class, on the last night of the voyage...'

'Magnificent?' she said uncertainly.

'Magnificent!' he replied firmly. 'Do not worry, dear Miss Lizzie, I am not unkind with my assistant!' He smiled mischievously. 'I simply require – perfection!'

On their way to her cabin, down the vacant alleyways, he laughed and put an arm about her thin shoulders.

'You are so like Alicia, and yet so unlike, Miss Lizzie.'

'In what way, Mr Salvador?' Delighting in, suffering in, the arm about her.

'You, too, are withdrawn and shy and a little dependent on me, as she was.' He felt the shoulders stiffen, and smiled. 'But this is only a temporary dependence, Miss Lizzie. You depend upon me much as a weary bird depends upon the ship's mast. It needs to rest for a while on the journey. Then it flies again, with renewed strength.'

She smiled back then, with such quiet beauty that he bent forward and kissed her cheek.

'Good night, dear Miss Lizzie. Sleep well. May God bless you – and her, whose journey appeared to be with me.'

The silver phantom crouched in the centre of the stage and cried out in inhuman terror. Her voice echoed through the corridors of Lizzie's restless night.

TWELVE

ON FINE DAYS the ladies strolled the decks, accompanied by gentlemen, and viewed the ocean through blowing veils.

Lizzie stood alone and pressed her handkerchief to her nose and mouth, looking out on to the everlasting sea. The *bagatelle* of a performance had assumed tremendous proportions. Salvador's programme altered daily, hourly. He was at this moment consulting various ship's officers to ascertain that certain illusions could be presented. Their co-operation was necessary. She had tried to intercede. Were they not being too ambitious? Had he not told her...?

'Do not dare!' he had cried, enraged at having his word brought against him. 'Nothing but the best for Salvador and for his audience. Nothing but the best. Please to go if you have less to offer. I manage alone.'

So she wept quietly, staring at the metallic water, because she could neither leave him nor bear with him. Her own efforts did not satisfy either her or the magician. He had wounded her on that score, too.

'So wooden, so lifeless. The hand drooping instead of announcing like a herald. The head held sideways instead of showing challenge. Oh, Alicia, Alicia!'

Then she had retreated, seeking comfort in privacy and tears. She could draw strength from disagreement with those she reckoned as enemies, but from a disagreement between friends she suffered loss and confusion. Manacled to royal railings, carried aloft by hostile policemen, held down by wardresses, she knew who and what she was. Charmed or scolded by Salvador, she became the creature of his mood, unsure of her worth.

Grief turned to resentment, resentment to an aggressive self-respect. At dinner-time she was collected and smiling: indifferent to his praise or blame. He might set a procession of fine meals before her, faultlessly presented, served with homage. He might light a thousand candles and order a cellarful of wine, dark as rubies and honey-scented. He might touch her glass with his and smile into her eyes as much as he pleased. But she would be resolute.

Salvador said, 'Forgive me, Miss Lizzie. In the early days Alicia, too, found me quite impossible.'

She had so closely identified herself with Alicia that she cried, 'And neither of us had anywhere else to go!'

Now he knew he had hurt her and his face became grave.

'I forget that you have troubles of your own, Miss Lizzie. You hope to escape from grief and instead you are bedevilled by this fellow!' He struck his white starched front, and produced six national flags one after another.

Lizzie endeavoured to hold on to her grievance, and failed. She began to laugh, and he laughed with her. The waiter smiled as he served them. Their neighbours turned and nodded, amused and hopeful. He had bridged their differences.

Still she said, bending over her soup, 'Mr Salvador, it is hardly fair to use your power to charm people as you do. But perhaps,' she added, spoon raised, 'we are just as much in the wrong to allow ourselves to be charmed!'

'That is my Miss Lizzie!' he observed. 'She administers the rebuke, and then turns it upon herself. I shall tell you something, my friend. You see this lighted room, these smiling people, this little ship sailing through the night with its cargo of pleasure-seekers? Illusion, Miss Lizzie! My charm, as you call it? Illusion! My art and craft, my profession? Pure illusion!'

She had paused, and was listening intently as though he would provide an answer to herself.

'So what is real in Salvador? There is much reality in you, Miss Lizzie. Who is the real Salvador?' He indicated their fellow-passengers, now eating, drinking, chatting. 'Observe his audience now. He ceases to entertain them, so they return to their own lives. He must entertain or he does not exist, this magician. Behind the illusions lies one reality – work. One learns magic as one learns another language. Five years of patient attention to detail, of patient practice, go into a routine of sleights – and sleight of hand is only a part of each magician's repertoire. Work is real, Miss Lizzie.'

He mused over his wine. The waiter took away their plates, attentive and deferential.

'Another illusion,' said Salvador, nodding towards his retreating back. 'He is paid to treat us as though we were gods. Do not imagine for one moment that he has not taken our measure, and judged us as Solomon himself would judge! Our servants are our masters, Miss Lizzie. They weigh us, and often find us wanting, in ships and in hotels and on railway trains and in cabs. They bow to us, minister to us, thank us. Illusion!'

Lizzie said shyly, drawn by his argument, 'Marriage is often an illusion.'

Salvador said, 'Oh, no, Miss Lizzie, marriage is reality even when it is *not* disastrous. Marriage is a legal contract between consenting parties. Look around you, observe these wives with their medals and badges of servitude!'

Lizzie, whose only jewellery was her plain wedding ring, said, 'I mean, we can be deluded in our feelings, before we marry.'

'Ah!' he softened, smiled. 'That I can imagine, dear Miss Lizzie, with your neat head full of fine notions, and your great heart full of affections. Yes, you would love deeply and mistakenly some poor fellow who finds himself momentarily a king in your eyes – and then discovers he is only a clown after all!'

'No, I didn't exactly...'

'You chided me for my charm,' said Salvador, attacking his steak as though it were a bull and he the matador. 'I have a reputation for being something of a womaniser. Illusion! I find most women delightful. I like and honour many. I have loved only three, and one of them is my sister.

'This society maims its women, Miss Lizzie, by considering them only as housekeepers and breeders of children. When you add property to this possible wife-and-mother you rob a woman of her natural dignity. Look around you! These are the rich. Find me one woman's face in this room which is free from deception. They smile, they laugh, not from amusement but from the desire to please or placate. They are marketing themselves.'

Lizzie said with some spirit, 'Perhaps some of them care for the gentlemen they try to please. We are not all for sale, Mr Salvador.'

He had not been thinking of her, but of his sister, and he continued as though she had not spoken.

'I gave her freedom. I gave her work, at which she excelled. I gave her love and security.'

Lizzie's temper had swivelled from south-west to due east. Her appetite deserted her. She drank a little wine.

'Mr Salvador, forgive me if I speak out, but wasn't her freedom an illusion too? She was free so long as she stayed with you, in your opinion. Was that freedom to her? You gave her work at which she excelled – I begin to understand how much it cost her to excel. Was her dedication to her work perhaps another illusion? Finally you gave her love, but that was brotherly affection and women need more than that. You gave her security? Did your security comfort her, or did she suffocate?'

The magician was very pale, very composed.

'I'm sorry,' said Lizzie honestly, 'but I can't help thinking that this mistake she has made – and from what I've seen of him I believe the mistake to be a great one – was made because she had been cared for too much.'

There was no pettiness in this giant. He drank his wine down, and the waiter hurried forward to refill the glass. He drank again.

'You used the word *mesmerise*, in connection with Fleischer, once,' he remarked. 'Alicia could have been mesmerised.'

He did not mean by Fleischer alone. He meant by himself, too.

'I don't want to hurt you, Mr Salvador, but it's better to speak the truth as far as we know it,' Lizzie replied, and then was silent and sorry.

He raised his glass, and nodded.

'Miss Lizzie, I admire you. I admire women of spirit whose truth cannot be bought.'

He was quiet for a few moments, moving the base of his glass round and round on the starched cloth.

The group of picnickers spread themselves graciously beneath the beech trees, and round the vast crumpled square of linen which had held the feast. Hints of epicurean delights were evident in the empty dark-green wine bottles, in ruined battlements of pastry, in carcases and cores and crusts, in the rolled apples and oranges and the plucked skeletons of grapes.

The closing of this girl's parasol announced the end of a late summer afternoon in 1899. She paused in front of Salvador and smiled into his face frankly.

'But are you not going to have your likeness taken, too?' she asked. 'Surely, after all the entertaining you should join us?'

'Oh, certainly, if you command me, madame,' Salvador replied, and looked around to make sure he was offending no one.

He had recently triumphed in London, as part of a music hall programme, and would have returned to Europe modestly pleased had it not been for the Prince of Wales's friend. She, having an eye for talent and the belief that we should help one another, had invited the magician down to her country house for the weekend. The Prince was there, of course, very affable and hearty, and needing to be constantly amused. Nothing had been promised to Salvador, but he understood that the royal favour could mean an extended booking at a better theatre with special billing. So he kept at a respectful distance, without being servile, and was rewarded by being overworked.

'Get that magician fellow to show me a few card tricks!'

Salvador was on the brink of an international reputation, but had not yet arrived at it. So his position in the house-party was difficult. Everyone was most polite, but only the girl chose him as a companion and drew him into the group. The others set this down to her eccentricity and wilfulness. As she was also young and lovely they excused her.

Now they made room for the magician, who would have been left standing at the side, and he stretched himself on the grass at her feet. He was intensely aware of her presence. He sensed the shape of the rose pinned to her muslin dress. He glimpsed the frill of her parasol, her small kid shoe. Her kindness had rendered his nights wakeful and his mind uncertain. He who had gloried in his freedom was no longer free. His captivity both chafed and delighted him.

The titled young man at the tripod ducked under his black cloth hood.

'Absolutely still, everybody!' he cried.

Straw boaters and striped blazers. Garden hats garlanded with wild or artificial blossoms, one gentleman in his waistcoat and shirt-sleeves (he had begged permission of the ladies before divesting himself of his jacket). Leaves and light and water and...

'Smile, please – and hold it!'

Click. Time held still and held fast in a scrap of celluloid.

'She was so free, so unbroken in her flight,' Salvador was saying. 'I loved her for that spirit. They were trying to market her, of course. She was young, she was beautiful, she came of what they called "the right sort of family". And she would have none of it. She spurned them. She sought me and chose me and loved me. She loved me before I was famous – another illusion, Miss Lizzie, in which powerful men indulge. They are not loved for themselves but for their money, their image. She loved me in spite of convention, in spite of the difficulties which beset an attractive single girl. We thought with one mind, loved with one heart, spoke with one voice. The quality of that loving is part of me, as though life had drawn a circle round us in the summer of 1899 and said, "This is perfection." I thank God for her, and wish her well.'

Lizzie said wistfully, 'What happened to this lady, Mr Salvador?'

He spread out his hands and let them fall.

'Suddenly we did not meet any more. Her family may have realised, and taken her away. Or, as I believe, *she* realised – and left me.'

'Realised what, Mr Salvador?' said Lizzie mystified.

'That this love affair was perfect in itself. That it could not have grown. That it was complete, and would only be spoiled if we asked anything more. She, with her unfettered spirit, could never have moulded herself to me or to any man. I, with my work, in my perpetually homeless, perpetually travelling state, had no future to offer her. She was what I have called few other women so far – a fine human being.'

'I suppose,' said Lizzie slowly, 'I only understand a more ordinary sort of love.'

'There is no ordinary way of love, Miss Lizzie. Love takes you up and crushes you and lets the pieces fall. It is both marvellous and fearful. It alters everything so that life is never the same again.'

Lizzie sought among the humble emotions of her existence for a consuming passion, and did not find it.

'I should have thought,' she said finally, '– though I'm no expert, of course, Mr Salvador – that love could build something and grow, if it was love.'

'I have not found that, except with Alicia. And, as you said, that is a brotherly affection and women desire more than that!'

'I believe it to be possible,' said Lizzie with supreme faith, supreme because her memories were unlike those of Salvador.

'Just look at *you!*' Eddie accused, as she tried to undress behind the shelter of the wardrobe door. 'Talk about forcible feeding, it looks more like forcible starvation to me. Not a scrap of flesh on your bones, and you were never what I'd call a fine figure of a woman anyway! You've made a proper mess of yourself, with all those fancy notions, haven't you? Keep away from me!' Peevishly, as she crept into her half of the bed, 'You give me the creeps, looking like a blooming scarecrow. What sort of an armful do you think you are for a man?'

'You must have loved him very much,' said Salvador kindly. 'Perhaps you still love him more than you know, Miss Lizzie.'

'Love who?' she asked, sad miles and sad months away.

'Your husband, Miss Lizzie.'

She shook her head with quiet emphasis.

'Oh, no, Mr Salvador. When I talk about love I talk about something I've never experienced, only I believe it exists. There's the truth again!'

She smiled though she felt more like crying.

'Perhaps your love is another illusion?' he suggested lightly, with more wit than wisdom.

She rose, keeping herself controlled, though her voice shook a little.

'Perhaps *all* love is an illusion, Mr Salvador, in which case there seems precious point in living at all – since love is the best part of us.'

'I did not mean to hurt you,' he cried, 'but what you describe is not love as I know it.'

'My father,' said Lizzie, trembling, 'is going off thousands of miles to a strange place. All he's got is a change of clothes and his courage. Do you know why he's doing that?' The magician made a placatory gesture. 'Not for the fee. Not for glory – he's solved hundreds of cases in his time. He's going because his wife was pushed under an omnibus. Shall I tell you about her?

'We don't get on, she and I. We respect and love each other, but we don't understand each other. She's elderly and no longer pretty. She's had four children and brought them up on

126

a policeman's wage. She means more to my father than anyone else in the world, and he loves *me* well enough.

'Mother came from a working-class family. She couldn't afford to be wilful. They lived hard, but they built something between them that lasted more than a summer, Mr Salvador. Something that sends him off in his old age to defend her and justify himself. That's love! When *you* talk about love beware that you're not creating yet another wonderful delusion!'

DEFYING THE BULLETS

Ha! Ha!! Ha!!! – The barrel is not founded – the bullet is not moulded, to bring him to destruction – No! he defies the deadly ball, and holds at naught the "WINGED MESSENGER OF FATE". *Bring your own bullets.*

> The 1615th time of MR BARNARDO EAGLE performing this extraordinary delusion.

THIRTEEN

Saturday, 3 March 1906

HE HAD TRAVELLED a long way. He had been a long time
travelling. America went on for ever. It travelled with him:
a companion of infinite scale and variety and of all weathers.
There were cities stacked high as Babel, there were mountains
which dwarfed the cities. Plains stretched out ahead of him,
dotted with minute communities. Bitter cold in New York,
snow in Chicago, winds in Salt Lake City, mild spring now as
they journeyed down Nevada and into the promised land.

The Central Union and Pacific Railroad catered for all con-
tingencies. This great engine bore a snow-sweeper as a knight
bears his shield. It took on distance and hazard with a stead-
fastness that Lintott revered. Its plume of steam rose like a
banner, its whistle heralded approach. By day it hammered
out territory and presented him with a picture landscape. By
night it rocked him to sleep in a curtained bunk. Its wheels were
an orchestra possessed of a humdrum repertoire. It was a few
minutes' company for that solitary woman leaning on the fence
of an outlying farm. It bore down on these little stations with
a noisy stir of excitement, with the majesty of an army, an
air of romance. For where had it been and where was it going
to in the boundless space? And the rails which had been
forged and laid in man's sweat ran on and on across the endless
land, connecting arrivals with departures.

The vision of the United States of America had been godlike, the conception far from immaculate – since humanity is never perfect – but the idea captured Lintott, and mirrored his own audacity. People had come from the known to the unknown and grappled with it. They had ventured in small worlds of wheels, wood and canvas to explore the infinite, to achieve the impossible. They had begun with nothing and aimed for everything. Somewhere between their wagons and those dreams lay America.

Round him were the Americans, who shared one nationality and all nationalities. Their roots had been uprooted, newly-planted. They understood what they wanted and who they were, but not what they had been. There was no tradition from which to draw strength, on which to base rules. They started with a blank sheet and worked their own design. Watched by the old world, they were often puzzled how to make a new one. They were visionaries who saw Paradise gained. They were adventurers who sought Eldorado. They were gamblers who held a straight flush. They were buccaneers who sailed a high sea and damned the consequences. They were nomads in search of home. Because each of them must depend upon his neighbour, because each stranger must be a brother, they cast off the social shackles which bound other countries. They held out their hands and offered their hospitality.

Lintott's only refuge was the identity of Frank Teale, widower and retired locksmith. The rest of him lay at their benevolent mercy. They would not let him be, so he joined them in rueful good-humour.

'Pardon me, sir, but are you British? My folks came from Kent. Maybe you knew them? Name of Crabtree. You travelling alone? Hey, May-Ellen, this gentleman is from the old country. Now I am Oscar Crabtree, and this is my wife, May-Ellen, and these are our kids. Shake hands, boys. Your name, sir?'

Lintott knew the routine by heart.

'Frank Teale. Call me Frank, Oscar.'

'If that isn't great! Now why don't you come right on over

and join us? May-Ellen here bakes the best apple-pie in the whole U.S. of A. Yes, sir! Here, you just try a mouthful – what did I tell you? Good, ha?'

'My compliments, ma'am. Thankee.'

'We are a nation of apple-pie and sandwich eaters, I'm telling you. We make the best sandwiches in the wide world!'

Into America's cooking pot the nations poured their recipes, and having assimilated them America produced a few of her own. The palate was a global one. Lintott wished they could make tea properly. Nobody but the English could brew a good pot of tea. He relinquished this homely luxury, however, with no more than a sigh. Time and space were too vast to encompass with a packet of Brooke Bond.

The engine shuttled them on. They had covered the length of Great Britain five times over when it roared into Oakland with a final triumphant blast on the whistle, a final spurt of steam.

I shall hear those blessed wheels a-drumming in my head for days, Lintott thought. He stepped off stiffly, Gladstone bag in hand.

Another boat to take for the last lap. A ferry-boat, broad-bellied, sharp-nosed, with a stout black funnel, fretful to leave the jetty and show them how it rode the busy waters.

A cool blue day like an English spring. An immensity of sky on which bright clouds floated. A sense of isolation and unimportance, and yet the feeling of being part of a great adventure. The usual hotch-potch of passengers pressed against each other. Top hats, billycocks and peaked caps. Fine feathers, humble shawls. Tailored broadcloth, Levis. The rich, those who could be rich, those who would never be rich but nourished hope. For America was the land of equality and opportunity, and the nettle of success had only to be grasped with courage.

Beneath the sky, like promise, lay San Francisco. A confetti of houses sprinkled her many hills. A multitude of citizens lived within wood frames or stone palaces. Today she was colour and light and air, smiling.

Lintott stood outside the Ferry Building and fell disgracefully in love. In his pocket lay the address of a rooming-house, culled from one of his several passing friends. He hesitated between a cable car and a horse carriage, but opted for the carriage since he was unsure where the cable car went.

'Where to, bud?' asked the driver.

Lintott consulted his piece of paper.

'Mrs Olson's rooming house. Fifth and Mission.'

He had arrived.

The frame house hustled its neighbours in the friendliest fashion: a lady past her prime, but intent on your remembering her glory. The flight of steps had been trim, the columned porch topped by an ornamental balcony. Now paint peeled from the busy fretwork, the net curtains were almost white, the bay windows not quite clean. This image carried over, as it were, into the landlady. She meant to be genteel but fell unaccountably short of her intention: a little blown about the hair and overblown everywhere else, and yet kind.

Lintott had prepared to put himself on Christian name terms here, too, but Mrs Olson kept at a distance for professional reasons. She surnamed her gentlemen lodgers to their faces and behind their backs. It was easier to give notice that way, when necessary. So, as Mr Teale he was most earnestly questioned, and his recommendation by one Joseph Dooley read at arm's length.

'Yeah, Mr Dooley. I think I remember him,' uncertainly. 'I didn't know he could write this good, if it's the Mr Dooley I'm thinking of! Did you write it for him?' Suspicious.

'I helped him with the spelling,' said Lintott, amused, 'but he worked most of it out for himself. A very independent gentleman, Mr Dooley. Honest and straightforward, I'd have said, but quick on the temper and heavy with the fists.'

'I been had before, you see,' said Mrs Olson, concentrating on the letter.

'Well, ma'am, if you don't want me I shall have to find somebody that does.'

She fingered a strand of hair back into its cottage loaf shape.

'Who said I mightn't want you? Mr Dooley? He don't know nothing.' That decided her. She smiled. 'I keep a nice house, Mr Teale, and I have to be real careful who comes here. All my guests act respectable. Did he drink?'

'I dare say he enjoyed his glass, ma'am. Yes.'

'I don't mind nobody enjoying a drink but I mind when they get liquored up. I had a heap of trouble with the demon drink, Mr Teale.'

'I shan't get liquored up, ma'am, I can promise you that.'

'And no complaints about the victuals. The girl does her best.'

'Certainly, ma'am.'

She ruminated. There was something eluding her.

'Board and lodging, ma'am?' Lintott hinted.

'Sure. We all eat together. Soup, hash and pie for supper tonight. Five dollars a week, pay in advance, week's notice either side. Washing extra.'

'Thankee, ma'am. Understood and accepted.'

'You want to see the room? The girl'll bring you up some hot water. I cain't run around like I used to!'

Lintott tutted sympathetically and prepared himself for his temporary quarters, but he need not have feared. The room was clean, if a little cluttered.

'Very pleasant, ma'am,' said Lintott, relieved and delighted.

His praise reached her. She looked at him properly for the first time.

'I kept a nice house when my late husband was alive,' she said.

'Ah,' said Lintott, in kindness, 'you still keep a nice house, ma'am, only he ain't with you.'

'Are you a married man, Mr Teale?'

For two reasons he decided to be a recent widower. First, it would be one more screen behind which he could hide. Secondly, it would explain why he was travelling to the other side of the world.

'My wife died, ma'am, last year. We'd saved a bit, and I

seem to be spending it roaming round. I can't settle somehow.'

'Well, you're not alone,' said Mrs Olson, 'everybody in this city belongs some place else. Like they say, you may be new in San Francisco but you're no stranger. How long do you plan to stay, then?'

She was friendly now, interested. He must keep the balance between them: amiable but not too intimate. He invented another fiction.

'I'm not too sure of that, ma'am. I ain't here because I stuck a pin in the atlas, as you might say. I have some reason for coming this far. A relative of mine came over here some years ago. I shall be walking round asking about him.'

She stood musing, hand on hip, unsurprised.

'You should try the newspaper offices,' she said at last. 'Maybe they'll let you look up back copies, gossip columns, things like that. Why, we had a gentleman here from Europe that was looking for his daughter. All he knew was her married name, what she looked like twenty years ago, and where he last had a letter from. He took it out to show me, Mr Teale, and it was so worn that you could hardly read the words. He used to come back here, night after night, almost too tired to eat. *Mr Stojkovitch*, I used to say, *take it easy on yourself*. But he found her, Mr Teale, and all was well.'

'Thankee again, ma'am,' said Lintott sincerely, but his mind was busy.

'You're welcome, Mr Teale. I'll send the girl up with hot water. Supper will be in a half hour.'

Washed and spruced once more, Lintott followed the sound of china, and came into the dining-room. The other residents greeted him and each other as good friends of long standing. Lintott replied in the same vein. The food, like the house, the landlady, and his room, lacked elegance but was adequate. Mrs Olson presided over a tureen of Dutch onion soup which she ladled into willow-patterned bowls and served with crackers. A pitcher of iced water stood in the centre of the table. A shy thin girl with red hands and elbows removed crockery and brought on the food. They ate a quantity of corned beef hash with poached eggs and cabbage. They chewed in appreciative silence, passing beer mustard and apple sauce politely, reaching for chunks of hot bread. They demolished two vast blueberry pies and a quart of Italian ice-cream.

The serious business of the evening being done, they drank coffee in Mrs Olson's parlour and engaged in conversation. Lintott, bemused by travelling and eating, had difficulty with his persona, and was called upon twice before he answered to the name of Mr Teale. However, he rallied sufficiently to receive a great deal of advice on how to find his missing relative. Apparently this was a mobile nation.

'Here today and gone tomorrow, sir,' said the man called Mr Rafferty. 'The newspaper offices are your best bet, but if you have such a thing as a likeness of the gentleman then show it around. Ask questions. Somebody will know something. You would be astonished, sir, how far perseverance goes!'

'Thankee, sir. I'll bear that in mind,' said Lintott with sleepy sarcasm. 'Ma'am, if you will kindly excuse me ... ?'

As he closed the door softly behind him, listening, he heard Mrs Olson.

'Mr Teale has been recently bereaved...'

He looked round the little room, which was not swaying or rumbling over iron rails, and thanked God for it. He unfastened his tie, dropped his collar-stud into the china saucer provided for it, opened the wardrobe door to hang up his suit. Naphthalene balls rattled along the paper-lined drawers as he pulled them out.

None of your moth corrupteth here, Lintott reflected. Everything in American apple-pie order. Draw the blinds down and shut out the dark. Have a chat by the fire over the tea-cups. *God Bless Our Home* on the wall, with a spray of violets in the top left-hand corner. Late husband's photograph on the sideboard. Say your prayers and sleep sound. All's well with the world. Only, it ain't! Don't I know that?

He folded his underwear neatly and pulled his night-shirt over his head. He settled his nightcap comfortably over his ears. His muttonchop whiskers bristled benevolently.

The candle shone on the polished dressing table, to be reflected radiantly in the swing mirror. It reminded him of Alicia, though he could not have explained why. He thought of her as a child, though he was unable to explain that feeling either. Something pathetic, vulnerable, about her. Well, well, he would begin the hunt on Monday. Tomorrow was the Seventh Day, and for once he would hallow it!

The clamour of an approaching bell brought him to the window. Running up the blind he saw horses galloping three abreast, saw the black gleam of helmets. He heard hooves and wheels, the cry of *Jump her lively, boys!* The firemen were there, here, gone. He peered for the flames but could see none. Nevertheless they had not been summoned without cause in this wooden quarter of the city. These buildings south of the Slot were as close and dry as sticks of kindling. Set a match to any of them and the rest could run wild with fire in minutes. He paused, sobered by the thought, and closed out the night again.

Twin plumes of flame quivered as the candle found its image in the glass. Sleep tight and God bless, Lintott counselled himself, and blew out reality and reflection with one breath.

FOURTEEN

Monday, 5 March 1906

SAN FRANCISCO HAD SHONE for Lintott's first afternoon, glittered for his first evening. This Monday morning she was still smiling, and the Inspector set course briskly for Market to get his bearings. Once he had placed himself by means of a major thoroughfare, he reckoned, he could add to it in other directions. Mission was south of the Slot, and Market Street was the Slot itself along which the cable cars ran, with horse carriages allowed to bowl alongside, and the motorcars of the rich making an occasional incursion.

Way down to Seventeenth, rubbing shoulders with Mission District, teemed a cosmopolitan hive of Spanish, Italian, German, Irish and Negro families. The further west you walked the shabbier the area became, but if you headed east then you were most aware of increasing prosperity. Here grew those vast towering structures Lintott had first glimpsed in New York, called *skyscrapers*. The Call building reared eighteen storeys high, to be topped by the tallest office in the West, the James Flood. The Crocker and Chronicle stood side by side: a giant flat-iron, a giant cube. There was the Palace Hotel where Salvador and Lizzie would stay in six weeks' time. And so on and on, along a battery of street lamps like iron candelabra, until you came at last to the Ferry Building on the Bay.

Here Lintott stopped and nodded twice or thrice to himself. He knew Market Street now. He could have returned to it ten years later – if he were still alive, if it were still the same – and know it again.

The eating-house where he stopped for his mid-day meal was a crowded, busy, shabby place. Sawdust on the floor, kicked cane chairs, scratched tables with stained cloths. Two overgrown girls scurried to and fro, bearing tin trays heavy with steaming food. They looked as though they had been there for ever. The savour of meals past and present was so condensed as to provide sustenance while he waited. One of the girls halted at Lintott's table, balanced an empty tray on an angular hip, prodded a stray hairpin into her topknot, and said all in a word, 'Whaddayawant?'

'I beg your pardon, my dear?' Lintott enquired, leaning forward to hear better.

Misunderstanding his movement, she became an iron signpost pointing to a notice behind his head. Good-natured, puzzled, thinking perhaps that the menu was on the wall, Lintott put on his spectacles and read KEEP YOUR HANDS OFF THE WAITRESS. He was resigned to indignities, but not prepared to waste time on them.

'Just you fetch me a plate of pot roast, my girl,' he said sternly, 'and none of your nonsense.'

She disappeared, silenced. Lintott stared through the smoke and steam at another notice, fascinated. PLEASE USE SPITTOON. Brown streaks in the sawdust marked the places where aims had fallen short. He took off his spectacles. Better not see more than he need, while he ate.

A lascar slid into the chair beside him with one long lovely movement.

'Wanna buy a bracelet?' He hung and swung on the words.

'No, thanks,' said Lintott shortly.

'Wanna buy yourself a good time?' The same rhythm.

'I just want my food in peace. Scarper!'

The lascar was not particularly tall, but of such leanness as to seem all supple bones. The heavy-lidded eyes moved slowly, the heavy mouth dominated the face. He was beautiful in a primitive fashion, and filthy. Lintott could smell stale sweat and curry.

'Wanna buy yourself a dream?' It was a song, an invitation.

'Clear off, will you, friend?' said Lintott, but more mildly. He had noticed the knife in the belt, the long nervous fingers.

'I gotta sister,' persuasively.

'So've I,' said Lintott with desperate humour, 'and she's nothing to boast about, neither.'

The man was puzzled, not yet angry. But give him time and another couple of refusals, Lintott thought, and he would act first and never consider it after. Fortunately his predicament had been observed. The owner finished wiping down the counter and padded over to Lintott's table. He was a truculent, big-bellied fellow. The lascar became a sinuous movement towards the door.

'Git!' said the owner briefly, fists on hips.

The lascar got.

'Thankee,' said Lintott civilly.

'That's okay, okay. You British? My grandmother came from Leeds. Yes, sir. We Britishers must stick together.'

He looked as though a few other nationalities had helped to stick him together since his grandmother touched the American shore. The eyes were distinctly oriental. Lintott shook hands.

'You carry a gun, buddy?' was the next remark.

'No, sir, and never have.'

'Know how to use one, buddy?'

'No, sir, I do not.'

'The hell you don't? Round here you can use a gun like a lush can use a drink! Want to know why he scat?' He moved one corner of his apron. His Colt lay delicately in its holster, the handle within finger-reach.

'Well, it's a bit late in the day for me to learn, ain't it?' said Lintott sensibly. 'So I shall have to manage without.'

The man regarded him with sorrow, and urged him to eat his food as though he were the warder in a condemned cell, bringing the last breakfast. Strangely enough, Lintott did relish his meal. The long walk had sharpened his appetite. He had seen worse eating-houses in Whitechapel, or as bad. He could do nothing with or about a gun. If it were indeed essential then he was staking shorter odds on survival, that was all. He felt better, if anything.

'You have to be losing afore you think you're winning, John Joseph!' Bessie's voice chided in his head.

He stirred the pot roast tenderly with his fork.

I'll get back to you, my lass. Never fret.

He left Market at Geary and came into the smooth lawns and cool trees of Union Square. The St Francis Hotel flew a flag from each of its three turrets. Lintott paused to take his bearings, and was aware of two presences in a doorway: man and dog.

San Francisco carried its cargo of mendicants like any other city, and he had observed with detached pity the same spectacles which confronted him in London. The crouched and palsied creature offering a tremulous tray of matchboxes: the legless man mounted on his trolley, cap in hand: the silent blind holding out a tin cup, beseeching. Physical mutilation or suffering, destitution, were common to them all. But America had a distinct advantage over England – California. Like swallows, the American mendicants were able to migrate. A fortunate group of nomads, they displayed their afflictions in the sun. These were the professionals, the ones who realised that deprivation could be a way of life.

So Lintott turned, feeling for a dime, and was greatly surprised to meet a pair of steady blue eyes and a serene face.

'Afternoon!' said Lintott heartily, and patted the dog's head, and laid his dime in the cardboard box.

The man did not touch his forelock nor launch upon pathetic explanation. He sat cross-legged on his piece of blanket with an ease and composure which impressed Lintott. His face was tanned and clean-shaven, his eyes clear and untroubled, his frame neat-boned and spare-fleshed.

'Folks call me Scotty. My name's McTavish.'

'Frank Teale,' said Lintott, and held out his hand. Scotty's fingers were light, dry and firm. 'And what's this little chap's name?' he asked of the curly-haired dog whose breed seemed undecided.

'She's called Patch.'

Patch was as naturally friendly as Scotty was naturally dignified. She jumped up against Lintott's legs and barked acquaintance. Scotty brought a ball from his pocket.

'Throw this up in the air for her and see what happens. Go on. Just throw it.'

The sun shone down on the oasis of Union Square. The clouds were laundered, the sky was dolly-blued. Lintott tossed a small green rubber ball into shining air, and Patch leaped up and caught it in her mouth. The two men smiled at each other. Then she lay down again on her share of blanket and put her nose on her paws. She had earned the dime.

'I wanted to see Nob Hill,' Lintott explained.

Scotty smiled, understanding.

'It's a great place. Several blocks, and every block a palace.'

'That's what I'd heard. That's what I wanted to see.'

'The great names, the great places?' Scotty asked, without blame. His life-style reckoned them unimportant. 'Crocker, Huntington, Hopkins, Stanford – the Railroad Kings. Flood, Fair, Mackay and O'Brien – the Bonanza Kings. In San Francisco we have millionaires like dogs have fleas! Alvinza Hayward – looks like a gentleman, swears like a trooper. Wells and Fargo, the Transport Kings. Alvin Adams, bearded old Ben Holladay. Reese, Cotton, Tobin. James Ben Ali Haggan. Ralston, Sharon. How much royalty can you take?'

'How many names do you know?' Lintott enquired, keen.

'More'n the history books will remember half a century from now. All big, all rich. Some of these I mention are dead and left a fortune behind. Like forty million bucks' worth of fortune, which is a lot of fortune. This is the city of gold, friend. The ladies sprinkle flakes of it in their hair, pour their afternoon tea from it, serve dinner on it, wear it, spend it, think it. The city smells of money, that's why she's the American dream, friend. They got a lot of names for her, like the city of love, but love don't count for nothing compared to the nugget. How old am I, friend?'

Lintott measured the youth of his open face, the wisdom of his eyes.

'Around forty?' he hazarded.

'I'm more'n that, friend. I been around a long time. I remember the '70s real good, that was when they went crazy, that was when dough became something you threw off the platform of a railway train. I seen an Irish washerwoman in a shawl pinned together with a diamond brooch. I seen miners wearing watch chains made of gold nuggets. I remember when some rich kids salted Sacramento with two thousand dollars' worth of gold dust to kid the Easterners. In 1869 the spike they drove into the rails of the Pacific Railroad, to celebrate the meeting of East and West, was made of gold. When Delmas Demas bought the *Call* newspaper he had five men carry baskets full of gold into the office, as a deposit. On Nob Hill they eat off gold and silver plate like we eat off of china.'

He took a handful of biscuit from his pocket, and Patch ate out of his hand as he talked.

'The dress circle at the Opera is called the "Golden Horseshoe". When you gamble in Portsmouth Square, or most places, you don't pass paper bucks across the baize, you roll gold. Before we had the official Mint here there were private mints. They turned out fifty-dollar octagonal slugs, twenty-dollar double eagles. The first classy paper we had was the *Golden Era*.'

He uncovered a dish of water, and Patch drank, wagging her tail.

'D'you smoke?' he asked Lintott, offering a rolled cigarette.

'My pipe, of an evening mostly. Carry on, sir. I'm a-listening.'

'What can I tell you? I'm telling you nothing. Just walk around, friend. Talk to the people, smell the air, watch and listen a little. That's what I do. That's what I done most of my life. This is what I own in all the world, friend,' and he indicated the blanket, the dog, and the cardboard box.

144

'Where do you live?'

'I have a friend. I have a lot of friends. I live by crumbs from the table, and in San Francisco they let fall crumbs of gold. Sharon's daughter had a dowry of two and a half million bucks, which was the price Crocker paid for his mansion. Their horses are stabled better than most people are housed. They have gold cages for gold birds.'

Fluttering, on the edge of the box. Fire, fire, fire.

'They will give a dinner, as they did at the Palace for Sharon, where the bill of fare was engraved on a forty-dollar silver plate, as a memento for every guest. They import chefs from Paris by the boatload. They import the finest food and wine from the best places. They have private Pullman cars on the railroad, and the trains stop where they say stop. If they get tired of San Francisco and the local power they can spend a million bucks getting themselves elected to the Senate, where they watch over us – on account of knowing all about life and how it is lived.'

But he spoke without bitterness, with an irony that reached without hurting. Lintott weighed him, judged him, found him to be wanting in and for nothing.

'Mr Bela Barak?' said Lintott.

'Ah!' Scotty smiled without reproach. 'You could've saved me the list!'

Lintott, feeling slightly embarrassed, found a greenback in his wallet. Scotty held up one small-boned hand.

'If that's for information about Bel Barak I don't want it, friend.'

'You mean you won't tell me anything?'

'I mean you don't have to pay me a buck. You have a reason to ask about him. You don't need to pay for a good reason.'

Lintott nodded. They understood each other completely. He laid the dollar humbly in the cardboard box.

'I'd appreciate you accepting this, as one friend to another,' he explained.

Scotty stroked Patch's head.

'You'll find his house on California. You can't exactly miss it. He had it custom-built ten or twelve years ago, and it cost over three million. Do you know what a French château looks like?'

'Yes, I do, as a matter of fact.'

'Well, that's what he thinks he got. But I travelled too, and I seen the genuine article. It was a little too simple for him, you see, so a half dozen architects kind of improved on it. But somewheres, buried deep, is a French château, friend.'

'I've seen quite a bit of the world myself,' said Lintott proudly. 'Late in life, mind you, but I've seen it. Oh yes.'

The sun was warm on his hands and face.

'I've travelled most of the world over,' said Scotty.

Lintott saw him covering territory with Patch on her lead; the blanket and cardboard box in a bundle on his back.

'So you don't belong to San Francisco then?' he asked.

'Sure I belong to her. She won't let me go that easy. There's more than gold to San Francisco, like maybe sea fog and frying fish?' He was smiling, making fun of her. 'She's a lady dressed for the grand ball, only maybe she has a ladder in that silk stocking and those gloves could be cleaner. Know what I mean?'

He lifted a harmonica to his lips and blew a tune softly. Then he answered Lintott's question another way.

'Sure, I walk off sometimes, because that's the way I am. But I come back.'

'I shan't be able to come back,' said Lintott soberly.

'How do you know you'll get to leave?' Scotty mocked.

'Because only six foot of earth would keep me here, and I hope it won't come to that. See you again, Scotty. Thankee.'

'Be seeing you, friend.'

Again he lifted the harmonica, smiling. As Lintott walked away he heard 'The British Grenadiers' being rendered with considerable panache. Touched, he marched in time to it, until he had marched out of earshot.

Iron balconies, iron fire-escapes, painted cream. Trees and white railings and pigeons strutting red-legged on the sidewalks. Steam rushing from the round heavy man-hole covers in the centre of the street. Wrought-iron gates with ceremonial bearings and crowns. Palm trees in courtyards. Garbage cans and backstairs. Pink and beige brick, painted wood. Grilles against the windows which stood level with the pavement.

Lintott had continued up Geary until he struck Jones, and then began a manful ascent. Post, Sutter and Bush were almost reasonable. He gathered breath at Pine. The next gradient was near vertical, he would swear to that. There was no option in this city of hills but to climb. To the left Pine swooped up and down, to the right he glimpsed the Bay. At California he stopped to rest.

It's just as well, he reflected, to find out where I am. I hope I don't have to run after anybody, or away from anybody, up these here mountains. Now where might his place be? I'd best watch out in case somebody's looking from behind a curtain. Still, the best place for a mouse to hide is under the cat's chin!

No one troubled to look out. Seclusion had been built into Barak's French-styled château, and beauty and simplicity built resolutely out. The original graceful sweep of pale stone, massive yet unobtrusive, had queened a hill and a valley in France. This turreted and castellated monster had closed its shutters, presumably against the unseemly spectacle of a Germanic stronghold on one side and a mock-baronial hall on the other.

No one looked out, but the mistress of the household was contemplating life within.

FIFTEEN

THE GOLD CLOCK beneath the bell glass struck once, twice,
thrice. The lady society editor stood in the centre of Mrs Barak's
private sitting-room, which was as vast and high-domed as a
cathedral, though furnished in the style of a Venetian palace.
She was used to waiting for rich ladies, and her patience had
been strengthened by the knowledge that they could not afford
to cross her.

Francesca, framed in the doorway at the far end of the room,
paused for a moment. Then she swept forward, smiling, holding out her hand.

'This is very kind of you, Mrs Barak. I know how valuable
your time is, and how many calls you have on it.'

Cards on a silver tray. Embossed invitations.

'Why, I am just so happy to see you again, Mrs Strauss. Shall
we sit by the fire?'

The society editor said, 'Do you mind if I take a few notes
as we talk, Mrs Barak?'

'Of course not!' Softly, automatically.

Mrs Strauss poised a sharpened pencil.

'First of all, may I say welcome back? San Francisco has
missed your sparkling entertainments these last months, but
you are looking great. What a very charming tea-gown you
are wearing, Mrs Barak. Our lady readers would simply love
to have details. Thank you,' scribbling. '*Écru* lace over white
satin, trimmed with *vieux rose* velvet. Parisian, I guess? I guess

right! An indispensable garment this time of year for the society hostess.'

From the crystal chandelier the ladies would have seemed exquisite dolls in conclave.

'I should have loved to interview you before you went abroad last Fall, particularly since you were away so long. The rumours that fly around! You know what people are like? I laughed most of them off, but a few words from you, dear Mrs Barak, and I'd have had a little more ammunition for them! Why, I even heard from one source that you and your husband had a serious difference of opinion. I told them I found that very difficult to believe.'

The graceful lady surrounded by symbols and tributes of marital devotion said, smiling, 'We never quarrel, Mrs Strauss. My husband is just too good and generous to me. I can tell you confidentially that I regard myself as a very spoiled person. I only have to ask for anything ...'

The day's tribute of red roses bloomed by her chair. She bent one towards her and sniffed its scent.

'Now that's exactly what I told them,' said the society editor, shrewdly observant, 'but when Mr Barak returned without you, after all, what was I to say? I put on my little thinking cap and said you were visiting with your illustrious family in Virginia.'

'You were so right,' said Francesca. 'I hadn't seen them in such a long time, and I just love going home when I can ...'

'And you still call it home? Now I think that is just lovely, a really fine sentiment, Mrs Barak. Home. Because, of course, Mr Barak's multiple commitments do not allow him to accompany you ...'

'As often as he would like to ...'

'Your family, the Sinclairs of Virginia,' tasting the words as though they were especially fine sugar plums, 'have only visited you here once in your six years – is it really six? My! – six years of marriage ...'

'My father has so many obligations of his own. I guess I shall just have to go on being their visitor!' she added gaily.

'And those little whispers about an estrangement between

your family and Mr Barak are nonsensical, of course...'

'I love my mother and father, Mrs Strauss, and they love me!'

Sincerity for once being manifest the society editor dropped the topic and picked up another.

'A little bird told me that you had not been feeling so good lately. I thought you were maybe visiting London, England, to see a Harley Street specialist again...'

'I was tired after the summer season, and you, who attended all my parties, can vouch for that, now can't you, Mrs Strauss?' Laughing, hiding.

'I certainly can, Mrs Barak, and I thank you most sincerely for those invitations. But you have visited specialists here and in Europe, in recent years. Is it still that riding accident which bothers you, I wonder?' She laid down her pencil. 'This is not for the column, Mrs Barak. I deal in society news, and I am a good friend to have because when those crazy rumours start I can scotch them like rattlesnakes!'

Mrs Barak's eyes turned a darker blue. Then she smiled.

'Why, yes, Mrs Strauss, that riding accident left me with a little spinal trouble, as you know. Now and again I hear of somebody who might be able to relieve it. So far I have been unlucky, but I guess I shall keep on trying.'

Mrs Strauss said, with a show of sympathy, 'The trouble is not too painful I hope?'

Francesca replied, 'Just an ache. Nothing very serious.'

'And I was hoping you might have exciting news for us all...' the society editor said blandly.

She had heard, from every source which furnished the empty nursery upstairs, of that magnificent monument to Barak's posterity. She saw from Francesca's expression that she must go no further.

'...about your brilliant reception in London, Mrs Barak.'

Francesca replied obediently, 'My husband was unable to accompany me on my autumn shopping expedition, owing to business obligations. But as soon as he could join me he gave me a little party to celebrate our reunion.'

One of the drugged swans on the trough had surfaced sufficiently to bite Fleischer's hand. She had watched the blood run, and had been kind.

'A little party?' echoed Mrs Strauss, laughing. She wagged her finger. 'I was told about that prodigal little party of yours by Mrs Harvey N. Baldwin of Philadelphia, who had the honour to be present!'

Francesca laughed too, spread her pretty jewelled fingers, and cried, 'Then you know how spoiled I was!'

Still smiling, she pulled the beaded bell-rope for tea. Yet the society editor had not extracted every morsel.

'I believe that Farquharson and Wheelock's of New York can expect an order from you for a court dress in the near future? When is the presentation to their English Majesties expected, Mrs Barak?'

'Why, surely I would go nowhere but to Farquharson and Wheelock's for a court dress,' Francesca drawled gently, 'but you are somewhat ahead of me on schedule, Mrs Strauss. My presentation at the English Court is not in my mind!'

'Oh, really? I understood that Mr Barak had approached not only two titled ladies in London society, and three prominent politicians in Washington, but also the American Ambassador in London, with regard to sponsorship ...'

The butler in striped trousers and swallowtail coat knocked softly at the door and entered. He had been imported from England to make sure that Barak was getting value for his money. He motioned the footman to bring a trolley in. The footman was followed by a demure parlour-maid. Between the three of them they would serve a genuine English tea.

Francesca, given time to consider strategy, decided on apparent frankness.

'As soon as I have definite information you shall be the very first person to hear!' she confided.

They must now speak only of Mrs Barak's social programme and wardrobe for each occasion, while servants were present.

'I believe you have a new addition to your lovely stables

out at Belmont?' cried Mrs Strauss. 'I had not forgotten your Palomino! Orange Belle?'

Now Francesca awoke and became animated. The society editor watched, and smiled drily as Mrs Barak remembered to comment on her husband's indulgence of this costly whim.

Swapped for a horse! she thought grimly, and wished she could write the truth and use this phrase as a title.

'Now did you or your husband think of using the stable name "Belle" with your particular horses? If I recollect aright his wedding gift to you, six years ago, was "Southern Belle". Then you had "Midnight Belle", I believe? "Carnival Belle", and so on. That is, if I recollect ...'

She recollected accurately.

'That was my husband's loving notion,' Francesca confided charmingly.

She had evaded the problem of a future presentation at court, so must concede a gobbet for the gossip columnist.

'He called them all "Belle" after me! But I should just hate you to print that – it sounds so conceited!'

'It sounds like you are a very lucky and happy wife, Mrs Barak,' said Mrs Strauss, dutifully scribbling, 'and I don't know that I can promise to keep that little secret from our readers!'

The clock struck four insistently. Servants and trolley withdrew.

'My, how time flies!' cried the society editor, assembling herself for departure. 'Well, now, I do hope that the next time we talk with each other you will have news of a royal début! I know the Lord Chamberlain's office is exacting in its requirements, but I should have thought ... your wonderful old family in Virginia ... your rich and influential husband ... I say to everybody, "Mrs Barak not only *keeps* thoroughbreds, she *is* a thoroughbred" ... and now I must just thank you once again for ...'

'So the gossip-lady admired your tea-gown, madame?' Genevieve asked, helping her mistress out of it.

'All gossip-ladies should be horse-whipped!' said Francesca, deceptively sweet of tone. 'And just you keep that little remark between the two of us! Genevieve, as soon as I have gotten through this latest round of socialising, you and I are going down to Belmont. Anybody who wants to see me can make the journey! And I shall be out every day, riding. The way I feel right now I might just ride to Mexico!'

'Madame, make sure, if you please, that you do not offend. The last occasion was an unhappy one for both of us.'

Francesca looked away, looked down, as she always did when disguising what she felt, when pursuing her own course in spite of disapproval.

'Oh, that was very different, Genevieve. This is just fun.'

The French maid sighed and stared down her long nose. Her plain face and black dress set off Francesca's beauty and lace.

'Madame should remember that she has certain powers and I have none! If anyone should one day need a goat-scape...'

Francesca giggled with relief.

'For heaven's sake, Genevieve, the word is scape-goat!'

'Madame knows very well what I mean.'

But Madame had borne her share of affliction that afternoon, and was laughing with the gaiety which sounded nearer despair than delight.

SIXTEEN

Mrs CLAUDIA STRAUSS was so busy writing the interview in her head that she nearly fell into the arms of two men, and snarled her foot in the dachshund's lead. The shorter, greyer fellow, whose accent was English, whose face was fatherly, steadied her by the arm. The other, an impudent creature in the livery of the Barak household, smiled as he caught sight of her ankle and petticoat hem.

'Thank you, sir!' said Mrs Strauss to Lintott, and then to the footman, 'Shouldn't you be exercising that dog instead of your mouth, young man?'

'Yes, ma'am,' he replied, grinning, 'but don't you remember me?'

She took a pair of eye-glasses from her reticule and peered at him closely. She smiled, changed, gave him a coquettish little push.

'Why, Denver Peabody, how in the world could I forget *you*?'

'It's the uniform,' said Denver. 'When I come to see you I was wearing my own clothes.'

'Well, Denver, any time you have any little item of news for me you are welcome to a Bourbon, and you know that!'

'I may be along later this week,' he said, and raised his eyebrows.

'You will surely be welcome,' she repeated, bowed to Lintott, and proceeded stylishly upon her way.

Denver Peabody's eyes followed the trim waist and straight back. He winked at the Inspector.

'That lady is Claudia Strauss, the biggest pen in town,' he explained. 'She is some person, I can tell you. I think she'd be willing to hold hands with me, but she's too smart for that!'

His accent was a curious mixture of southern American and London cockney.

'Oh, yes?' Lintott replied. 'A lady journalist, is she? Widowed?'

'No, she has a husband of sorts, who acts like her chaperon. Being a wicked pen our Claudia has to keep as clean as Caesar's wife, otherwise somebody might write a little something about *her*! So, when I get my Bourbon, old Mr Strauss will be sitting there, and only when she gives me my tip for the information will she squeeze my fingers!'

'How long have you been over here?' Lintott asked.

'A coupla years. I had to disappear for a while, and a kind lady raised the passage money for me, steerage.'

Lintott whistled sympathetically, but his eyes were sharp and cold.

'Denver ain't an English name,' he observed mildly, 'though Peabody is a good 'un.'

'I was Dennis, but Denver sounded smarter. I picked up the lingo pretty fast. I guess you wouldn't know I was English, would you?'

'Not if I was an American, perhaps,' said Lintott drily, 'but being English I catch one or two words now and again as remind me of London!'

He looked at the dog, he looked at the footman in his livery of green velvet and gold brocade, complete with buckled shoes and cuff frills.

'I think I ought to buy you a drink somewhere,' he said, 'but I don't know where. That is, if you want a drink. I ain't forcing myself on you, it's just that I'm by myself here, and...'

'Sure,' said Denver, 'I understand, Mr Teale. I felt that way myself when I arrived. Now I like it, because nobody knows me and I can just have a good time.'

'Then where do we go?' asked Lintott.

The footman's tongue protruded between his lips briefly. He winked again.

'You just want a drink?' he asked.

'That's all,' said Lintott firmly. 'A drink and a friendly chat.'

Denver Peabody found a dark little bar.

'I wouldn't have believed,' said Lintott, 'as a city could change street by street, like this. One minute you're with the millionaires, the next...'

Denver was warming, in spite of his sophistication, to the presence of someone from the old country. His American accent faltered and then disappeared. He became the cocky, friendly lad who had a way with the ladies. Lintott listened and recorded, wishing he had access to his London colleagues.

Petty larceny, he decided, and got in with a mob as was too big for him. Probably framed. Lucky to get away with it. No great harm in him. No great good, neither!

'We're right on top of the red-light district here,' Denver was saying. 'The nobs as live on Nob Hill – that's our lot – they keep their fancy pieces on Russian Hill. But when they feel like a bit of the other they only have to step next door! All this, round here, is the Upper Tenderloin – the best slice of the joint!' He laughed heartily, and dug Lintott in the ribs. 'You'd be surprised how big the vice district is, Frank. North by Broadway. Here, half a mo', I'll draw it for you!' He dipped his forefinger in the Bourbon and marked the table top. 'North by Broadway, South by Commercial, West by Powell, East by the waterfront – and then there's Morton Street if you like peepshows and that. Morton Street's rough! Now this line separates the Upper Tenderloin from the Barbary Coast.'

'The Barbary Coast,' mused Lintott, who breathed underworlds as others breathe clean air. 'Who runs that, then, Denver?'

'You'd be surprised! Who do you think?'

Lintott's eyes were pinpoints.

'How should I know?' he said mildly. 'I don't know my left hand from my right, in this place.'

156

'I'll tell you the inside story,' said Denver, and Lintott knew why he had left England.

Talks too much, he thought. Anxious to impress folks. Fair gift for speculation, so pushes out a bit further. Even happens on the truth now and again, and that can be dangerous.

'She's too new, you see,' Denver was saying, jerking his head at some vague point which represented San Francisco. 'She's only got a surface on her, and underneath there's a regular old pig-sty. Mrs Barak, that's our mistress, comes from what you might call gentlefolk, for all they're American. But *him*! His mam was a washerwoman, and his dad was a miner who struck lucky. He don't mind the dirt, so long as it's on somebody else's hands. You'd be surprised how much we know, downstairs!'

Oh, no, I wouldn't, Lintott thought. That's why I made your acquaintance, my lad. That's why you're drinking my Bourbon!

'He's got what the Chinese call a *boo how doy* – a bodyguard. Oh, that ain't what they say he is. We call him *Mr Fleischer*, and treat him like fine gold because we know better than to cross him. But we know why he's there. He carries a gun, don't he? He don't live with us – well, I don't suppose the mistress would stand for that. No love lost between her and him, I can tell you. He drives round in a new Cadillac.'

'Married, is he, this Mr Fleischer?' Lintott asked amiably.

'No! Blimey! Him? He'd freeze a woman to death.'

'A Cadillac, did you say? That's a bit beyond me. What does it look like?'

'You can't miss it, Frank, believe me!' Denver was deeply impressed by the marvel of the modern age. 'It's kind of a dark red, and big, with brass headlamps and black leather seats. This year's model...'

'I know nothing about automobiles,' said Lintott mildly. 'But you got side-tracked, Denver. You were going to tell me who runs the Barbary Coast.'

The footman's eyes were small and black and bright under his powdered wig.

'One day,' he said, on another track of conversation, 'one day, Frank, I am going to be somebody. And do you know why? Because I keep my eyes and ears open and the ladies like me, and I'm kind of smart. I'm just biding my time.'

'Certainly, I don't need to be told that,' said Lintott, smiling. 'I knew you were a sharp lad when I saw you. He'll go a long way, I said to myself, because he's smart, and he knows more than he says.'

'I got no proof, mind,' Denver cautioned, 'but I've watched that Fleischer, and I've watched the master and mistress – Claudia Strauss only gets the tit-bits. That Fleischer lives with Aunt Patsy on Mason Street, and Aunt Patsy keeps a parlour-house – a ken full of judies!' Lintott smiled at the homely phrase. 'Now he ain't interested in women, like I said, so I reckon he keeps an eye on things for Aunt Patsy. She's the respectable sort, don't like a rough house. I got a friend on Mason as told me that Fleischer keeps an eye on any number of places like Aunt Patsy's – for a consideration. But if they was his – know what I mean? – he could retire tomorrow. He don't. He goes on holding a gun for Mr Barak and driving him around in the Cadillac. So I think our gentleman has a finger in this little pie, and that finger's name is Fleischer. Oh, my Gawd!'

He had glanced at the watch in his satin waistcoat pocket.

'See you sometime!' he cried, pulling the dachshund to its feet. 'Come on home, honey. No walkies today. Hey, thanks for the drink.'

He was putting on his American *alter ego*. He waved a white hand. Lintott nodded and smiled. He paid the barman and went out. Enough was enough, for one day. He heard an exuberant clatter and clamour behind him, and accosted an elderly man in a black beret, carrying a string bag.

'Excuse me, sir, but where do I get on one of these here trams of yours?'

'Corner of Jackson. Just there, bud. You a Britisher?'

'Yes!' shouted Lintott, and sprinted before he could hear that the man's aunt came from Edinburgh.

Breathless but triumphant, he swung himself up the step and sat on the wooden bench in the open part of the car.

'How much?' Lintott asked, feeling in his pocket. 'And where are you going?'

'A nickel. Hyde and Wharf. Hold *on* there!'

Lintott held on, by means of the rail, and consulted his plain watch. He would see where they went, and if it was the wrong direction then he could come right back. No harm done. Supper was at six o'clock.

The cable moved noisily in its slot, chuntering along at an unsteady nine miles an hour. The driver, the Dummy as he was unfairly called, stared straight ahead and played a skilful concert with his three gear levers. Occasionally he called out, as one might shout 'Land ahoy!' to fellow voyagers, 'Hold *on* there!'

Lintott suddenly clutched his hat as well as the rail. The car launched itself recklessly round the corner into Hyde, and everyone swung to the left with it, and then levelled again as it made the straight. Lintott could not help feeling that they had survived more by good fortune than good management. The Mexican at the controls wore a fearsome aspect, as of a man willing to risk death. His peaked cap was pulled well down over one black eye. A black moustache drooped sardonically in an impassive dark face. A jailbird, past, present, or to come, if ever the Inspector saw one. They were in his hands, rattling along, stopping at Pacific and Broadway to pick up more passengers. So far, not so bad, apart from that lunge into Hyde Street. Vallejo, Green, Union, Filbert. He was beginning to enjoy himself. Ladies and children sat safely in the closed car, as was right and proper. Not much danger, then, if that button-booted, feather-hatted cargo of the gentle and timid ventured aboard. The male adventurers were now standing on the step in front of him, crowded next to him. A lady paused, uncertain, peering into the crammed car. Lintott lifted his bowler hat, gave up his seat and took his place next to the young and middle-aged bloods on the iron step.

And off again, in this ornamental glass coach with its gold

trimmings and gaudy scrollwork, to the Wharf – wherever that might be. Somewhere on the sea.

At Greenwich they crested the final run, and Lintott stared into the pitch of the Bay from an incredible height, at a scandalous angle. In spite of the warmth of the day he felt the blood leave his face, the sweat start to his hand. Suppose it got out of control and they hurtled faster and faster towards destruction? He expected he could jump off without breaking more than a leg and arm in the process, but what would stop his own spinning descent after the spinning transom? He wanted to clutch the Mexican by his dark sleeve and ask him whether he had considered the matter seriously. Instead, he shut his eyes, took a stronger grip on the rail, and allowed himself to be dashed to his doom. The Mexican arched backwards superbly. Carefully they trundled nose-to-rail down the sheer drop. Lombard, Chestnut, Francisco, North Point. Straightened out, and rolled mildly into the terminus.

Never would have believed it, Lintott thought, and wiped his hands and forehead. He got out and read their destination. POWELL, HYDE and MARKET. Better than he could have expected. The Mexican smiled slowly as Lintott paid his fare for the return ride and took his stance by the rail.

'Ain't you had enough, buddy?' he enquired, friendly.

'I reckon I've only just started,' Lintott replied, good-humoured.

He clapped his hat tightly down and braced himself like an old San Franciscan. They were off. Pitching up and down hills, lurching round corners, tilting perilously over cliff-falls, clanking along the straight. The Mexican pulled and pushed with a strength and sureness quite admirable to behold. They were safe with a driver of that calibre and understanding. He had survived for years. Lintott suffered a schoolboy's regret as they drew up in the Market terminal. An elderly schoolboy, he gave them a hand in pushing the car round on the turntable, nodded at them in a comradely fashion. They had been through much together.

'They talk about throwing these cars on the garbage,' said

the passenger who had pushed shoulder to shoulder with Lintott. 'They say they're obsolete and oughta be replaced with a subway.'

'Fiddlesticks!' said Lintott, and was astonished to hear himself so loud and passionate. 'Rubbish!' he added, in a lower and more moderate tone. 'There's a lot of life in these here trams yet.'

'Sure! Anyway, who wants a subway when he can take a look around?'

Lintott shook hands with him, was suitably amazed and impressed when the man told him he had a cousin whose mother was born in Devon, and regretted that he did not know the name of Brewer, nor the village of Chagford.

Making his way back to Mission he edited and highlighted the journey for Bessie's future benefit. He savoured her expressions of horror.

'Nothing to it, Bess,' he would tell her, some fair day. 'Took it in my stride as you might say.'

San Francisco was undoubtedly showing off to her new courtier. Her evening sky was apricot and gold. The crowded frame-houses, south of the Slot, jostled by warehouses and factories, interlaced with railroad yards, became most beautiful in Lintott's eyes.

Sure, I belong to her! Scotty had said.

Well, thought Lintott, I shall just have to belong to her back in London! Better not let Bessie suspect, neither, or the fat'll be in the fire!

The following morning San Francisco decided to pamper Lintott no more. He padded off to study newspaper gossip columns and the Social Register in the wet. Nor was the rain like any he had experienced before, for it fairly lashed down, striking the ground with such force that it bounced back in miniature waterfalls. His trousers were soaked to the knee before he had gone a hundred yards. Furthermore, an insidious wind carried swathes of rain in different directions. Lintott strode on, black umbrella held before him like an ineffectual shield, and was not dismayed.

He had decided to play the simpleton, to build up the portrait of a kindly man on a hopeless mission. In Mrs Olson's eyes he was a grieving widower, grasping at a pretext which would fill his heart and time. To the office staff of the *San Francisco Examiner* he became yet another madman.

Sharp-witted, almost young enough to be his grandsons, they registered amusement and incomprehension as he told them about his missing uncle. They knew the sorry side of humanity too well, they saw too much and had to form a personal philosophy in order to cope with it. So Lintott and his fictional uncle arrived upon them in the form of wry entertainment. They were kind, they were courteous, they gave him cups of coffee and permitted him access to yesteryears' revelations. They watched him, fascinated, as he plodded patiently through reams of old newspapers, culling information about Bela Barak and his life-style. They asked him questions, now and again. He never failed to delight them, and himself, with his replies.

'Pardon me, Mr Teale, but was your uncle a gold-miner?'

'No, sir, he was a tin-miner.'

'I mean, when he was out here, Mr Teale, did he mine gold?'

'I wouldn't know about that, young man,' glancing up blandly over his spectacles. 'I think he came to advise them. Does it make a difference, then?'

'Sure, Mr Teale. If he struck out on his own he might have struck lucky. He could have a heap of gold, right now.' Hesitation. 'If he's alive, that is.'

'Won't make any difference to Uncle Fred. Never parted with a brass farthing in his life! He ain't dead as far as I know, neither.'

'Oh, really? How – how old might he be, Mr Teale?'

'Let me see now. Last time I saw him was way back in 1870. He'll be ... oh, going on eighty-nine by this time!'

'That's some age, Mr Teale!' Awed. 'Are you sure he's alive?'

'Positive. We're a very long-lived family.'

'Oh, sure, sure. Uh! Pardon me, Mr Teale, but if you find the old gentleman – what then?'

'Take him right back home with me,' said Lintott gravely. 'I can't have him roaming round California at his time of life. There's no knowing what sort of trouble he might get into. I've seen a few things round here as I don't care for, I can tell you. And he was always easily led!'

They would disappear into the back office, choking and incredulous. Lintott heard suppressed comments, suppressed laughter. He smiled, and read on. He reckoned San Francisco could carry one more eccentric.

He discovered more than Bela Barak in William Randolph Hearst's *Examiner*. He found a vitriolic crusade against the Southern Pacific Railroad and robber barons who built castles on Nob Hill and lived by bribery and corruption. Mind you, the classified advertisements of the same paper were invitations to exploit another commodity. Lintott was to learn later that this newspaper had been dubbed 'The Whore's Daily Guide and Handy Compendium'.

'Plays both sides against the middle!' he observed to himself.

The *Examiner* was, in the end, more informative about Barak than any other newspaper. Nevertheless, he worked through samples of the *Chronicle*, the *Bulletin*, the *Call*, the *Daily News*, the *Evening Post*, and the *Globe*. He suffered only one bad moment, and it was a human episode which touched him as much as it alerted him. At the *Daily News* a young reporter named Ed Gleeson, introduced to the saga of Mr Teale's long-lost uncle, stopped by to have a word with Lintott.

'I've been thinking, Mr Teale. Maybe we could help a little,' he offered. 'I could write him up if you give me the facts. Folks like a family story. Somebody might read the column and remember the old guy from somewhere.'

Lintott was alarmed and ashamed at once. It took all his natural cunning and apparent simplicity to ward off Gleeson's kindness. The Inspector shook him warmly by the hand, anyway, and thanked him.

'Any time,' said Gleeson. 'We're here to help, y'know.'

Lintott drank his coffee and wished it were something stronger. Getting so sharp I'll cut myself, he thought!

Barak loomed grandly from the pages of the *Commercial Encyclopaedia*. His appearance was so impeccable as to seem a blueprint for the kind of citizen America looked for. He was described simply as being a 'Capitalist'.

Which covers a mort of ground without specifying it, thought Lintott.

> Born 1857 in Sacramento, only son of Aaron Barak who made the foundation of his fortune in the early gold-mines. On the death of his father in 1880, Bela Barak came to San Francisco where he now holds directorates and offices in a large number of corporations and companies.

So he does, my word. Take a look at them. Mines, railroads, banks, real estate, land, hotels, gas and electricity, lumber, coal and iron and steel, water, telephone and telegraph. You could set him up as a city on his own!

> Prominent in social as well as financial circles, he is a member of many clubs, among them the Pacific Union and the Burlinghame. He is a pioneer of the promotion and resources in the development of California.

With a fat percentage of those resources drifting into his own pocket, I'll bet my boots!

> He has given liberally to many charitable institutions, endowed schools, hospitals, and other public beneficiaries. He can always be found ready to lend his influence and to contribute freely to every public enterprise instigated for the betterment of his native city. Mr Barak was married in 1900 to the beautiful and accomplished daughter of Mr Philip

Sinclair of Virginia, Miss Francesca Sinclair. They reside in California Street, Nob Hill, in a wonderful French-styled château which is the envy and pride of the élite of San Francisco. He is fond of out-of-doors sports, and is a popular member of the Saint Francis Yacht Club. His favourite recreation is his long yachting excursions along the north shores of San Francisco Bay, in his schooner yacht, the *Adventurer*.

He should have called it the *Pirate*! That would have been nearer the mark. So that's Bela Barak?

Lintott folded his spectacles thoughtfully.

Coincidences do happen, he told himself. It's quite possible that Mrs Barak had a slap-up row with her husband, flounced off to London, was followed by Fleischer both before and after Bela Barak arrived there, and Fleischer happened to see Alicia Salvador again. For whatever reason, Fleischer did a little kidnapping on his own account.

Loyalties are a funny thing, too. It's possible that Barak and Fleischer think a deal of one another: master and man. I've known more than one relationship of that sort as worked better than brother and brother! So Fleischer only has to sidle up to Barak and ask him for a bit of help and cover-up, and Barak says yes.

But it does seem too much of a coincidence and a convenience to me! I wish I knew what they'd quarrelled about. I might have a clue to the rest then.

INTERMISSION

DUO BRILLIANTE!
Violin and Piano Forte,
accompanied on the
Patent Concertina.

From a herald advertising Mr Sutton
at the New Strand Theatre, London

October 1905

BELA BARAK SAID, sitting in the Regency chair in Francesca's bedroom, 'How do you like your console mirror, honey?'

She lifted her hands to her hair, in the way of women since time began, and admired her reflection.

'I think it's the most beautiful mirror in the whole world, Bel!'

'It should be,' he said, looking at his purchase. 'I paid all of five thousand dollars for it.'

The mention of money was distasteful to her. She frowned momentarily.

'That wasn't what I came to see you about,' he continued.

He rose and paced the room, brooding.

'Your family did worse than lie to me,' he said softly, 'they kept back the truth. I have paid one hell of a lot to find out the truth about you.'

She turned away from his black stare and said, 'Honey, when are we going to take a vacation together? It seems about a hundred years since we took a real vacation...'

'Listen to me, honey, and don't you interrupt me. I have something very important to say. Your family made me feel like dirt, did you know that? I felt they were doing me a favour even letting me look at you.'

He had ordered Genevieve out as soon as he entered the room, and his wife was in her frilled wrapper with her hair down. She now picked up a silver-backed brush and began uncertainly to draw it through her long black locks.

'Put that brush down!' he shouted, and snatched it from her hand and pitched it across the floor. 'With all the money I have, and all I offer you, you can still use those old brushes?'

Her exquisite pallor was now marked. Her eyes shone most brilliantly.

'I should hate for you to damage that brush,' she said composedly. 'I really care for this set, Bel. It belonged to my grandmother.'

She had walked past him to retrieve it and now stood by the window, head bent, examining the chased silver for signs of ill-treatment.

Barak's eyes were contemplative of his injuries.

'I couldn't figure it out,' he said to himself, and rubbed his heavy jaw and rubbed his greying head. 'Once I married you I thought we should be in the right circles socially. But no matter how much money I spent, how many people I knew, I just could not get things going. Oh, sure, I can buy my way into most places, but I lacked class. That was why I sat around in Virginia, taking all those nice smooth smiling faces on trust.'

Francesca said lightly, 'I thought you sat around because you liked *me*, Bel, not my connections!'

'I was crazy about you!' His emphasis stilled her. 'And who were you crazy about? Tell me that!' Since she could not answer he continued, 'I thought that if I was good enough to marry one of the Sinclair girls – and though they were cool they were friendly, your family! – why, I thought I was good enough to go any place I wanted. So I married you, Francesca, and suddenly nobody who was anybody wanted to know us. Why?'

She stood motionless and colourless, smoothing the silver with one waxen finger. She did not look at him, while he looked nowhere else but at this poor and powerful bargain.

'Why?' he demanded. He laughed and shook his head from side to side, without humour or kindness, 'Because of the whispers. Have you ever traced a whisper, Francesca? It costs an awful lot of money...'

Suddenly she flung the brush at him, crying, 'Will you for heaven's sakes stop talking, just once in a while, about money?

It's so vulgar. Did you know how vulgar it was? How vulgar all this is...'

Her gesture at the room indicated the ostentation of his tributes to her. He could not understand for a moment what she was saying, and cut across the hysterical flurry of words with a diatribe of his own.

'Whispers. That's all. No facts, no names, no places. But don't you think for one moment that I won't get the truth from somebody...'

'You wanted me to have gold hairbrushes. Why does everything have to be gold? Have you any idea about anything at all...?'

'I thought I was just not good enough for them. Oh, my God. And all that time, among those china teacups that belonged to everybody's damned grandmother, they were whispering about *you*...'

FANTASMAGORIA

Will introduce the PHANTOMS *or* APPARITIONS *of
the* DEAD *or* ABSENT, *in a way more compleately
illusive than has ever been offered to the Eye
in a Public Theatre, as the Objects freely
originate in the Air, and unfold themselves
under various Forms and Sizes such as the
Imagination alone has hitherto painted them* ...

advertising de Philipstal, Lyceum Theatre,
Strand, London, 1803

SEVENTEEN

March–April 1906

'AND NOW, NOBLE LADIES and gentlemen, behold!' cried Salvador, passing his hands over the golden crucible. Fire leaped. 'I bring you visions from the past. I bring you the dead mysteriously arisen. I bring you – *phantoms*!'

The gold brocade gown, stiff and rich as a bishop's cope, gave Lizzie a curiously imposing air. She had become a priestess, assisting at a sacred ritual, as she handed Salvador the dark bottles of blood, of alcohol, of vitriol. The crucible blazed against a background of black silk curtains, illuminating Lizzie's costume and the magician's white shirt front.

'*Voilà!*'

Smoke poured up and massed into a menacing cloud. Thunder rumbled, lightning flashed, strange music haunted the theatre. The tolling of a bell, the tolling of Salvador's voice, announced the apparitions which formed in the air. Ghosts hovered and glared, were released into the auditorium to the accompaniment of shrieks and exclamations from the spectators, spread out and vanished. The final spectre was a clown who disappeared with a bang and made everybody laugh in relief.

Salvador was laughing as the smoke cleared. Lizzie was smiling broadly. She indicated his skill with both hands extended. They applauded heartily. He spread out his arms to garner the applause. Lizzie and Salvador both bowed low and smiled at each other.

'Thank you, noble ladies and gentlemen, thank you! Before I try to amuse you with another little illusion I must say how very pleased I am by your reception of this one. Some years ago, in Mexico, I was arrested by the police for doing the same thing, and spent a few hours in prison before the kind consul released me...'

Lizzie unobtrusively moved away to check the next lot of apparatus. No one noticed her, they were spellbound by the magician. As he had told her, they watched what they were meant to watch, and were mystified by what they had not observed. Her heart was light, her carriage proud these days, for she performed to the satisfaction of Salvador, herself and their audiences. Her face and smile had become serene.

'I wonder,' Salvador was saying, 'whether some kind gentleman...'

He had taken up the pack of cards and was fingering them in anticipation. She observed his movements with indulgence. At breakfast-time he would fan them out on the table, tipple them back upon themselves, run them up his sleeves. *Always practice, always perfection*, he would say to himself. The work behind the magic was formidable, relentless, never ceasing.

In Manhattan, as soon as they had arrived, Esmerelda had accompanied Lizzie to a wardrobe dealer's shop and advised her in her choice by means of halting English and eloquent gestures. They selected a necessary minimum of clothes to meet different climates and occasions. The cream silk costume, bearing seven smoked-pearl buttons on each sleeve, was laid away in readiness for California. The brocade gown had been hanging high up on a line at the back of the shop. Lizzie had pointed, Esmerelda had nodded emphatically. It was their final purchase. Now Lizzie possessed some style and quality.

'You wear your elegancies with much elegance, Miss Lizzie,' Salvador had said in quiet pleasure, for her unobtrusive flowering was the greatest compliment she could have paid him.

Strangely enough she did not feel smarter, but she felt more a part of the surface life of hotels and railway trains. She was flying steadily now, after preliminary trembles and tumbles, with the regular birds of passage. She could sense the personality of an audience: tonight it was particularly relaxed and sympathetic. She could sense the aura of a theatre: this one was older, more intimate. She was learning how to travel. She was learning how to travel on.

The clock had ticked off the weeks. She stepped out of cabs, trod the lobbies of great hotels, ate late suppers with the magician, raised blinds on new mornings and looked on to new streets, new cities, new states, new worlds. The vitality in the air suited her. She moved faster, talked faster, thought faster, over here. She coasted on a perpetual current of energy like a paper boat. The dryness sometimes caused her to exchange a mild electric shock instead of a handshake.

At the coming of darkness the skyscrapers were alight: storeyed brilliants pouring out their cargoes of fun-seekers. Life was riding high and riding by; life spangled and spiced, one long fixed smile to indicate that the good time was for ever, that someone was awake all night over here.

'And now, noble ladies and gentlemen, we shall see whether ...'

The evening was a culmination of small and great triumphs, her own and his. She moved from one routine to another, smoothly, at her ease. She rode with him on the wings of his triumph. She saw that he was tiring. As he shrugged on his jacket, the back of his shirt was wet. Still he smiled, still he was magnificent. I, Salvador, Salvador, Salvador! Arms outspread, head flung back, feeding on the applause. Then he was turning to indicate the tall fine figure in its gold brocade who was herself, or the illusion of herself, she was not sure which. She bowed gracefully. They clapped her heartily. The magician came over and took her by the hand, led her to the footlights, indicated that they should give of their loudest and best.

She was smiling, trying not to cry at his praise and theirs, for life had been small and hard and dull and was now glorious, and she did not know what would become of her without him.

Supper was served as usual in Salvador's suite. The old people had gone to their beds, all duties done. The gold-framed glass over the fireplace reflected the white damask napery, the shining silver, the roses in their little vase. The waiter served them with unobtrusive skill and courtesy. This was their setting.

'We shall manage very well now,' said Salvador. 'Thank you.'

The man saw that everything was to hand, bowed and withdrew. Lizzie had bought an amethyst gown for evenings, and was deeply in love with its elegance, and in love with herself in its elegance. She drank her wine and admired the sleeve falling away from elbow to wrist in chiffon frills.

She permitted herself to say a little of what she felt for the magician.

'You brought me out of exile, in a way, as you brought Alicia.'

Pouring more wine into her glass, he replied, 'I wish to be a magician of life as well as of art, Miss Lizzie.'

Enclosed in a magical universe, she said, 'However shall I go back to what I was?'

'You will never go back, Lizzie. You can only go on.'

'But where to? Where to?' she asked earnestly.

'To wherever you belong – wherever that may be!' He saw that between wine and fatigue and excitement she was near tears, and cried, 'To Babylon!' And as she smiled, and wiped her eyes, and shook her head, he leaned forward and said tenderly, as to a child, 'How many miles to Babylon, dear Lizzie?'

'Three score and ten!' she replied, smiling, chin trembling.

'Shall we get there by candle-light, dearest Lizzie?' he asked gravely.

'Yes,' she said with conviction, '*and* back again!'

'To our journeys, wherever they may lead, whatever they may bring, both separately and together!'

He lifted his glass. She touched her glass to his. The candles shone in their silver sconces.

'Have you ever been in love, Lizzie?' Salvador asked.

'Yes,' she replied. 'Yes. Just once.'

'You never address me by my name, though I call you Lizzie.'

'Oh, I'll call you by your name, if you like,' she said, and pushed away her plate and drank her wine, and could neither eat nor breathe properly.

'We can love more than once, Lizzie, and in many different ways.'

'Can we?' she asked, and added with her old strength and humour, 'I should have thought that once was enough, Felix.'

'Why?'

She had come so far, and so hard, that love meant more pain than joy to her.

'It costs so much,' said Lizzie. 'It costs so much – like learning magic.'

She remembered four lines of Chaucer, and quoted them as a compliment to him who made magic, though by now she was talking of her unfinished self.

The lyf so short, the craft so long to lerne, Th'assay so hard, so sharp the conquering.

He regarded her with compassion, with interest, with admiration.

'Such magic is worth the cost, worth everything,' said Salvador.

She shook her head, bewildered and afraid.

'I don't know, I'm sure,' she said. 'I don't know. I don't know anything at all, any more. I just go along with you, that's all.' She added, 'I hope that's the right thing to do. It seems right.'

'It is absolutely right,' said Salvador, 'for both of us, Lizzie.'

Now, magician that he was, he used his personal magic in order to reach this strange and lonely woman. He longed to comfort, to please her, to make her bright and whole. He was as much a victim of his desire as she was. So he cast down his napkin and came over to her.

'Don't touch me,' said Lizzie, terrified, and put out her hands to hold him away.

'But why not, why not, my love?'

'Because I can't stop you,' she said, 'and I don't know what will happen.'

'Whatever happens will be right, Lizzie.'

'Are you sure?' she questioned. 'Suppose *I*'m not right for you? I was never right for Eddie. He liked women different from me. I think ..'

'Hush, Lizzie, hush,' said Salvador, and unpinned her shining coil of hair.

'But suppose?' she asked pitifully.

A morning breeze played hide and seek among the filmy curtains. She heard the day begin to unfold before her like a play on which the curtain has just risen. Six o'clock. A hushed and hurried tread outside the door, a sound of shoes being returned in a high state of polish. An early tray of tea being carried to another guest in another suite. Blinds rolled up in the house opposite. Awnings rolled out against the first beams of the sun. A Negro voice singing. All these were significant to her as they had not been.

Her body was at ease in its envelope of flesh. She could wander the room with her eyes, in silent completion. The glass over the fireplace would reflect a new friend. She turned noiselessly, carefully, towards the magician and lay as closely as she dared without disturbing him. Her fingers reached out and touched his face gently, reassuring themselves that he was there. She had no notion when he would make love to her again, nor whether it would ever be the same again. But she had a great confidence in him, feeling that whatever he was, whatever he did, would be right. In his sleep his hand sought hers, stroked her arm and shoulder, rested on her breast.

She watched the guardian eyelids flicker, the carved mouth respond. She moved into the circle of his arms. Half-waking, his voice was deep and slow, intent on framing the syllables of her name. Lovers have little need of conversation. So she hung upon the sound that was to come, that would express his reason for holding her, for loving her again, for continuing to love for ever and ever or until death sundered one from the other. He, in a maze of dreams, spoke of love past.

So said, 'Francesca?'

And turned away to sleep again.

THE CURIOUS SPY GLASSES

Secondly – He will produce his justly celebrated CURIOUS SPY GLASSES *which distort and misrepresent all Objects that are looked at through them, and occasion in the Company* A SUDDEN AND SOCIAL DISMAY; *such as has never before been witnessed in this country.*

Satirical broadside sold
in London in 1794 – based on
the extravagant claims of
PINETTI

EIGHTEEN

March–April 1906

THE MAROON CADILLAC had just been parked outside Bela
Barak's mansion on California Street. Her long body was
polished until it scintillated like a ruby in the sun. Her brass
headlamps glittered. Her gleaming black leather upholstery invited the rich to relax while they were driven.

Small and anonymous in this place of towering Babels, Lintott had gone without breakfast to note the start of Hank
Fleischer's day. The Cadillac was proving to be a better lead
than he had expected, for Fleischer was devoted to her appearance and drove her slowly that she might not be splashed with
mud. Also he was addicted to punctuality and orderliness.
He parked in precisely the same spots, glancing at his gold
watch to check the precise times of arrival and departure. He
followed the same routes, ate at the same restaurants, stopped
at the same bars. His daily life was a reaffirmation of the
previous day.

A little cluster of men now came out of the French-styled
château to escort Bela Barak, hand him his brief-case, open
the Cadillac's door, see him safely and comfortably settled, to
bow and withdraw. Fleischer glanced at his watch. Eight-thirty
exactly. He cranked up the engine, jumped in. With regal splendour the automobile glided past Lintott, so near that he could
see the rapt expression on the scarred man's face.

'That's all very well,' said the Inspector to himself, noting that they drove down Powell Street, 'but if I can see *him* he might well see *me*, sometime!'

He took out his notebook and wrote down another item in his quarry's schedule. He reflected that the dossier he was compiling on Fleischer would be based on the man's virtues: reliability and dedication to duty. The irony was pleasurable to contemplate. Another irony, equally fruitful for the Inspector and almost as pleasurable, was Barak's inability to be anything but a prominent public figure. Lintott could pinpoint Mrs Barak's social round. He could almost make out her daily programme for her, from reading the daily gossip columns, noting present and future public events and the visiting personages who must be entertained. Sometimes the Baraks were together in the evenings, sometimes apart. She used the black Cadillac, and a chauffeur drove her.

Barak too, for all his power, was trapped within a schedule. Lintott knew, for instance, that Fleischer had just driven him to his office in Market Street. Barak would be incarcerated there until lunch-time, with Fleischer in the vicinity as driver. The lunches were a puzzle to Lintott at first, until he realised that Barak had only half a dozen favourite restaurants and would be at one of them for a couple of hours each day. He never lunched with Fleischer, but entertained business colleagues, politicians, visitors. Meanwhile Fleischer waited by his shining Cadillac, and polished her absent-mindedly with a yellow duster, or removed specks and splotches.

At six o'clock each evening Fleischer reappeared and drove Barak to his mansion on California. There he stayed for an hour, presumably drinking Bourbon and talking business. Then the time seemed to be his own, and he toured the Upper Tenderloin slowly and splendidly in the ruby car, stopping at different houses. Lintott had not quite decided how Fleischer ordered these visits, for he would stay longer at some places, or neglect a house for a few days while he kept a near-constant eye on another. Certainly Lintott could not hope to cover every hour, every excursion, but he was noting down an increasingly large and detailed programme. Only, in none of these details, in nothing of this framework, lay a single clue to Alicia Salvador. She seemed, this time, to have vanished for good.

The barber's shop was a leisurely place to be this shining morning. A long lean man with a sharp face lounged in the doorway, exchanging conversation. He wore a canary-coloured silk shirt studded with imitation diamond studs. The four chairs were full but no one was waiting. Lintott sat down and looked at a copy of the *Police Gazette*, while collating the snippets of talk which ran criss-cross through his mind.

'...another fire down Mission last night. You know something? We have no pipe system good enough to fight a big fire? Sometime we are going to have a fire that Chief Sullivan can't stop...'

'...hear that the Mayor is in some sort of trouble. His salary does not equate with a house on Fillmore Street...'

'...needs cleaning up. Say, you could have a man murdered for the cost of a bottle of Bourbon anywhere along the Tenderloin...'

'Did you hear about the shoot-up at our place last night?' asked the man leaning on the doorjamb. 'Funny how that guy Bassity never stays home. You would think he owned enough girls without playing away...'

'Okay, sir, your turn!' commanded the lanky boy with the freckled face.

Lintott stepped into the chair and was ceremoniously swathed in white.

'You want a hair-cut, sir?' asked the boy.

From the corner of his eye the Inspector saw a ruby Cadillac draw up to the sidewalk, and stop. Fleischer jumped out, stood for a moment looking around, spotted the man in the doorway, and began to walk slowly towards the barber's shop.

'I want – a shave,' said Lintott, heart thundering. 'A good long shave, son. Be quick will you, like a good lad? I've got a lot to do today.'

'You want me to shave round these?' the boy enquired, indicating the luxurious growth of muttonchop whiskers.

'I want them shaved off!' said Lintott urgently.

The boy twirled the creamy brush round the soap dish. Then he tilted back the heavy chair at an alarming speed, and lathered Lintott before he could sputter a protest.

'Go to it, Sammie!' called the man at the door, hands in pockets. 'You've got to learn how to shave a guy sometime!'

He turned quickly as Fleischer laid a hand on his arm. The scarred man raised his eyebrows and nodded in the direction of the Cadillac. They went off together without so much as a farewell to the rest.

'Business calls!' said one barber significantly.

Scarlet with importance and concentration, the boy had stropped his razor until it winked, stretched a portion of Lintott's weathered cheek between two fingers, and scraped away a generation of habit.

'These did kind of go out with the Ark, sir,' he began conversationally.

'I had them – for above – thirty years,' said Lintott pitifully, as the boy started on the other half of his face.

'That's what I was saying, sir. Shall I thin the moustache, too, sir?'

'Do what you like, son,' said Lintott mournfully. 'It don't matter now!'

The talk ran criss-cross.

'That was Hank Fleischer, wasn't it? I thought so. I knew him by sight when he almost had the seat out of his pants, and no scar...'

'Must have been ten years back, when he worked for Bassity. He's come up in the world since then. I guess that's why Bassity teases him – like shooting out the chandelier at Solange's place last night. Hank keeps an eye on Solange.'

'Bassity will find one of his places on fire, some fine day!'

'I reckon that was why Fleischer picked up Al just now. Isn't Al the bouncer at Solange's house?'

The young barber wiped Lintott's face, parted his hair on one side, snipped with the very points of the scissors, and set him suddenly upright. He was slightly breathless at his own success.

'Well, bless my boots!' said the Inspector, looking at a younger, smarter, sharper Lintott.

'Now you can call yourself a regular 1906 gen'l'man, sir!'

An elderly baby swaddled in a white gown, Lintott stared at his reflection in the mirror. He was thinking what an excellent idea it would be to look unlike his usual self.

'You've done a rattling good job, my lad. Can you trim my hair to match?'

'Style it some, sir? Scalp massage, sir? Oil shampoo?'

'Whatever you think best!' replied Lintott recklessly.

'It was Bassity that scarred Fleischer. Those two guys hate each other's guts. One of these days they are going to fight for the Barbary Coast crown...'

'...did you know that General Funston asked for a dynamite squad, in case of a big fire? Washington said sure, but could City Hall give a thousand bucks for a vault to store the high explosives? City Hall wouldn't give a nickel!'

'...city government. Why, they would eat the paint off a house...'

'...needs a clean sweep...'

'Hello there, friend?' murmured Scotty demurely, and Patch barked and leaped.

'Morning!' said Lintott, disappointed. 'So you recognised me then?'

'Mr Teale, I have kind of a talent for knowing folks, though you look very different, I will say that.'

'Ah! Nice weather for the time of year, ain't it?'

'In San Francisco it is mostly this kind of weather, friend, though we had a rainy winter. I hear you are looking for somebody!'

Lintott's opaque eyes flickered. He stood at his ease, smiling down on the wanderer and his dog, and pondered the remark.

'I was listening to a bit of gossip today, Scotty, about a man called Bassity and another called Hank Fleischer. Now who might they be? I admit,' said Lintott, with his most engaging smile, 'as this is pure curiosity on my part!'

He brought out a bag of broken biscuits for Patch, whose head moved to one side in contemplation of this extravagance. He laid a dollar tentatively in the cardboard box.

Scotty smiled enigmatically, and recited, 'Jerome Bassity, real name Jere McGlane, is the uncrowned but indubitable King of the Barbary Coast. He is also the hind leg that helps wag City Hall. Our Mayor is a very tricky and charming guy by name of Eugene Schmitz. His playmate, less charming but equally tricky, is an attorney by the name of Abe Ruef. These three gentlemen are said to run San Francisco, and they and their associates are certainly till-dipping up to their shoulders, friend. Bassity is a big mouth that nobody can close, though they try.

'Hank Fleischer, by a strange coincidence, has a connection with your favourite millionaire, Bela Barak. The story goes that Fleischer worked for Bassity, around ten years ago. He found girls and kept an eye on them. Then he and Bassity had a fight, and Bassity laid open his face with a kitchen carving knife. Mr Barak, out of the kindness of his great heart, happened to hear of this and handed out a charitable buck to Fleischer, which the scarred man multiplied according to the advice of the parable. Only he multiplied it in a trade which no parable likes! Hank Fleischer is the Cathouse King of the Upper Tenderloin, friend. Jerome Bassity is Cathouse King of the Barbary Coast. And they would like to carve up each other and their business concerns in one big showdown, only the time is not yet ripe.

'This city, friend, is built on gold, railroads, and semi-lawful prostitution. If you want to open a French restaurant on Jackson Street then you oil the skids with Abe Ruef until the licence hangs on your Christmas tree, with love from Santa Claus. You serve good food downstairs, and charge for it. Upstairs you serve something else and charge still more! Right?' He added softly, 'I would know your face if you shaved off all your hair, friend. You can't shave off character!'

He contemplated Lintott calmly, and offered Patch a fragment of biscuit in return for a beg.

'If you have been observing Bela Barak and his friend Hank Fleischer,' he said idly, 'you will see nothing that can't be explained. Barak is well-known for his charitable concerns. Hank Fleischer may not be the sort of guy you could take out to tea with your dear old grandmother, but he is grateful and he worships his benefactor. Therefore, it gives him pleasure to carry the great man to and from the office, to have a gun in his breast-pocket in case thieves break into the Cadillac as it cruises down Powell, and so on and so forth!

'Gossip pursues even the mighty. There are some who say that Hank Fleischer is Bela Barak's front. That Barak set him up in the Tenderloin to make a profit, that the red Cadillac was bought out of those profits. Still more devious minds suggest that Barak owns both Bassity and Fleischer, and that though they do not like each other these public quarrels are a front. Which means that Bela Barak would own both the Barbary Coast and Upper Tenderloin, that he would use City Hall, that all these names are simply his cover. But this is gossip, friend!' He said softly, 'You are some kind of an English detective, aren't you, Mr Teale?'

'Yes,' Lintott replied composedly. 'Who told you that, Scotty?'

'It was my surmise. So my lips are now and for ever sealed, because I like you. I have a word of wisdom to impart. Bela Barak is a very important person and Hank Fleischer does not hesitate to use his gun. They both resent interference. Do you have a gun, friend?'

'No, nor any use for one,' said Lintott stoutly.

'I never kind of cared for them myself,' said Scotty serenely. 'But I would learn to duck real fast, friend, if I were you.'

Lintott took his judgement into his hands, and added the possibility of his life.

'I need help, Scotty,' he said simply.

The blue eyes surveyed him, lighted on a passing acquaintance and lighted up in greeting.

'Morning, Colonel!'

'I'm looking for a young lady by the name of Alicia Salvador. She eloped with this Fleischer, from London, over two months ago.'

'Morning, Miss Lucy!'

'She left a note for her brother, saying she would be back in a few days and explain everything. He never heard a word, nor saw her. Are you listening?'

'Morning Mrs Svenson. Miss Svenson, you're looking mighty pretty! Sure I'm listening, Mr Teale. Only I don't want anybody to know I'm listening, get me? What is more, friend, I am not powerful. I know an awful lot and I have no power. So I must be careful, or Miss Patch and myself will be asked to leave – and San Francisco is our home, friend. Morning, Susan, how's your Mom?'

'Have you heard anything about Fleischer and a young lady?'

'Only that he don't like them, friend. Young ladies, that is. He has one great love in his life, which is his Cadillac. He has one great god, who is Bela Barak. For women he has no time, except maybe as a commodity.'

The city changed her mind and climate in moments. Clouds, suffused with anger, loomed on a sallow sky. Wind scoured Powell Street, scooping off hats and whipping skirts. Lintott came into the doorway for shelter, suddenly shivering.

'Should've put my topcoat on,' he explained, 'but she was shining away, earlier!' Nodding at the gusts of temper in Union Square.

'She's like that. What a morning, Mr Riordan!' He put an arm round Patch, who was nuzzling his jacket. 'What kind of person is she, Mr Teale?'

'Ladylike, a bit on the childish side, small, fair, pretty. An artist in the theatrical line. Her brother and friends have taken care of her, shielded her as you might say. Not the flighty sort, the deep sort.'

'Mr Teale, if Hank Fleischer brought that young lady into the city I should have heard a whisper, or three. A hundred people will talk to me in one day. Some guy will say, "I been decorating a lady's apartment up on Russian Hill. Isn't that

great? We need the dough, on account of having a new baby!"
Another guy will tell me, "Say, there is a new lady in such-and-
such on Russian Hill! I delivered the groceries this morning
and talked with the maid!" The porter will drop by and fill in
a few more details. These scraps of news by themselves mean
nothing. To me they form part of the picture. Your Alicia Salvador is no part of the present picture in San Francisco.'

'Then where is she?' Lintott asked. 'She's been travelling
under the name of Mrs Fleischer. Whether she's married to him
or not I don't know. But what has he done with her?'

Scotty stroked Patch's curly head and pondered.

'Friend, this is only a notion, and does not answer your
question – directly that is. Why should she belong to him?
Barak has used Hank Fleischer as cover for over ten years.
Maybe he is doing it again. If anything leaks out this is
Fleischer's little lady, not his.'

'Wait a minute, wait a minute!' cried Lintott, as all the
pieces flew apart and reformed.

Rain plastered their clothes to their skins. The streets were
wind-tunnels. Clouds darkened and climbed until a giant
sprawled over San Francisco and clutched the skyscrapers to
his breast.

'Bela Barak is crazy about his wife, but she is far from
crazy about him. I guess the monster is human at base, so he
falls for a nice quiet little lady who probably thinks he is a
great guy. All this is supposition, friend. I am merely talking
through the hole in my head.'

'Suppose away, friend. I'm listening!' said Lintott.

'Last fall the Baraks had such a bust-up that the lady swept
right out of her Venetian-style drawing-room and over to England. Hank Fleischer was posted off after her – which is why
Bassity has been Mr Uppity of late, but Fleischer will sort
him out in time. Yes, sir, the cathouses had to stumble on
without their guiding light, but that is the way of the cruel
world! Could you stand in front of us with your back to the
square, friend? That way we have a little shelter and you
can't be seen so good!'

Lintott, teeth rattling in his head, obliged. Scotty and Patch huddled together on the damp blanket.

'When I have said this I am going home,' said Scotty. 'The lady does not intend for me to have a nice day! So the Scar found Mrs Barak, and Barak followed. That much I knew. I also heard about the reception in her honour. He bought her another horse. It is one hell of a guilty conscience which costs so many thousands of dollars!'

'The Salvadors travel from place to place, though,' Lintott observed. 'It ain't easy to strike up a friendship, let alone a love affair, on the move.'

'The Baraks travel also, friend. They were in Europe last year, for instance. She goes ahead, he follows. When people become involved with each other time and distance is no object. Your little lady and the great Barak only needed a spark, not a twenty-four-hour furnace. They may have corresponded and Mrs Barak could have found a letter. No lady likes a rival, however much you buy for her in consequence! So they quarrel over this letter, this rumour, and she goes to London, England, to confront the little lady. Only Bela Barak has other plans, like bringing her over here and setting her up in an apartment eventually. How does that sound to you, friend – though you are the expert!'

Lintott nodded, meditating.

'I ain't proud,' he said. 'I can take a hint when it's a good 'un. Would you...?' offering five dollars.

'I'm not proud, either,' said Scotty, accepting them with a grin.

He gathered up his blanket and his box and fixed a lead on Patch's collar.

'So where is Alicia Salvador now, then, do you reckon?' Lintott asked.

'He could have taken her to his place in Belmont, which is very large indeed, and all watchdogs and iron gates controlled by mechanisms, friend. You could not only hide an entire harem of ladies there, you could almost lose the Southern Pacific Railroad!'

194

NINETEEN

GENEVIEVE SAID HURRIEDLY, 'Madame, I regret troubling Madame, but Mrs Fleischer is here at Belmont. She is lock in the tower rooms, over the rose garden. Is it not strange?'

Francesca's cheeks were brilliant from the morning ride. She sat down at her dressing-table and began to draw off her gloves, finger by leather finger.

'It surely is,' she said, thinking. 'Surely is, Genevieve. But how in the world did you find out?'

The maid shrugged, lifted her eybrows, pursed her mouth. How does one explain what is surely a gift for collating hints, words and silences, a change in the atmosphere or the routine?

'I am much alone, except for Madame. I see, I hear, I put two and three together. Then I find for myself. It has always been so.'

Francesca untied her stock slowly and thoughtfully.

'I forget Madame in my chatter,' said Genevieve, letting down the black braids. Her hands were cold. 'Please to excuse!'

'Now take a few deep breaths, Genevieve!' As the maid reached for a hairbrush and dropped it. 'What scares you? Leave my hair alone for a minute. You are going to be banging my head or your knuckles with the back of that brush if you don't take it easy!'

'Pardon, Madame!'

'Now what ails you?'

'She is strange in the mind, Madame. I speak to her through

195

the door. Sometimes she is sensible, sometimes not. She is lock up all day, every day. She does not know how long she has been there. They bring her food, they care for her, but that is all. I think she goes mad with solitude.'

She clutched the silver-backed brush as though it were a spar. She was endeavouring to control her fears, her tears. Francesca watched her, frowning.

'Whatever is going on around here?' she asked herself. 'If she needs treatment she should be in a hospital, not locked up. Why in heaven's name bring her here, anyway? Genevieve, did you ask her about Mr Fleischer?'

'She make no sense, madame. I am so sad for her. I weep, I weep!'

Weep she did, a spare plain woman in her middle years who was much afraid. She wept for more than the imprisoned girl. She wept for her own imprisonment, reliant on the whim and will of her employers. She wept even for her mistress's imprisonment, for her unwise attempts at escape, for her blithe reliance on the power of beauty.

Francesca patted her shoulder, offered her a handkerchief.

'Now you just listen to me, Genevieve. We both feel the same way about Mr Fleischer, and that's for sure. But he kind of cares for Mr Barak and Bel likes having him around. For myself I will say this – if he so much as set foot on my father's back porch he would be horse-whipped! I guess he asked Bel to let this poor little thing stay here, and Bel has so much to think about that he would just say yes! Not thinking to ask me. But she must have been here all the while, Genevieve, and I am about to alter that. Whether Bel likes Mr Fleischer or not he is just going to have to make him see sense. For heaven's sakes, Genevieve, supposing Claudia Strauss got wind of a strange lady being kept here at Belmont! What could she make of that little item, I ask you?'

'What is Madame doing?' asked Genevieve, terrified, as Francesca rapidly pinned up her braids.

'I am this minute going to telephone my husband and get things straight, Genevieve. And I don't eat one bite of breakfast until I know just where we all stand. I can promise you that.'

She switched up the skirt of her riding habit and left the room. Behind her followed the maid, weeping and protesting in vain.

Bela Barak said, 'Now tell me all about it, honey, and take your time.'

On his writing pad he scribbled, *Find Hank Fleischer and bring him here immediately*, and pushed it across his desk to his secretary.

'Honey, you amaze and astonish me,' he drawled, in that gravelly voice which could inspire either fear or confidence according to its tone. This fine morning he was bent on placating her. 'There seems to be some kind of misunderstanding on Hank's part. Like Genevieve says, the lady is a little unbalanced. She should be in hospital. Maybe he was afraid to tell me, or maybe he tried to and I brushed him off. I've been over-busy of late. Honey, I can promise you that I am sending Hank down to Belmont right away to sort things out. I will not have you worried by poor Hank's family problems. My back is broad enough, God knows, to take on his troubles as well as mine ... sure, I know what Claudia Strauss would say – she's said too much already and I wish I knew some way to close her mouth!' The sudden edge on his tone silenced the voice from Belmont.

'Now listen to me, honey,' he said, dark and quiet, 'I am taking this problem right out of your way, so don't you worry me about it any more. Eat your breakfast and forget it. Right? I want to say two or three little things before I ring off. I let you go down to Belmont, which means I am on my own up here. Remember that! Then, I admit I was pretty shaken up by the way you left me in the fall, and I reckon I treated you like a queen. Nobody could say I spared a nickel to make you happy. Now could they?'

It was Francesca's turn to placate. He listened, satisfied.

'The other thing is about Genevieve. I know you think a lot of her, and she's been maiding you since you were a girl, but she is becoming a problem and I don't like that. She must mind her business from now on, honey, and if she does not then you must tell her. If you can't stop her nosing around everybody else's life then I shall. Is that understood?'

He nodded to himself. His voice changed from winter to mild summer.

'And have you been for a ride already? You have? How's Orange Belle going? Say, if she is that good we can breed from her later on. Honey, I tell you what. I know you don't care for Hank, though that rough exterior conceals an honest heart, so why don't you go out for the day on Orange Belle? Ride over and see the Spencers. You haven't seen Dolly Spencer in quite a while.'

He changed again, becoming protective of his property.

'Mind you take one of the grooms with you. I won't have you riding alone. And get back before nightfall. I'll ring you just before dinner to make sure you're back safely. Go eat your breakfast now, like a good girl, and forget all this. I'm taking care of everything...'

He hooked up the receiver and sat thinking for a while, hands folded. His huge shoulders hunched over the problem. His black eyes brooded. He did not like to be crossed, to be called to account. He looked up as Fleischer came silently into the room.

'Belmont wasn't nearly big enough for both ladies, Hank,' he said quietly.

Fleischer said, sliding into a leather chair, 'It's that French maid, I guess, Mr Barak? I thought so. You know your own business best, Mr Barak, but that long-nosed lady is going to nose out something we can't cover up, sometime.'

'Then scare her off,' Barak ordered, picking up a sheaf of papers from his desk. 'My wife will be out all day. Go down to Belmont and take Alicia Salvador some place else for the present time.'

He began to read. Fleischer ran one finger slowly down the scar, thinking.

'Where do I take her, Mr Barak? She is a very strange person.

She says very strange things. I can't take her to a hotel, now can I, Mr Barak?'

Bela Barak laid down his papers and looked steadily at the scarred man. His voice was deep, his eyes benevolent, his demeanour princely.

'Hank,' he said softly, 'do you remember what I said to you the first time you came to this office, with your face all sewn up?'

Fleischer's brown eyes were alive. The scar moved tenderly with his smile.

'You just looked at me, Mr Barak, like you are looking now. And you said to me, *Hank, I want the Upper Tenderloin. How are you going to get it for me?*'

'And do you remember what you told me, Hank? Because I do – every word!'

Fleischer recited, 'I said, *Mr Barak, sir, leave me to figure that little thing out!*'

Barak smiled now, resplendent with power.

'You keep Alicia Salvador safe for me, Hank. I am only asking you to put her under wraps for three more weeks. Right?'

Fleischer rose obediently, though his unease was evident. He set his brown Derby hat thoughtfully on his head. He paused a moment, looking at Barak.

'Take care of everything for me, Hank,' said Bela Barak.

In Union Square the old men sat in the sun, threw bread to the birds, waited for meal-time. The city was radiant and seemly under her blue canopy.

'Morning, Mr Teale,' cried Scotty, tanned and smiling. 'Your friends seem to be moving around lately!' And he left a minute folded note in the cardboard box and picked up the dollar bill.

'I know what you mean,' said Lintott. 'I read Mrs Claudia Strauss's column!'

'A very entertaining and well-informed lady,' Scotty agreed politely.

'The lady's maid sounds as though she's disappeared.'

'The Barak wires got jumbled,' said Scotty ironically. 'Our friends gave two totally different reasons for the maid's absence, which you will see if you read between Mrs Strauss's suspicious lines. Naturally Mrs Strauss, knowing that the maid accompanied her mistress to England last fall, believes this to be the result of yet another marital upset! That is what she evidently hopes, anyways. You and I could possibly work on a different theory.'

'I wish I knew where that maid was,' said Lintott wistfully.

'I guess Mrs Barak would like to know, too. They were kind of attached. She came with Mrs Barak from Virginia. Sometimes a personal maid is the only friend a rich lady has, Mr Teale. Which is a somewhat sad surmise!' He smiled on a passing acquaintance, and added, 'Have you thought any more of that visit to Belmont, friend?'

'I've found out where it is. I took a trip into the country, as you might say. The lady has a regular ride afore breakfast.'

'You been sleeping rough, friend?'

'I wrapped up warm and dry,' said Lintott sturdily.

Scotty inclined his head in salute.

'Friend, it is time we were parting. Before you go I have something to tell you which will be of interest. You asked me some days ago where you could find a little entertainment in the evening. Morning, Mr Keroian! Did I ever tell you about my Aunt Patsy?'

'The name sounds familiar, very familiar,' said Lintott sharply.

'She is a very respectable lady. No vulgarity allowed in her establishment at any time, in any place. No hard liquor, no profanity. Her daughters, though strictly good-mannered and all brought up in the Catholic faith, are very obliging girls and their wardrobes are suitable for all occasions. Visitors are required to have an introduction, and any gentleman wishing to pay court to any of the young ladies must have the means to open a charge account.

'On Sundays, after church, favoured gentlemen callers are served tea and cake while Aunt Patsy plays hymns on the harmonium. That lady would not harm a fly upon the wall, sir. But the insect would no doubt be charged a standard rate for resting its wings!' He chuckled to himself. 'The humour is included, friend. No extra cost. Good luck and God Bless!'

In a quiet corner of the bar Lintott set his steam beer before him, and looked askance at the great collar of foam. He eyed the drip pan under the spigot and tasted warily. The White Horse was noted for its beer. He answered the bar-tender's unspoken question.

'A bit different to what we drink in England, sir,' he remarked, wiping a quantity of froth from his newly-trimmed moustache, 'but very refreshing!'

The man nodded, and attended to other customers. The place was filling up at lunch-time. Lintott put on his spectacles and reached for Scotty's note.

Aunt Patsy's lodger has his wife staying with him now.

The address on Mason Street was well-known to Lintott. He had seen Fleischer's Cadillac there first thing in the morning, last thing at night. Aunt Patsy's parlour-house was the nearest place to home that Fleischer would ever know.

TWENTY

Friday, 6 April 1906

WHEN ONE LEAD FAILS TRY ANOTHER had been Lintott's motto. He saw his work as an intricate jigsaw puzzle, and proceeded with each case in much the fashion he would have assembled a multitude of wooden pieces. Use the straight-edged facts and make a frame, then fill in what you could. If those trees refused to come together start on that church. If sky was difficult put in people.

So, after great cogitation in Mrs Olson's parlour of an evening, puffing away at his pipe until he seemed to be generating a miniature sea-fog, he had temporarily given up the idea of rescuing Alicia from Mason Street. He had no means of either doing it or getting safely out. Consequently he turned his attention to the weak spots in Barak's formidable defences, and padded round them hopefully. The relationships in the Barak household formed and reformed in his mind: a mysterious quadrille.

Barak and Francesca. Barak and Fleischer. Francesca and the maid Genevieve. Francesca and Fleischer.

Husband and wife. *They* (Alicia and Barak) *may have corresponded. Mrs Barak could well have heard of this. Maybe they quarrelled over a letter, a rumour?*

Master and man. *Barak has used Hank Fleischer as cover for ten years. Maybe he is doing it again. Why should she* (Alicia Salvador) *belong to Fleischer?*

Mistress and maid. *She came with Mrs Barak from Virginia.*

They were kind of attached. Sometimes a personal maid is the only friend a rich lady has.

Mistress and man. *That scarred tom-cat was a-following her when she went out alone. No love lost between her and him, I can tell you.*

There were two teasing formations which remained as question marks. Master and maid? Barak would accept Genevieve provided she did not get in his way. The maid obviously understood her mistress rather better than Barak did, which would make her position in the household a difficult and delicate one. Lintott knew something of ladies and their closest servants. Genevieve would be wholly for her mistress. Any hint – and servants were the first to smell a liaison in the wind – any hint of an Alicia Salvador would be discovered and reported to Francesca Barak by Genevieve. Therefore it was possible that Alicia had been at Belmont, that Genevieve had been a risk, that Barak had removed that risk.

Maid and man? The two opposing forces. He working for his master, she for her mistress. They would hate each other. She would also fear him. He was adept at vanishing ladies. Therefore, if Barak had given the orders Fleischer had carried them out.

Francesca Barak. A lady bought and sold in the marriage market, coming from an old Virginia family, could not afford socially or financially to acknowledge and challenge her husband's transgressions. Fleischer was a different matter. She could despise and even delicately harass him. She could blame Fleischer when she dared not blame her husband. Therefore?

'Well, well,' said Lintott, knocking out the ashes from his pipe. 'I seem to have made a regular old furnace of this here parlour, ma'am. I beg your pardon most sincerely. Should I open a door or a window or something of that sort?'

Mrs Olson laid a hand upon his sleeve.

'Mr Teale,' she said, 'I have been watching you, though you may not know that!' He knew it perfectly well, but assumed astonishment. 'Mr Teale,' she continued tenderly, 'when a gentleman, or a lady for that matter, is thinking of past happiness, their thought should be respected.'

'Very kind,' said Lintott, moving courteously away from her. 'Most understanding, ma'am. I'll just fan the door to and fro for a bit, shall I?'

'Memories are sacred, Mr Teale,' she said, looking fondly upon him, 'but they who have passed on do not demand that our days be spent in mourning. There is always tomorrow, Mr Teale.'

'My own thoughts exactly, ma'am. Always tomorrow. Very well put, if I may say so. Which reminds me, ma'am, I shall be off for another day or two.'

Her face was disappointed with this reply.

'Somebody as I met today thinks they saw my uncle in San Mateo, ma'am!'

Mrs Olson recovered gallantly.

'The room will be ready and waiting for your return, Mr Teale.'

On the stairs the man called Rafferty caught him up and made some excuse to speak what was on his mind.

'Mrs Olson thinks a great deal of you, sir. She would be sorry to have you leave us.'

Lintott said, 'You've been here around five years, haven't you, sir? I thought so. Mr Rafferty, my wife – my late wife – is the only woman as I ever cared for. Some men are like that. I shall be going back home fairly soon, when this here goose-chase of mine is over, whichever way it goes. You're staying here, Mr Rafferty. If I were you, sir, I should see as my carpet slippers was on the other side of that parlour fire-place soon after! Get my meaning?'

Rafferty wrung his hand.

'I hope you find the old gentleman, sir,' he said fervently. 'Good night and God bless you!'

His quarry was approaching at a cracking pace, and alone. Lintott moved away from the giant redwood tree which had been his lodging house and shelter, and stood where both horse and rider could see him. He spread his arms to indicate that they should stop, and remained there very still and calm to give the lady confidence in his intentions.

They were slowing from a gallop to a trot. She drew rein some yards from him. She was looking for signs of a gun.

'I ain't going to harm you, nor kidnap you, nor shoot you, ma'am, if that's what you're thinking!' Lintott shouted into the clear morning air. 'But I should like to beg a word with you, if you please. About your maid, ma'am. Miss Genevieve.'

She clicked her tongue softly to the Palomino, who stepped forward as delicately as though the ground were floes of ice.

Lintott looked up at the fine broadcloth riding habit, the snowy stock and diamond pin, the black braids beneath the hard hat, the porcelain face flushed with exercise. Spoiled and spirited, he thought.

He inclined his head, bowler hat held reverently to his chest. 'Mrs Francesca Barak, I believe?'

'You are correct in that assumption, sir,' she answered, and her mouth curved into a smile. She could not help her answer sounding like a compliment to his manhood. 'May I ask your own name, and what you want with me?'

'It ain't impertinence, ma'am. I mean nothing but good. I think we might be able to help each other, and I'm taking my life in my hands by so much as speaking to you. I'm in trouble with Mr Fleischer.'

She frowned slightly. She was trying to assess him. He saw her make up her mind to take a chance on him, and inwardly applauded both her caution and the gamble.

'She gets restless, standing still, sir,' Francesca explained of the Palomino. 'We are a long way away from the house here. We can walk her under the trees while we talk, if you so desire.'

'I'm obliged to you, ma'am. Thankee.'

She dismounted lightly before he could help her, switched the long skirt of her riding habit up, and stood beside him. He was not a tall man but she barely reached above his shoulder. Her voice was unconscious courtship, her beauty a constant delight.

Regular charmer and no mistake, thought Lintott. In spite of his resolution, which never wavered, he enjoyed her presence.

'I should like to tell you the truth, ma'am, but I should need your word of honour that you didn't repeat anything as I told you.'

'You have my word, sir. Mr Fleischer is no friend of mine. Though,' she added automatically, 'he has been a good friend to my dear husband.'

'Understood and accepted, ma'am. Your husband don't come into this,' Lintott lied cheerfully. 'My name is Inspector Lintott of Scotland Yard, London, England – where I had the honour of first seeing you in a theatre box at the Coliseum. On the third of January, this year, at a matinée performance given by Mr Salvador and his sister.'

Her erect carriage did not stiffen, her easy pace did not falter, but her face expressed some disturbance.

'Mr Fleischer approached me after the performance – I believe you must have left afore it finished, ma'am? I didn't notice you there at the end. You'll excuse me saying as you're the kind of lady folks do notice.'

'I was feeling a little faint,' she said, and paused and spoke words of endearment to the Palomino. 'Yes, I recollect I felt a little faint with the heat.'

'Quite so, ma'am. Well, that afternoon Mr Fleischer obviously had in mind what he carried out in fact. He took Miss Alicia Salvador away with him, some two weeks later, and she hasn't been seen since.'

The effect on her was more dramatic than anything he could have supposed. All the morning colour fled her face.

'You ain't feeling faint right now, are you, ma'am?' he enquired anxiously. 'I can help a lady as is dizzy, but a lady and a horse might be a bit beyond me!'

She smiled a little then, at his concern and his humour, and a dry humour of her own tinged the reply.

'Inspector Lintott, a Southern lady only faints at appropriate moments, and in the most graceful places. This would hardly apply now, would it? I ask you!'

The last three words were delivered with her usual energy. They continued to walk: man, woman and mare. Francesca was as pale as the Palomino's mane, but composed enough to pick up their conversation.

'I understood that the lady was his wife, sir.'

'Ah! that was understood, certainly, by everyone involved. But nobody actually knows whether she was or not, ma'am. Her brother, Mr Salvador, says she was not – but then, he's prejudiced and he don't know everything.'

'I met him years ago in England,' said Francesca lightly. 'He was entertaining at a house-party. I was one of Lady Maud's guests. We spoke with each other a few times. I did not even know he had a sister. When I attended the matinée at the Coliseum I assumed she was an assistant. I had no notion that she had disappeared. I most certainly did not know that Mr Fleischer's wife was Miss Salvador.'

'But you did know that he was keeping her at the house here, in Belmont?'

'Surely!' She was recovering quickly enough for Lintott to suspect that he was moving away from the point which concerned her personally.

'Your maid Miss Genevieve found her, didn't she, ma'am?' Very direct.

Francesca's pretty mouth opened, and shut.

'Fleischer frightened Miss Genevieve, didn't he, ma'am?'

'Sir, you are making assumptions!' Attempting to block the questions.

'Oh no, I ain't,' said Lintott, sure of himself now as her pallor increased. 'I'm telling the truth, ma'am. Now recollect, we're speaking of Mr Fleischer. Your husband don't enter into this. Mr Fleischer took the young lady. Mr Fleischer either smuggled her into your country house, or trumped up some tale for your husband as sounded all right. Mr Fleischer frightened your maid, and probably had her taken away some-where for a time while things quietened down.'

Francesca's colour began to mount again. She gave him a triumphant, reckless smile: the smile of a successful conspirator.

'Now that is all you know, Inspector,' she chided. 'So far you are right, and no further. Surely, Genevieve was scared half out of her wits. But she came to me and told me what he said, and *I* sent her away somewhere while he smoothed down a little. He had reckoned without me,' she added proudly. 'The way I was brought up, sir, we looked after our servants right down to the smallest darkie. I was having no white trash threatening my own personal maid, sir.'

Again she flashed him that wide reckless smile, and Lintott grinned back.

'Ah!' he said, half in warning, half in admiration. 'You want to watch that spirit, my dear, it might get you into trouble sometime. What's more,' he continued, 'you shouldn't ride so wild. You could fall off and hurt yourself!'

She laughed aloud now, throwing back her head, blue eyes brilliant.

'I don't care one little bit, sir!' she said. 'Why, I am just so *bored*! When I was a girl I had such a good time. I loved my family, and I had my own horse – not nearly so beautiful as *Belle* here, but I loved her too. And we laughed and rode and all. Now it seems there is nothing but paying calls on folks I don't care for, and wearing all my jewels, and having this white trash around me that my father would whip off the back porch!'

'Mr Fleischer took Miss Salvador to San Francisco with him,' said Lintott, sticking to the point, though a smile was evident as he listened to her. 'Look, my dear, that young lady ain't exactly right in the head, did you know?'

He had disturbed her again. She looped her skirt more firmly over her arm, and spoke to the golden mare. He noticed that she had the trick of turning away from anything that troubled her. He talked on as though she had answered his question.

'Yes, I expect Miss Genevieve told you, didn't she? Well, it worries me, ma'am. But if Mr Fleischer knew I was looking for the poor girl he'd turn his gun on me faster than I could wink! That's why I wanted you to keep this conversation secret. He's a very nasty bit of work as ought, by rights, to be behind bars for a few years! Where did you send Miss Genevieve, ma'am?'

Now she gave him her attention, because she knew he was seeking an address.

'How could she help you, sir?'

'Ah! you're too quick for me by half!' cried Lintott, shaking a paternal finger at her. 'I think she could give me some information on Fleischer as I could use against him. So I could prise that poor girl away from him without a lot of trouble. We don't want trouble, do we?' he persuaded her.

'What could she tell you, sir?'

'I don't know,' said Lintott frankly, 'but it's worth a try.'

'I won't have her getting scared again, sir.'

'We could meet in a church, say, near where she's staying. I know a bit about French ladies,' said Lintott comfortably. 'She'll be a Catholic lady, won't she? Likes going to church to make her confession and that? Yes, I thought so. What's the harm of me being in church at the same time, having a word with her? You could get in touch with her, ma'am, and explain. I'll make sure nobody's following me, either before or after. If we can get this Fleischer put away, between the three of us, ain't it worth a bit of a risk?'

'Put away?' she asked, puzzled.

'Even if the young lady was his wife, which I doubt, the law ain't going to let him treat her like that,' said Lintott. 'If I can get evidence – which don't involve either you or your good husband...' the adjective *good* had soothed Francesca, and he noted the effect.

'Oh! I should surely like to see that gentleman in jail where he belongs!' she cried, in hope.

'Of course you would, my dear. A spirited young lady like you, as looks after her own folks! So if you'll give me a description of the lady, and let me have the name of the church where we meet ... I don't have to know her address, that way, do I?'

'No,' she breathed, completely at rest. 'Well, you have my word on this, sir!'

She held out her fingers and he first kissed, and then shook them to make sure no foreign code of good manners had been offended. He printed his own name and address and cautioned her to destroy it when used.

'I'm in your charge, remember, ma'am,' said Lintott. 'So just you take care of me like your family took care of those little darkies, mind!'

She laughed again. The patroness.

'Now I know nothing about horses,' Lintott continued amiably, 'but this here's a beauty, ain't she?'

He ventured to pat Orange Belle's arched neck. She switched her silver tail, and looked on him with pride and pleasure like her mistress.

'If you see she's a beauty you know all about horses!' cried Francesca, charming him. 'Now you just act like my stepping-block if you please, sir. Lock your fingers like this,' illustrating, 'and hold them so's I can mount.'

She placed her little boot in the cradle of his palms and sprang lightly into the saddle. She had enjoyed their conversation, frightening and puzzling though much of it had been. She liked this plain and sturdy man. So she smiled on him most splendidly.

'You think I ride too fast?' she demanded. As he nodded good-humouredly she said, 'Then watch us right now, sir!'

She turned the mare for home, clicked her tongue, touched the heel of one boot gently into Orange Belle's hide, and they were away. He heard her voice trailing back on the wind.

'Is this fast enough for you-u-u-u!'

He shook his head, slapped his thigh with his bowler hat, and began to think of the journey back to San Francisco.

TWENTY ONE

LINTOTT STOOD JUST INSIDE the heavy door, closed it noiselessly, and bared his head. The reverence of this gesture was belied by his air of purpose. Treading softly through the thick soft silence of the church, he was looking for Genevieve. Few were here at this time of day, and those few were all women absorbed in private prayer. As he crossed the centre aisle Lintott made automatic obeisance, and again stared keenly round.

The Virgin held her child, for ever smiling in a blue reverie over her wax tributes, thanks and pleas. Candles guttered and flared on iron spikes, forming fantastic stalactites. Lintott took a candle from the box, paid his cents, lighted and impaled it, padded on: observant and stealthy as a cat in the half-dark. He paused behind a slim veiled woman, slipped into the pew beside her, knelt.

Rising, sitting back, he whispered without looking at her, 'Is it Miss Genevieve?' She nodded. 'I am Inspector Lintott of Scotland Yard, as you've been expecting.'

She sat next to him and smoothed her dark skirt. She was spare and plain and much afraid.

'Do you object to talking in a sacred place, Miss? We could go somewhere else.'

'No, no,' she replied hurriedly, quietly. 'I feel safe here.'

Partly concealed by a pillar, partly disguised by twilight, they spoke in hushed tones. She wished to unburden herself of her fears, to tell him of Barak and Fleischer and her mistress's intervention on her behalf. It was the spinsterish rambling of a woman who has only been wanted for her ability and her usefulness. Lintott let her talk herself out while he listened and cogitated. When she lapsed into silence, and knotted her thin hands in her lap, he spoke again.

'I've always respected a lady's intuition, ma'am, and I'd more or less come to the same conclusion as yourself. I thought that Mr Barak brought the young lady over here for his own reasons. I didn't so much as hint that to Mrs Barak though!'

Genevieve put a gloved finger to her mouth.

'No, no, no. Never. Hush!'

'Exactly,' said Lintott. 'However, something else has come up which sets a different light on the matter. Did Mrs Barak happen to mention the young lady's name when she wrote to you about this here meeting?'

Genevieve shook her head.

'Ah!' said Lintott. 'It don't matter, of course, miss. Tell me, you're very close to Mrs Barak, ain't you? I thought so. I saw you were the sort of lady as would attach herself to someone of Mrs Barak's quality.'

He was feeling his way round to the questions he really wanted to ask. His whisper, soothing and insistent, built up a metaphorical house of cards round Genevieve which he would presently blow down. She listened, dark face averted. Her confection of a hat had once belonged to Francesca and she had altered it cleverly to suit herself and her position in life.

'You're a French lady, ain't you, Miss Genevieve?' Lintott pursued, delicately complimentary. 'There's an air about French ladies. I don't know how to describe it exactly. Very elegant, anyway. I can see you and Mrs Barak getting on like a house afire, what with her elegance and yours, miss.'

'She was always the high spirits, the do-not-care, sir!' Genevieve confided. 'I tell her. Her *maman* tells her. She does not listen.'

'I warned her about riding too fast,' Lintott mused. 'She rode off like a streak of lightning – just to show me!'

The hint of a smile was on her mouth. She nodded emphatically. That was Madame!

'Acts first and thinks after,' Lintott purred, watching the maid. 'Only it catches up with her in the end, don't it? Catches up with her, and with *you* too, because you know all about it. Why ever did you both stay at Claridge's, my dear? It must have been the first place he looked!'

'I tell her, I tell her. She does not listen!' Whispering frantically.

Lintott placed a warm hand over her two cold ones.

'Don't upset yourself, my dear. You're quite safe here with me. But that's why you're frightened, ain't it? That's why your mistress went to all that trouble to hide you until everything blew over, isn't it? That's why she went off with you to London in such a hurry, isn't it? They couldn't very well threaten *her*, could they? Not with her family in Virginia, and all the high society round, and the gossip columnists waiting for a bit of scandal. But they could try to get the truth out of you because, in their view, you don't matter. And once you talked you could have set the cat among the pigeons, couldn't you?'

She was weeping silently, gloved hands over her face, all her faithful, feeble defences down.

'She don't think from beginning to end, your mistress,' Lintott mused, absent-mindedly patting Genevieve's shaking shoulders. 'She takes things at face value, and that's a great mistake. Trouble blows up and she runs off to London. Her husband gives her a reception and another horse, and tells her he's sorry for losing his temper, and she comes flying back again, all smiles. You find out something that seems wrong, Fleischer threatens you, and she whisks you off to Telegraph Hill. If they both come, cap in hand, tomorrow, and say it was a mistake, she'll have you back home again afore you can put your bonnet on!'

'No, no, no, no!' Hysterical.

'Here, here,' Lintott said kindly. 'You mustn't take on like this. That's why I'm with you, my dear. I'm going to see the pair of them put behind bars if I can, and you're going to help me. So you may as well tell me your side of the case, and then I'll know how to go about it.'

Still she hesitated, out of loyalty.

'Didn't your mistress tell you the name of the young lady, then?' Lintott questioned softly. 'I will. It's Miss Alicia Salvador. The sister of Salvador the magician!' Her face was sallow with comprehension. 'You wouldn't probably know that he had a sister,' Lintott continued mildly, 'but Mr Barak and that Fleischer found out all right. They found out a lot more, too. The first time they threatened you, afore you and Mrs Barak hopped it to London, they really wanted to know. But this time they were just trying to scare you off. They want you out of the way, out of your mistress's way, so they can finish what they started in London. You're as safe as houses, in Telegraph Hill, my dear!'

She wiped her eyes on a scrap of handkerchief and sat very still, very quiet, staring ahead of her at the crucified carpenter.

'I haven't come here to ask you a lot of questions,' said Lintott amiably. 'I've come here to tell you the truth, Miss Genevieve. A long time ago your mistress met Mr Salvador in England. He was entertaining the guests at Lady Maud's place. Your mistress was then as she is now, only younger and more foolish, wasn't she?' A trembling nod. 'She and Mr Salvador liked each other. I know him and he's cut out of the same cloth as your mistress – he does what he likes, when he likes, and picks the pieces up after!' She was nodding with each sentence, as his monotonous, soothing voice sauntered along. 'She made a public fool of herself, didn't she? Spoiled her chances on the marriage market over there, and fluffed them up over here, too. Didn't she?'

She was now spent of love, of loyalty, of fear.

'Yes, and yes, sir,' she said tiredly. 'Whispers, rumours. Everyone is still friendly, but the doors are closed. Madame is beautiful, she must marry, only the old families and the good families do not wish the daring Miss Sinclair to marry their son! Then this rich man comes from San Francisco. He worships her like a queen. The Sinclairs think this is the answer. On the East Coast Madame is finish. On the West Coast she can begin again, and in style. But something is very wrong. The Mr Barak wishes to use her connections so that he can be the great gentleman, not the rich mountebank. He wishes to be accepted by all those who would no longer accept even Madame.'

'What a blessed muddle!' said Lintott drily. 'He married her for the very thing she couldn't give him. She married him in order to escape what he most wanted. Did she see Mr Salvador in London, personally I mean?'

Genevieve shook her head.

'She wishes only to look at him. She goes secretly, without me, to see him. Only the Mr Fleischer follows her.'

'And had already found out what he wanted to know, and worked out how to punish Mr Salvador,' Lintott mused. 'All for the sake of a bit of a scandal as was over afore Mr Barak met her!'

Genevieve said, 'The consequence is not over, sir. The consequence is never over.'

'Is your mistress still fond of Mr Salvador, my dear?'

'She is unhappy with her husband.'

'I can see a mort of unhappiness ahead for everybody concerned,' said Lintott grimly, and did not know that his daughter would be part of it, 'but the important thing is to get the only innocent party out of this here mess. That's Miss Alicia. Aye, she's paying for all their selfishness!'

They were alone in the church now. One by one the women had prayed for strength or succour, and departed. A tear wandered down Genevieve's nose.

'You're all right, my dear,' said Lintott. 'All you have to do is to lie low and keep quiet. That's what they want. Just give me a few minutes' start, afore you follow me out.'

She nodded, sitting without hope. He strode past the mild Virgin in her perpetual reveries, genuflected as he crossed the centre aisle, slipped out of the church, slipped into nothing, into nowhere.

Fog had moved in through the Golden Gate, and the city was submerged in a billowing white ocean. This was no London Particular, yellow, smarting, blinding, but a milky muffled dream through which he walked like a dreamer. People and buildings appeared with the tenderness and unreality of dream images. Flower stalls swam out of focus, their blooms curiously subdued.

'What are you playing at, madam?' Lintott asked San Francisco.

She answered him with yet another vision. White horses formed out of the mist, drawing a glass bubble of a coach. Black pompoms quivered, black top hats gleamed dully. Within the carriage a rainbow of wreaths shivered in time to the muted roll of wheels.

The hearse streamed out of nothing, into nowhere.

Lintott walked slowly, relying on his sense of direction and his knowledge of the city's grid network to fetch him safely home. He paused at the intersection of Lombard and Stockton. Remembering that Stockton came up into Union Street eventually, he headed south.

He had encountered no enemy but his apprehension grew. His fears were as elusive, as intangible, as the soft and silent tide flowing about him.

He heard Barak's voice saying *Everybody has some price.*

He don't mean *price*, Lintott thought suddenly, he means *value*. We all have something or somebody as we value most. He *would* get it confused with price, now wouldn't he? But, my word, he knows where to hit hardest.

A thought struck him, and he cut straight down into O'Farrell Street and found the Orpheum Theatre. Posters of the magician graced the entrance. He went to the box office and made his enquiry.

'Are there any seats left for the first night of Mr Salvador's show?'

'There are no seats, no bookable seats that is, for any night of Mr Salvador's performances, sir. I'm sorry. We're sold right out.'

'That's good, ain't it?' Lintott asked, faintly perturbed.

'Very good. We had a whole lot of block bookings.'

Lintott stuck his hands in his pockets and turned up Powell Street into Union Square. Apprehension sat in his stomach like a meal. He glanced into Scotty's doorway. They were there, despite the sea-fog, in quiet companionship.

'Hello!' cried Lintott, heartened by the familiar after the strange. 'This here mist is a right old how-de-do, ain't it?'

Scotty stroked Patch's head, leaned forward and put a folded note into the cardboard box. He did not look at the Inspector.

Uneasy, Lintott exchanged dollars for the note. Scotty's lips moved.

'We are being watched, friend. Pass by, friend. Sorry.'

Lintott flushed up, strode on. Sharp left down Powell, across Market. His neck prickled. He turned sharp right and stood inside a doorway. No one passed him, or stood uncertainly on the corner. He waited, shivering in the cool air, for over an hour, then hurried home to Mrs Olson.

In the privacy of his lighted room he spread out Scotty's note. It read, *Contact Reverend Terence Caraher, Church of St Francis, Chairman of the Committee on Morals.*

Tomorrow, Lintott thought wearily. Tomorrow.

GRAND EXPOSURES

*Barney, when we last met I merely ruffled
your feathers, this time I'll pluck you
clean ...*

John Henry Anderson, Sr, to Barnardo Eagle

TWENTY TWO

Saturday, 14 April 1906

THE PALACE HOTEL, pride of San Francisco, was a place of
contrast like her native city. Naturally, she was the most
luxurious hostelry in the West, many said in the States, and
some insisted in the world. She sprawled magnificently over
two-and-a-half acres, boasted eight hundred rooms, reared seven
stories high. She was far too large, and ostentatious to the point
of vulgarity. Her grand court was pillared and paved in marble,
domed in glass, elegant in lamps and plants and iron gates,
spacious enough for horse-carriages to be driven in from Mont-
gomery Street. The service was superb and tipping was expected to match. Yet, Lizzie observed, the clerk picked his teeth
and scratched his head while they were signing the register.

This mixture of the splendid and the casual appealed to
Salvador, who entertained the residents of the lobby with a
spontaneous burst of personal publicity, while Lizzie enquired
after messages. There was a letter waiting for her, as promised,
written in her father's neat square hand.

'My dear daughter,' the news was bad, then. Lintott became
formal when troubled:

On no account must either you or Mr Salvador attempt
to contact me in any way. I stress this for all our sakes, particularly for Miss Alicia who is in a dangerous position.
Just tell him I know where she is, and hope to bring good

news soon. Don't mention her danger. Something is brewing up here. If you can persuade Mr Salvador to cancel or postpone his engagement it would be best. If he won't then look out for trouble. If there is any – mizzle! This is not your problem, but his and mine. Take care now. I'll keep in touch. Expect me when you see me. It might be sooner than you think. Your loving father. X.

The kiss brought tears to Lizzie's eyes. Tears were near the surface these days. She was expending herself on living, as though life were soon to be taken away. She veered from one to the other mood as the wind changed.

The magician had finished his brief repertoire and turned to her for rescue.

'You must go now, Salvador!' she said automatically, and led him from his admirers.

The nearer they had travelled towards San Francisco the more pre-occupied Salvador had become. Like Lizzie, he seemed to sense that this was the end of something. If Alicia were found then Lizzie must go. If Alicia were not found then what would Salvador do?

He sat by the window of his suite, absent-mindedly putting his cards through their daily paces while Lizzie imparted her father's news. He answered her listlessly. She passed on Lintott's advice to cancel the engagement. He shook his head.

'Is there anything I can do?' she asked.

He smiled, roused himself, held out his hands and clasped hers.

'Lizzie, this evening I shall show you San Francisco!'

His tone was vivacious, his smile a placation. Although the gesture appeared to be affectionate it kept her at arms' length. He intended her to be amused so that he could be left in peace.

'If you're not too tired,' she replied stiffly, chilled by his remoteness.

'I am never tired!' he cried, severing himself from her completely.

She did not argue with him. She had expected that physical possession would bring them closer, but it had not done so. He was a curiously selfish man because he gave so much and received so little. He needed audiences, not a woman. He wanted to be admired by thousands, not loved by one. Alicia was closest to him because she served both magic and him, because she was wholly dependent upon him. Without Salvador she could neither work nor live effectively.

But I'm not like that, Lizzie thought. For all that I love him, that I truly love him, I am myself.

'What are you thinking, Lizzie?' he asked, aware of a change in her.

'I am thinking,' said Lizzie, with the fine tone and smile and style she had acquired over the last months, 'that as you are not tired, and I am not tired, I should like you to show me San Francisco!'

Salvador was not the answer to her problems, though he had given her a new way of looking at them, a new strength to cope with them. She would carry them with her, unwanted and ungovernable children, until she found her personal solution. This evening they must be laid aside. She would clasp the magician's arm and saunter, wearing her wide-brimmed hat on which the ribbon was only slightly faded; adjusting her cream silk sleeve so as to expose the subtle beauty of those seven smoked-pearl buttons.

The boy who had copied the *Mona Lisa* on the pavement in coloured chalks had scrawled this message next to his capful of dimes. *I love San Francisco but I want to see Paris before I die. Please help me get there!* A drunk was asleep on a bench. A young negro showed passers-by how to make coins disappear. An old woman in filthy grey shawl changed her stockings in a doorway, mumbling to herself, 'No time, no time. Nobody's got no time. Hurry, hurry, all the time!'

San Francisco was lit up for nightfall and ready to go. Restaurants and theatres were opening. Red lamps flared in the dusk. The Barbary Coast and the Upper Tenderloin were prepared to sell pleasure until dawn broke. A man could dance himself dizzy, eat and drink himself sick, gamble his income, his health, even his life if he were unfortunate. They would strip his wallet as long as he could pay, throw him out when it was empty; and the woman he had taken would take another client, and the barman would serve another customer, and the waiter would set another table, and the girls would entertain another audience. All night long.

Down the sidewalk strode the inevitable prophet, wearing sandwich-boards which begged COME BACK TO GOD, AMERICA!

'Oh, look!' Lizzie was crying, as some fresh fantasy caught her eyes, as some fresh picture charmed her.

The prophet turned and strode back. He stopped in front of them, blocking their way, pointing a finger of doom.

The chill that crept through Lizzie's limbs turned to trembling. She clutched Salvador's arm and stared and stared. As she paled, and her lips parted, the magician's sense of timing and occasion came to her rescue.

'Off with you!' cried Salvador, taking the leaflet that the prophet held out. 'You have frightened this lady quite unnecessarily!'

He drew Lizzie into a small café a few yards away, and ordered a glass of Viennese coffee which he laced with brandy. Satisfied that she was not going to faint or weep, he read the leaflet while she sipped the coffee.

Between the lines of exhortation were printed these words. *Follow me when you are ready. I know a quiet place where we can talk. Destroy this now.*

Salvador selected a fine cigar from his case, asked Lizzie's permission to smoke, and used the note as a spill to light the cigar.

She said, very low, very shaken, wiping her lips, 'It was father!'

'When you are ready,' said Salvador, 'we must follow him.

He wishes to speak to us. You must show no emotion, Lizzie. Do you understand?'

She nodded. She finished her coffee. Salvador put out his cigar. They rose and joined the crowds on the sidewalk. The prophet began to walk away, pausing now and again to thrust a leaflet into passing hands. They followed him, talking to each other, pointing out whatever attracted their attention.

The crypt was silent and dusty.

'Help me off with these here, will you, Mr Salvador?' asked Lintott cheerfully. 'I feel like a regular old tortoise!'

He had grasped the full implication of their relationship as soon as he saw them together, and put the matter aside for future consideration. Now he embraced Lizzie affectionately enough, though with a slight reserve that told her he disapproved.

'I dare say we can sit down,' Lintott continued, 'these barrels, or whatever they are, will do for chairs. Here's my handkerchief to protect your fol-diggory, Lizzie. You're looking very fine nowadays, ain't you?'

The meeting was not how she had imagined it. They were changed by their different experiences. The old father-daughter alliance had weakened. Here were two independent adults who had shared a past, and now viewed an uneasy present.

'I know what it is,' said Lizzie, smiling. 'You've shaved your whiskers off, Father, and had a different hair-cut!'

'Ah, well. Needs must, sometimes. Now we can't stay here all night, chatting, so let's get down to business. The reason I'm togged up like this, Lizzie and Mr Salvador, is because those two villains know I'm in the city. It's a pretty good disguise, thought up by Father Caraher – who runs a public campaign against vice. Your sister is being held in a house in Mason Street, sir, and the Reverend and I have a scheme for getting her out on Tuesday night. I shall fetch her straight to you at the Palace Hotel, and I'd advise you to have your luggage packed and your engagement at the Orpheum Theatre cancelled, and you can all scarper!'

Salvador said, 'It is impossible to cancel an engagement of this length and magnitude, Inspector.'

'Then I've risked myself for nothing,' Lintott replied quietly, 'because he won't let any of you get away if you don't go while you can. He'll take a pot shot at me, too, for crossing him!'

Lizzie said, into the tight silence, 'Father, why was Alicia taken? Is she Mr Fleischer's wife?'

Lintott looked at the magician.

'Miss Alicia has nothing to do with it – except as the innocent party, except as the victim.'

'Am I the reason?' asked Salvador gravely.

'Yes, sir. I dare say,' said Lintott with dry sarcasm, 'as you've forgotten all about it. It goes back seven years, to a titled lady's house-party in England. You met a Miss Francesca Sinclair there, and had a bit of a flirtation. I'm putting matters as delicate as I can. That little affair put paid to her chances on the marriage market...'

Salvador was on his feet, crying, 'She was a free spirit, a fine spirit. The marriage market meant nothing to her. Nothing!'

Lintott surveyed him, very quiet, very dry.

'Oh, didn't it, sir?' he asked innocently. 'I must have been mistaken, then. She married Bela Barak.'

Neither Lizzie nor Salvador had any colour in their faces. He sat down, quite wordless. She was very still.

'I haven't yet found out what triggered off the quarrel,' Lintott continued, 'because she and her family had managed to hush things up for six years. But the quarrel was over that – flirtation. He reckoned – Barak reckoned – that *you* were to blame. This is his way of punishing *you*, and he don't mind having my poor wife thrown under an omnibus, or your poor sister held prisoner for three months, so long as he makes *you* pay. If you choose to stay here then he won't mind hurting me, or Lizzie, or anyone else that gets in his way. So, sir, what are you going to do about it?'

Then the Inspector sat squarely on his barrel, and looked both hard and blandly at the magician.

'My friend,' said Salvador, 'I have much for which to ask your pardon, yours and others!' He spoke slowly, thoughtfully. He was endeavouring to find a fair solution. 'My decision to fulfil this engagement is not based on vanity. It is a responsibility which no one else can share or shoulder. I agree that you and Lizzie and Alicia, and the old ones, must leave San Francisco on Tuesday evening. I have plenty of money. We can make arrangements for you to travel as swiftly and comfortably as possible. But I shall remain, my friend. It is, after all, my fault,' he added, smiling. 'It seems fitting that I should pay the final penalty, whatever that might be.'

He looked across at the Inspector, and shrugged slightly. He had regained some self-respect, though not the whole of it.

Lintott now took time to ponder.

'Well, sir, that's to your credit,' he began, after a minute or so, 'only it leaves out an intention on my part, you see. Because I'm staying behind to help to get Barak and Fleischer convicted of kidnapping. I've collected a mort of information on the pair of them, as could come in useful for more than one purpose. I've heard that the United States Government is sending somebody down here to look into City Hall, and I want to be on the spot when that happens. So, Mr Salvador, you and me will stay behind and help each other as best we can. Lizzie and Miss Alicia and the old folks will leave.'

'Done!' cried Salvador.

'Just a minute,' said Lizzie. 'You've forgotten *me*! I'm not a piece of luggage, to be put on board a train and sent off! I'm staying behind as well, and for more than one reason. I'm not leaving either of you here. What have *I* got but you? Father, I've been working as Salvador's assistant as well as his secretary. He can't give a full-scale performance without a trained assistant, and I won't let him down.'

Lintott's opaque eyes flickered, and settled into their customary bland stare. He was both annoyed and delighted with his daughter.

'Well, the sentiment does you proud, Lizzie, but you've reckoned without the other three in your party. Miss Alicia will be pretty shaken up, and the old folks ain't exactly as nimble as they might be. You're the only one as can sort them out and trot them off!'

'There's no point in *any* of them going if Salvador is staying behind,' said Lizzie promptly. 'He's their support, their protection. He's all any of them has got that matters.'

The two men looked at each other, and at Lizzie. Her determination was unshakeable. Salvador smiled. Lintott laughed.

'Here, help me on with these, will you, sir?' he asked. 'We may as well have saved ourselves the risk of meeting! Still, we've sorted one thing out – we're going to face the music together. That's something, any road!'

TWENTY THREE

Tuesday, 17 April 1906

NUMBER 620 JACKSON STREET had become notorious enough to warrant a regular stop for the cable cars. Were there no ladies aboard, the driver would bawl cheerfully, 'All out for the whore house!' Its backers were powerful men, sufficiently well-known in their civic and political capacities to have their investment nicknamed the Municipal Crib, sufficiently ruthless to have neighbouring brothels put out of action so that the Crib might thrive. Saloon-keepers, policemen, favour-seekers, recommended its services to strangers. Its prostitutes were guaranteed immunity from arrest. Its protection was of an unusually subtle and tough quality, being apparently both state- and church-proof. Like other highly profitable concerns, the Crib kept its secrets, and there were names behind the known names that were too big to mention.

Round the corner, Aunt Patsy's parlour house on Mason was demure and expensive: a rich, respectable sister. Hardly the sort of place, one would have thought, to attract the wrath of religious crusaders. Yet on this mild April evening a motley band of the Reverend Terence Caraher's followers were converging upon the premises: bent on harassment.

Father Caraher's present interest lay in closing down the Municipal Crib. He had already vanquished the Nymphia and the Marsicania, infamous brothels in Pacific and Dupont Streets. So he sent a trusty lieutenant to Mason Street in his stead, and all the picketers who could be mustered. They ranged from the fanatical to the curious-minded. A few had turned themselves into walking placards. Some played musical instruments rather badly, and others sang to the rousing hymns equally badly. Behind them marched a sturdy figure in sandwich-boards, on which was written COME BACK TO GOD, AMERICA!

Aunt Patsy's shining windows were raised to let in a current of fresh air. Her starched white nets billowed on an evening breeze. The sound of a piano tinkled into Mason Street, playing a series of popular songs.

'Halt!' shouted the gaunt red-headed Irishman.

The gaggle of the godly stumbled against each other, and re-formed, apologising and earnest. The instrument-players warbled uncertainly into silence, followed a few bars later by their choir. Lintott slipped quietly away to the back of the house.

'All together now, friends!' cried the Irishman and brought down his arms as though he conducted a celestial orchestra. The faithful opened their mouths.

> *There is a green hill far away*
> *Without a city wall...*

The player-piano continued to pour its melody into the street.

> *For you don't know Nellie like I do*
> *Said the naughty little bird in Nellie's hat...*

As the voices mounted above the piano, and windows were thrown up and pretty heads poked out, and astonishingly brash questions were asked, Lintott stacked his sandwich-boards against the wall and walked into Aunt Patsy's kitchen.

'Hands up!' said Lintott, and brandished an empty double-action bulldog revolver which he had bought in Shreve and Barber's for two dollars seventy-five that morning.

The kitchen staff raised their hands above their heads, and the bouncer's cigarette fell from the corner of his mouth.

'The house is surrounded,' said Lintott curtly and untruthfully. 'Just you show me the room that Mr Fleischer's lady is in, and be sharp about it!'

The bouncer did not argue.

'And one move from any of you,' said Lintott menacingly, 'and he gets shot...' he thought of the next possible step, '...first!' he added.

He slammed the kitchen door behind him, and stuck his revolver in the man's back. The front door knocker was banging, banging.

Outside, they were singing *We do not know, we cannot tell, what pain he had to bear.* Inside, the piano rolled into a fresh tune *And I'm one of the girls! a girl to spend the chink!*

'Open that front door!' Lintott said to the bouncer.

As Father Caraher's volunteers streamed into the hallway, Aunt Patsy's girls screamed out of the parlour. They were clad in long white nightgowns, lavishly trimmed with lace. Their hair was dressed in long girlish braids. Behind them a number of gentleman callers, all good family men, pushed through the throng in an effort to reach the back premises and escape safely home. Behind her girls and her clients, Aunt Patsy, looking like the nicest kind of elderly female relative, urged somebody to fetch Sergeant Mulligan.

'For he won't have me worried like this,' she explained. 'I've been generous with the Orphans' Fund, and that bell you can hear ringing on a Sunday from the church opposite was bought by me and Madame Solange...'

My old man is one of the boys, and I'm one of the girls!

'Turn that thing off, will you? I can't hear meself think!'

'Walk not in the way of evil men, for they sleep not except they have done mischief!'

'Hurry,' said Lintott grimly. 'The faster the better!'

The bouncer hurried along the corridor on the second floor, unlocked and flung open the door at the far end. Lintott pushed him ahead, and stared round.

A big brass bed, a dresser, a couple of chairs, a gaudy carpet, a reproduction of *Eros and Psyche.*

The faintest sound behind the door alerted them too late. She must have waited, perhaps for hours, for such an opportunity.

'Miss Salvador!' shouted Lintott.

She was gone. Running, running, through the clutter of evangelists and prostitutes and clients. Past Aunt Patsy, and the heavily gilded tables and chairs and divans. Holding her ears against the cacophony of hymns and ditties. Out into Mason Street, under the burning crimson lamps. Running, running, into a world which had made her afraid. Exchanging one bedlam for another.

Lintott, pushing his way out to the sidewalk at last, stuffed his useless gun in his pocket and began to run after her, calling.

The Orpheum Theatre on O'Farrell, famous for Vaudeville shows, had given itself up to two weeks of magic. Photographs of Salvador's noble head smiled enigmatically at the passing populace. Coloured posters advertised the magician producing marvels from a flaming crucible, levitating a lovely lady, and ordering an astral hand to write messages.

At the Grand Opera House on Third Street, the Italian tenor Enrico Caruso was opening on the same night, with the Metropolitan Opera of New York in the *Queen of Sheba.* He was also staying at the Palace Hotel. Both giants had professed themselves to be desolated at the thought of missing each other's performance. Both of them had staged private performances in their joint hotel: changing suites, making entrances into lobby and dining room. Both were due for a disastrous first night.

The magician was prepared for all occasions, and had instructed Lizzie how to behave.

'First, every piece of apparatus must be checked both by you and by me. Secondly, we make friends with our stage assistants, and bribe them so heavily that they will take care of our performance themselves. Your excellent father has told me it would probably be useless to contact the police, and in any case it would be difficult to convince them of premeditated hostility. Thirdly, in case Bela Barak has thought of planting ruffians in the front rows of the stalls, with the intention of breaking up the equipment, or myself, or both, I shall erect an electrical fence along the footlights. I had to do that once in Italy, and it proved to be an added attraction! Fourthly, should missiles be thrown we have no defence, so I wish you to leave the stage and allow me to carry on. I have done that before, too. There is much jealousy in my profession! Still, the critics will realise what is happening, and give me public support in their reviews. The theatre owners cannot afford to have their artists bullied out of town, so they will support me too. Therefore, dearest Lizzie, the first night may be a fiasco but the others should be normal. Please to follow my instructions absolutely, because I know exactly what I am doing. Is that understood, my dear?'

She had nodded. Admiring his attitude, she sought to emulate it. But now, within half an hour of the curtain rising, she became nervous.

'Even after the first night, Felix, Father doesn't think it wise to Catch the Bullets!' she ventured to remind him, fearful that his confidence might over-reach his commonsense.

'I think,' said Salvador, 'that to invite the guns of San Francisco would be to court certain disaster! Which reminds me, Lizzie – neither you nor I is bullet-proof. If he has decided on that solution there is nothing we can do to prevent it. So are you certain in your mind that you wish to assist me in this perilous evening?'

'Oh yes. I have never doubted that.'

'I honour you, dearest Lizzie,' he said, and kissed her cheek.

They had nothing to do now but to wait.

'If we do not survive,' Salvador continued, half-humorously, 'there is no problem. The problems arise, always, with living on!' He was finding his way round a shipwrecking rock of a problem at the moment. 'Tell me, Lizzie, have you thought about what you will do when you go back home? Can you not, perhaps, breathe life into your husband? Take what you have learned of this larger world and infuse his smaller one?'

She was momentarily shocked at the import of his questions, and then dry and calm again as she faced them. She had thought often and deeply of this possible solution, even when she was most happy with the magician. But she had been lonelier living with her husband in her husband's environment than she could ever be by herself. The end of her relationship with Salvador would mean loss, but not total loss. In his ever-magical world she had discovered many sides of herself.

So she could pass over the stage which most women would pass through – that of tears and accusations, of fruitless analysis and empty promises – and answer him directly.

'Oh, I shan't go back to him,' said Lizzie. 'It would be wrong to go back. I shall find work of some kind when I'm home again, and it won't be sticking a patch on my old life and making do, either! I know it will be difficult, but at least it will be difficult and worthwhile – not difficult and nothing.'

Salvador nodded once or twice, accepting the answer which reminded him, too, that he could not be one person's entire universe.

So he said simply, 'You are very fine, and very good, Miss Lizzie! Let us now face the lions. Afterwards – perhaps your father, with Alicia?'

'Let us hope so,' she agreed, with both generosity and dignity.

There was such a strange atmosphere as they walked the corridor, a pent silence with the hint of mockery behind it, that they looked at each other involuntarily. The magician shrugged and straightened his waistcoat.

'We are some minutes early?' he suggested.

'Of course!' cried Lizzie.

'*Illustrissimo!*' Fredo whispered, appearing as he always seemed to – from unlikely places. 'Salvador! There is something very wrong out there!'

He mimed disaster of an unknown nature, an event unforeseen and unprepared for, a thing out of his reckoning. As his eyes rolled and his head wagged and he gesticulated with his short arms, the magician said, 'Tell me!'

Fredo answered, 'The house is empty, *Illustrissimo!*'

They could hear accumulated whispers of conversation from the stage hands who hung about, embarrassed, puzzled. Very pale now, the magician peered through a fold of the curtain, and then motioned Lizzie to see for herself.

The Orpheum Theatre was a mausoleum, brightly lit and freshly swept. In the orchestra stalls the musicians tuned up their instruments as quietly as possible, feeling understandably exposed. The conductor's tap with his baton was a furtive movement and made an indeterminate sound. In the front row of the stalls sat a handful of theatre critics, craning their heads, talking among themselves, turning over their programmes. Here and there sat a solitary viewer, sometimes two or three viewers, sufficiently scattered to make the absence of the rest more noticeable. Then nothing but empty velvet seats and a hollow silence, from floor to roof.

The manager was at Salvador's side, explaining what he could not explain.

'Block bookings,' he kept repeating. 'Whole rows together.'

'Just tonight?' asked Salvador.

'Every night, sir. Every single night. Block bookings. I was doing a real brisk trade from the day the box office opened. Sold out...'

'How many are there in the house tonight?'

'Maybe a couple of dozen!'

Salvador motioned Lizzie to take her position. There was no need now to check the equipment, to rely upon anyone or anything to help them, to be brave, even to be ultimately heroic. Bela Barak had divined the price of a magician, and cost him his audience.

Running, running, out of bedlam into bedlam. Hoarse voices, jocular remarks, a hand catching at her flying skirts, at her arms. Full tilt into a drunken man who whirled her in a mock waltz. Round and round, red lights flaring in the dusk and sending out fiery haloes.

The cable car clattered to a halt.

'All out for the whore-house!' called the driver, grinning.

Men were shouting and laughing, carrying her along with them through the crowded hallway, down the dim passages full of noise and chaos.

The room in which Alicia tried to hide was about six feet square, furnished in a dirty and ramshackle fashion with an iron bed, a marble-topped washstand and a kerosene stove. The Mexican girl had made a small altar of the window-seat, on which the Virgin held her child imperturbably. Within a border of garlands a painted motto on the wall read *What is Home without Mother?* A man's hat had been rested temporarily on the ragged mat. His boots were on his feet, and a strip of oil-cloth at the end of the bed prevented them from soiling the coverlet. A kettle boiled on the stove. By the tin wash-basin stood a bottle of Lysol.

The girl called, over the man's shoulder, 'He'll be through in a minute. Only a quarter. You cain't take your clothes off, only your hat...'

Closing the door of the cubicle, and running among the men whose feet wove uncertainly to their destinations, whose mouths framed obscenities, whose eyes surveyed women for only one purpose.

On the first floor a red-haired Jewess had a line of customers waiting, while her protector marshalled them. They took off their hats and held their money ready.

In and out, slamming and running, staring, evading the out-stretched hands.

The negress must have weighed two hundred and eighty pounds. Her client, butting at the coils of shining black flesh, seemed to be a parasite on a whale. On her wall hung a card embroidered in violets, which read:

Satisfaction guaranteed, or your money back.
50 cents each. Three for a dollar.

Down the corridors and up the flimsy stairs. Running.

Small-boned, black-eyed, pock-marked, the French pimp said, 'Lucille is a dollar. She comes from Marseilles...'

Painted faces, simulated passions, expressionless eyes. Tired, tired, tired. The men spending their money, spending themselves, without a name or a face or a fragment of loving-kindness to make any meaning of it.

'...and like a dude I hang my coat and waistcoat and trousers in this closet and when I come to put them on again there is only one new dime in the pocket and I say where is my watch where is my dough and she says run buster before there is trouble she says you have the car-fare home haven't you she says don't you make no complaint she says this room has a push-button which will bring a saloon bouncer around she says...'

The hallway grew longer and darker and closer. Now she was fleeing into nightmare, because there would be no retreat. At the far end she saw a solitary man emerge from another stairway, observe her, and lean against the wall, waiting. She could not stop, because where else was there to go? So she fled further and further into obscurity until the gaslight on the grubby wall illumined him. She saw the scar raised by a smile, and threw out her hands, and fell at his feet.

Fleischer picked up the girl as though she had been a sack of bones, and slung her over his shoulder. From Jackson Street to California was only four blocks, then he could cruise round in the Cadillac, waiting to pick up the other party who had caused so much trouble.

Breathless, sick at heart, Lintott made his way back to Mason Street. He had lost her, having almost found her. Now he did not know where to look, because her flight was purposeless.

Outside Aunt Patsy's the sidewalk had been cleared by policemen, and Father Caraher's volunteers escorted from the premises, threatened with breaking and entering.

'But we didn't break, Sergeant!' the gaunt Irishman protested. 'They opened the door to us and we just walked in.'

'Then just walk out, bud, or you'll be in court tomorrow morning!'

Wearily, Lintott plodded to the back of the building, keeping wary eyes and ears on possible watchers and listeners. It was quiet enough, solitary enough now. In the dark yard he put on the wooden message, and strode forth to the city to find – whom? Salvador would be in the middle of his performance. Father Caraher could be anywhere.

'I may as well just walk up and down for a bit, and get my breath back, and hand out a few leaflets!' Lintott muttered to himself. 'Where should I go that's ungodly? I've got quite a wide choice, come to think!'

Market seemed to offer a variety. So he padded stolidly along to the Midway Theatre, which was barred to young men under the age of twenty-one – and therefore a terrible attraction to them. He visited the Cinograph between Third and Fourth. He picketed the shops that sold cigars and cigarettes and shotguns, all adjuncts of Satan. He saw that Newman's Richelieu Café on Market and Geary was rolling out its beer barrels into the road, so that the newspapers could report 'Newman a Nuisance Again!' and give him free publicity. He scattered a few office boys playing cards by the Donahue Monument, and harming nobody. He was waiting for the Orpheum Theatre to close, for Salvador and Lizzie to return to the Palace Hotel. He was doing something useless, in order to conceal the fact that he could do nothing.

Close on ten o'clock a ruby Cadillac cruised along the sidewalk and stopped by the sandwich-board man.

'Like to go for a ride?' Fleischer asked, hand in breast pocket, smiling. 'He wants to see you. Down at Belmont.' He looked at the sandwich-boards. 'Better leave those here, don't you think?' he purred. 'They would kind of spoil the appearance of the automobile.'

So the boards stood woodenly on the sidewalk, without their human filling, mutely beseeching America to return to God.

TWENTY FOUR

FLEISCHER SAID, LOOKING at the road ahead of them, 'If you try to do something stupid, Inspector, like grabbing the wheel or jumping out, I shall gun you down. Right?'

'Understood,' said Lintott, moistening his lips. 'Anyway,' he added stoutly, 'I was always curious-minded. I want to know what happens next.'

Fleischer's scar moved as he smiled. His hands looked hard and cold on the steering wheel, the hands of a dead man. But he drove well, he loved driving this machine.

'Well, you are going to find out what happens next by kind permission of Mr Barak,' he said softly. 'You ever been driven in a Cadillac before?'

'No, nor in any motor car. I know nothing about motoring.'

Fleischer's eyes were expressionless, his mouth pale and set.

'You know nothing about anything, mister. You fool nobody and you are nobody!'

'Then I'm not worth worriting over,' said Lintott in anger, 'so you may as well think about your motoring instead!'

He had meant to jibe, but Fleischer took him seriously.

'This Cadillac is the latest model,' he explained with reverence, with the nearest approach to warmth Lintott had heard. 'Mr Barak likes everything to be of the best. He aims to buy one of your English Rolls-Royces as soon as she is ready. The Silver Ghost. You heard of her?'

Lintott shook his head. He felt old and tired and hopeless.

'She will cost the same price as a thoroughbred, and then we have to ship her over here, which will cost another heap of dough. Oh, she is a princess! A six-cylinder, seven-litre engine with a new classic radiator. They say she will run 15,000 miles non-stop. She's kind of under wraps, right now, but Mr Barak said we should have a Silver Ghost just as soon as they came on the market. Rolls-Royce have a lot of class...'

Lintott wondered what had happened to Alicia, who also had class. He wondered whether Fleischer would have treated her differently had she been an automobile.

'...call her a Silver Ghost because that is what she looks like. You know something?' Quite friendly, because this man was helpless, because he had touched on a secret passion. 'I have no use for women. My mother was a hooker on the Coast. Women are greedy, they are sick, they carry disease. Did you know that? All women are greedy and dirty and sick!' His hand gripped the wheel, and then became gentle and sure again. 'Most men are pretty stupid, too,' he added out of fairness. 'So I got no time for men or women. If you want a lady, mister, you buy yourself a Silver Ghost. If you want a man you can admire then you find yourself a Mr Barak. That is why I work for Mr Barak, and it is a very great privilege...'

I've been down in the London sewers with the likes of Fleischer afore, Lintott thought. I've played water rats. I've meted out a mort of justice, and what mercy I could. But this here country ain't like England, it's larger than lifesize – with the villainy to match.

'...I will tell you something you do not seem to know. Mr Barak is a king round here, and it's hard to become a king unless you plan it out. So he plans it out until he has an empire, and I am proud to say I helped a little in that direction. Then he gets himself some kind of queen, and he is not the sort of guy to stint a lady! Until she came along Mr Barak and I were like that!' He lifted two fingers from the wheel, and crossed them. His mouth was thin. 'But this lady comes along, and the next thing you know I am not good enough. No, sir!

Oh, sure I kept out of the way when he was entertaining classy people, because I am a rough sort of guy to set among the company. But I would be in and around the house, and he would call me and take off his shoes – as if he was like you and me – and say "Pour me a Bourbon, Hank, and pour yourself one!" And I would sit there and we would talk, like a coupla brothers together. Not always business,' he said anxiously, looking sideways to make sure that Lintott did not get the wrong impression. 'I mean, we would have a game of poker together, and he would tell me about himself and I would tell him about myself. I mean, we really *talked*!'

There was a time when I might have thought this showed a bit of heart, Lintott thought. But now I know that this man is evil, directed by evil, and committing evil.

'Then she came along, with all kinds of fancy credentials, and he thought he had *somebody*. She wouldn't have me around. He explained about that. Mr Barak explained. I knew it wasn't him – no, sir. I tried to be nice to her. Then I saw how she was treating a great man like Mr Barak, and then he had no family...'

'Grieved him, did it?' Lintott asked drily. 'Big family man, was he? Children round the knee and stories at bedtime, eh?'

'Sure,' said Fleischer, missing the bitter irony. 'Mr Barak would have been a great father. But no, she had to have everything her way and give sweet damn nothing. That was when I started to do a little detective work on my own account, but I did it for Mr Barak's own good...'

'Oh, my Lord!' Lintott groaned. 'I should think about ninety per cent of my cases had somebody saying that at the start! Why won't folks mind their own business?'

Fleischer shouted, 'Mister, you have a mouth on you that won't stay shut!'

Suddenly Lintott saw that the man was moved, that he could be made to part with information. What use the information would be to Lintott he didn't know, but out of habit he began to question carefully. His face became smooth and bland. He patted Fleischer's sleeve, and felt the hard thin arm beneath.

'Half a minute, now, Mr Fleischer,' said Lintott. 'You'll have to excuse me being a bit on the jumpy side, but then I've got reason to be jumpy, ain't I? All right, I don't like what Mr Barak does, but he's human like the rest of us, ain't he? That's fair enough. If you said something rude about *my* family *I*'d be vexed, too! So, looking at it from his point of view, like you say, if he gives his wife everything and she don't fulfil her share of the bargain – then you want to set things right for him. This here motor car runs well, don't she?'

The scarred man was silent, brooding. But Lintott was judging him now to some purpose.

'Yes,' said Lintott mildly, 'if things had turned out differently I'd be enjoying myself, riding about the countryside in style. Style's a funny thing, ain't it? This motor car has style, Mr Barak's got style – though I don't see eye to eye with him! – Mrs Barak's got style. That horse of hers has style. I quite see why he married her, you know. And folks can't always choose whether they have a family or not. It ain't right to blame *her*.'

Fleischer began to laugh without humour.

'I was forgetting, of course,' Lintott pursued, 'that you'd found out about Mr Salvador. I thought Mr Barak had put you up to it. I didn't know as you did it by yourself. Detective work comes hard on the feet, don't it?'

'For God's sake, do you think I am some sort of a Pinkerton slouch?' Fleischer questioned. 'I *employ* those people, mister!'

'I was forgetting again,' said Lintott, 'as you're by way of being a rich man yourself. Only Mr Barak's so big he blots everybody else out, don't he?'

'Mister,' said Fleischer reverently, 'you will never meet a greater man than Mr Barak. You will not meet a man as great as Mr Barak.'

'So he only has the best,' Lintott mused. 'The best house, the best wife.'

'Mister, do you know what she did to him?'

'Bit of a flirtation?' Lintott said, avuncular. 'High spirits and no harm meant. You take it too serious, Mr Fleischer.'

They were in Belmont. Lintott could smell the night scents

under the trees. He drew in long breaths of dark spiced air.

'She was pregnant by that cheap magician,' said Fleischer, very hard, very cold. 'The Sinclairs knew a doctor. She had an abortion and they hushed everything right up. But they couldn't hush the rumours. I tell you what else couldn't be hushed up, and I found that out. Mr Barak had paid just about every specialist he could find, and they all held out a little hope for him. Something was wrong with her, sure, but some fine day ... did you know he had a nursery made and furnished just right? Did you know how much he wanted his family, his dynasty, mister?'

'You said you found something else out?'

'She was scared sick when she knew that the abortion had finished her. She must have used every bit of Southern charm she possessed to shut those specialists' mouths. Because Mr Barak only got half a tale. But when *I* started, mister, I got the full tale. And I told him. And I found out that the man was Salvador, and I told him that. Then we figured out what we should do, and we did it. Because that cheap magician had to be punished.'

They were drawing up outside the white door, under the white marble pillars.

'We haven't finished with him yet,' Fleischer assured the Inspector. 'Tonight is only the beginning. But it's as if something was on our side, on the side of Mr Barak and me, because whatever you do goes wrong, mister. You scared the hell out of that strange kid tonight, instead of saving her like you intended. Do you know where she went? After all the trouble I'd gone to to keep her safe?'

He began to laugh again, shaking his head from side to side, cruelly amused.

'She ran right into the biggest whorehouse in San Francisco. Aunt Patsy put the word out as soon as the kid escaped. They were looking for her like I've been looking for you – all the time, mister. I picked her up off the floor, after she'd been running around the place. And she is as crazy as any person in the State Asylum...'

'Where is she?' Lintott asked. 'Where is she?'

'Locked up in the house in California Street, mister. The house you used to watch. Oh, mister, I could have picked you up about a thousand times, but you were amusing Mr Barak — so he let you nose around. Like I said, mister, you fool nobody and you are nobody!'

It was Barak the host who greeted Lintott in the hall of the great house at Belmont: Barak the host who shook Lintott's reluctant hand: Barak the host who ushered him inside and offered him a drink. Lintott accepted a large Bourbon and drank it down, grateful for the spurious heat, the unreal courage of alcohol. He needed warmth and courage, from whatever source.

'Okay, Hank,' said Barak, 'you can take off for a while. Have the Cadillac ready for later on, when I call you.' He asked genially, 'How's she going, Hank?'

'Great, Mr Barak, just great,' said Fleischer, and even the scar showed love.

Barak cut and lit a fine cigar, smiling at Lintott's open hostility.

'You know, you are the kind of stubborn old mule of a guy I just have to admire,' he began. 'Now I know what kind of man you think I am, and you are wrong!'

'Prove it!' said Lintott, with a glint of his former authority.

Barak threw back his head and laughed. In most other men Lintott would have relished that laugh which came spontaneously and fully.

'You kill me, Inspector,' said Barak, good-humoured. 'Would you believe me if I said I was both a very practical man, and a man of vision?'

Lintott moved his head as if asking again for proof.

'Why do you think I had Hank bring you here?' Barak demanded, amused.

'I don't know,' said Lintott.

Barak laughed and spread his hands.

'Because we are quits,' said Barak. 'That is justice, isn't it, like you have in England? I proved Mr Salvador guilty and I meted out the punishment he deserved. We haven't quite finished with him. Hank has something in mind, but then Hank does not understand about justice and mercy. Hank is sometimes just plain mean! I say that, loving the man and knowing he loves me. So we shall see. Pretty well everything went according to plan. I am big enough to say that you did a fine job yourself, in a way, Inspector. You were just not as smart and important as the empire you were fighting!' He smiled, as though he were writing out a personal reference. 'It *is* an empire, Inspector Lintott, I would have you know that. Here, let me show you around!'

Lintott stood up, and Barak laid one immaculately-clad arm on his shoulders. The Inspector bore both weight and implication without shrinking as they began to walk the house together.

'My father struck lucky when I was a little boy,' said Barak, black eyes softening as the miracle was reborn. 'I remember him saying to me, "Now your momma is a lady!" He was a very simple man. My mother was a very religious woman. Oh, she taught me to turn the other cheek, and lay up riches in heaven, and all that sort of nonsense...' Servants were moving silently to one side as the strange couple approached, bowing or bobbing a curtsey. 'My wine cellar,' said Barak, as the butler unlocked a Solomon's cave of grape. 'Only the finest wines in the world!' Racks of bottles ran from floor to ceiling into infinity. 'My kitchens!' Minions acknowledged his presence. He ignored them. 'My chef comes from Foyot's in Paris. Yes, Inspector Lintott,' as they returned to the vast hall through whose glass dome the moon shone, 'the Bible is full of misapprehensions. Turn the other cheek and somebody strikes that one also! The meek do not inherit the earth, it is the grabbers who do that! The poor are not blessed – you have only to look at them! And you can break every one of those ten commandments if you just have enough hard cash on you at the time!' He laughed at his own joke, and then said in a different tone, 'The entire building is air-conditioned of

245

course. We have an hydraulic elevator.'

They mounted the stairs which branched left and right.

'Did you happen to notice that my front gates opened automatically?' Barak asked. 'That is due to a mechanism concealed in the road. Pretty good, eh? The gates were taken from an Italian palace. My gardens are a copy of some laid out in your old country, by a man with a crazy sort of name – Capability Brown. Do you know I like that? I like your crazy old names!'

There was no sign of Francesca Barak in the house, but perhaps she had retired for the night. It was late enough, Lord knows!

'The fountains are copied from those at Versailles. My mother's tomb was designed by an architect on the lines of a tomb in Florence. People come to see it, you know...'

He walked and talked and flung open doors on vistas of corridors, on accumulations of possessions. The exquisite stood with the vulgar, the pure with the profane. He could not tell the difference. He only knew their cost.

'Every window in this house cost me two thousand dollars in drapes. The console mirror on my wife's dressing-table cost me five thousand dollars. They say that money can't buy everything – I say, come and look at this! Even the cuspidors are solid gold! The chandeliers in this room came from a doge's palace in Venice – I even have one in the stables. The marbles are Algerian. The ceilings are frescoed. I have French tapestries. Tell me, have you ever seen anything like this?'

'Never!' said Lintott drily.

'But the money is not enough. I have a responsibility also,' said Barak, quite astonishingly. He contemplated Lintott's raised eyebrows with some pleasure. 'You did not expect me to say that, did you? I take full responsibility. I am known for my good works. They write them down in books. There are schools and hospitals that could not exist without my money. That is charity, and I am a charitable man!' He extended his hand with the gesture of a medieval prince. Then it clenched. 'But if I take care of people then they must do as I say. Right?

If they cross me then I demand that they should be punished.'

The arm round Lintott's shoulder relaxed. He patted the Inspector's sleeve lightly to show good fellowship.

'These carpets are Persian. Somebody told me they were so rare they should be hung on the walls. I told him I was not so mean that I minded people walking on my rare carpets!' He laughed again, a full-bellied sound. 'This is gold plate,' he continued, 'and it is not for display. We eat off it. These are very old pictures and they all cost me one hell of a lot of money. She has kind of a pretty face, hasn't she?'

The Florentine lady smiled down on Barak's excesses, unmoved and tender.

'I don't make mistakes when I buy things,' Barak told himself.

It was as though Lintott silently examined Barak's conscience, for the man defended himself, unasked, unaccused.

'*Knock and it shall be opened, ask and it shall be given*, my mother used to tell me. Now that way all you are going to get is grazed knuckles and a sore throat. Shall I tell you what you do? You knock the door *down*, and you *take*!'

He shook his head, ruminating. He had remembered Bessie, and must somehow make this right with the image of Bela Barak.

'Now Hank went a little too far with your wife, Inspector Lintott. All I said to him was to warn you, so you would know you must not cross me. You think I liked hearing about what happened? Do you know what I said when Hank told me about your wife? I said, "Hank, I am now about to order the most wonderful flowers that lady has ever seen. I am now about to give that poor lady the greatest and most beautiful experience!" That letter I wrote, those flowers I sent, were *sincere*!'

Lintott held himself proudly aloof from that brotherly arm. For he had given her greater riches than these, and none could be bought because all were beyond price. His old strength was running like a river. His old cunning returned.

'I don't exactly know what you're trying to tell me,' said

Lintott, seeming puzzled. 'I just want Alicia Salvador back. I want Mr Salvador left in peace while he's here. I want a safe conduct, so's to speak, when we all leave. There,' said Lintott amicably, 'what do you say to that?'

Barak began to laugh again. Then he stopped. He frowned.

'Look, Mr Lintott or Mr Teale, or whatever stupid name you call yourself, I hold *all* the cards. I tell *you*. You do not tell *me*. Ever!' He held out his closed hand. 'I have San Francisco in here. Who will take it away from me?'

'There's no reason to have that attitude,' said Lintott reasonably. 'One thing at a time, Mr Barak. San Francisco is no concern of mine. Alicia Salvador is. Your Mr Fleischer says she's insane. Now we don't want a scandal, do we? I only mention two names to you, to show that I know what I'm talking about. Father Terence Caraher and Mrs Claudia Strauss! Do you see what I mean, sir? Now I don't blame Mr Fleischer for exaggerating a bit, because he'd lay down his life for you, which is a very touching sentiment to think on. But he hasn't had his eye on me since I arrived, whatever he's told you. I've got notebooks of information on you and him, collectively and together, both private and business details.'

He had to hold Barak in a fine balance, to make him listen. Too much force and that black rage would boil. Too little authority and Barak would throw him out. Nor must Lintott seem equal. Nor dared he appear too inferior.

'Now those notebooks are in the hands of somebody as I can trust, and if I don't turn up before morning with Miss Salvador they'll be handed over to the San Francisco District Attorney – Mr Langdon. There is other information, I say this as delicate as I can, about Mrs Barak and her difficulties in the past, as will be handed over to Mrs Strauss if anything unfortunate happens to us. Now, Mr Barak, I'll speak as plain as I may. This sort of thing is beneath you, really, ain't it? It's too small for you to bother about. Yes!'

For the man was mad, not certifiably so, but most definitely mad.

'You see, sir,' Lintott continued affably, 'you show me round this here palace – I don't think palace is too large a word for it? – and you show me all you've done, and the charitable concerns and that, and I'm wondering why you ever worried about the Salvadors. It don't make sense. Then, when I ask you if I might just wind up my bit of a case, you start talking about San Francisco.'

Lintott chuckled and shook his head. Barak was watching him.

'Mr Barak, sir, San Francisco is too big for me to understand. If you run it, as you do, then that's your business. All I want is to get my party safe home and you'll never hear another word from me. As you said, you've seen justice done and you've called it quits. I understand that, sir. We may be on opposite sides of the fence, Mr Barak, but we hold the same principles!'

He stood there blandly, and smiled at the king in a most catlike manner. Barak took a turn about the room, thinking.

'What about these notebooks?' he asked.

'I'll have them mailed to you, by arrangement, as soon as we're all on the ship for England,' said Lintott, helpful.

'That's not good enough. What guarantee do I have?'

'Well, *we're* all here, ain't we?' said Lintott. 'Your Mr Fleischer can watch me put them in some neutral public place, like – well, a safe at the Palace Hotel. Somewhere you can get them on a certain date. We shall have to work that out, so's to cover both sides. In the meantime, we ain't going anywhere, and I'd be only too glad if we were!'

He was giving the impression of someone artful rather than intelligent: a nuisance, not a real threat: a time-server.

'Most of the troubles in life come through misunderstandings,' observed Lintott piously. 'You thought I'd crossed you, didn't you? Not a bit of it, sir! I crossed you in London, I admit that. But then, I was punished for it, wasn't I?' His eyes gleamed for an instant, and were opaque and mild again. 'And, sir, you were the first to admit as Mr Fleischer's little episode with my wife went further than you intended.' Barak put one hand solemnly upon his breast. 'So, as you say, everything's ironed out. I never crossed you here, sir, I was just trying to find Miss Salvador. I dare say that *her* trouble is a bit more than you intended, too?'

'That,' said Barak heavily, 'was *your* fault!'

'I admit it,' Lintott replied, 'freely, sir.'

'Okay,' said Barak in a lighter tone, taking another turn about the room, 'I reckon that will suit me pretty well, Inspector Lintott. I don't want the difficulty of keeping Alicia Salvador in either of my establishments. I've sewn up the Orpheum Theatre so that her brother won't perform to more than a handful of people, each night and every night that he is here. Hank wanted to break his hands,' (Lintott tutted) 'but, like I say, I mete mercy out with justice. So you take that poor girl, Inspector Lintott, and see her safely to the hotel. Sometime tomorrow Hank Fleischer will contact you – that notion about a safe in the Palace is pretty good – and those notebooks will be put in a neutral place. I shall work out the details myself, and expect you to abide by them.'

He was genial now. A genial prince. He held out his hand, and Lintott shook it as heartily as if he meant good fellowship.

'I'll get Hank to drive you home, Inspector.'

'You're very kind, sir. I appreciate you listening to my point of view.'

'And I hope you will assure Mr Salvador that, though I was displeased with him, I did not intend his sister to be disturbed to this extent.'

'I'll explain as it was my fault,' said Lintott obsequiously.

Fleischer, recalled to duty, said, 'I thought we were going to keep him here, Mr Barak, until we'd finished the last details?'

'Hank,' said Bela Barak in gentle reproach, 'you always go too far.'

'And sometimes not far enough, sir, if you'll excuse me saying so,' Lintott observed slyly. 'I should like to show you, sir, the extent of my confidence in you. I was not picked up helpless, as you might think. I came of my own accord.'

Fleischer's hand crept towards his answer to life's problems, which resided in the holster on his breast.

'Never mind doing that,' said Lintott in a different tone. 'Why didn't you search me?'

As they both stared at him, he took out of his pocket the empty Shreve and Barber revolver.

'Never take anything for granted, my lad!' he could not resist adding.

Then, afraid that they might check the gun and find it had no bullets, he shook his head from side to side in the friendliest fashion – and handed it politely by the muzzle to Fleischer.

'So you'd best keep that in your pocket until we get to San Francisco,' said Lintott, being fair and honest with his captors. 'Then I'll have it back, if you don't mind, sir. Some of those streets are downright dangerous at night!'

TEMPLE OF FIRE!

Positively The Last Night of that wonder of the present day, The Fire King, Who, in addition to his other extraordinary exploits, will exhibit himself in a Temple of Fire!

From a theatre bill advertising Chabert.

TWENTY FIVE

Wednesday, 18 April 1906

'WHAT A MAN, EH?' said Lintott, in admiration, as they headed for the city. 'Why, Mr Fleischer, if it wasn't for the fact as he's upset my client I'd be inclined to join you in your opinion of Mr Barak. I'll say this much – it's a pity he ain't on the right side of the fence. Excuse me speaking out, won't you? It's my way! Yes, sir, a great pity. Still, you and him ain't complaining...'

So he was friendly and loquacious with the scarred man, who answered in monosyllables.

Now, at California Street, they padded up the silent stairs, along the hushed corridors, into a remote turret. Sullenly, Fleischer unlocked the heavy door and stood back.

In one corner of the room Alicia crouched, arms extended, face lifted, eyes fixed.

'Miss Salvador?' Lintott ventured.

She neither moved nor spoke, looking on some terror beyond the solitary terror of her pose.

'It's Inspector Lintott, my dear,' said Lintott compassionately. 'The man with the special handcuffs. You remember me, don't you? I've come to fetch you home, my love.' He walked cautiously towards her, extending his hand. 'I'm taking you back to your brother, miss. He ain't far from here, and looking forward to seeing you again like – like I don't know what! You're safe with me, my love,' he said with homely conviction.

She was wearing what Lintott recognised as being an English

255

housemaid's Sunday best: a chocolate-brown cloth dress braided in lighter brown, with cloth-covered buttons. Her pale hair lay in a pale tangle past her waist. In her white mask only the eyes were alive. The Inspector approached her, one cautious step at a time. He grasped her cold hands in his warm ones. She allowed this, but moved her head from side to side in negation, staring past him.

'Yes, yes,' Lintott soothed. 'I'm taking you back to your brother. I'll just put an arm round you, if you'll permit the liberty. You needn't fear me, my dear. I never hurt a woman in my life, not even when she asked for it!' She was swaying on her feet, but his arm was fast about her waist. 'There we are. Right as a trivet, ain't we? Tight as two ticks. Yes.'

So he half-coaxed, half-carried her, comforting as he would comfort a child. She allowed him to lead her until they were outside the front door. Fleischer stood by the Cadillac, smoking a cigarette, waiting. Alicia stiffened, and put Lintott's arm from her.

'Listen!' she said softly. 'Listen!' Then she crouched to the ground, arms extended in her former pose and whispered, 'No, no, no, no, no...'

The early morning wind fluttered her hair, the moon shone on her mask of sorrow. A mime, she stretched out her hands in supplication, lifting her head to hear what she must transmit.

Lintott felt the hairs rising on his flesh.

'Yes, yes, yes,' she answered the unknown, 'old, very old, older than evil. Oldest. In the beginning, and in the end...' and she clasped her arms about her knees and rocked to and fro on the cold stones.

Fleischer stepped forward, unsmiling, and smacked her across the face. Stepped back. Lintott closed his eyes for an instant, held his temper in check, put an arm about her again. He felt a sudden strength surge into the girl. She was on her feet without his aid: a dreadful prophetess.

'Death!' she cried, wheeling on the scarred man. 'Death by burning!'

Fleischer said between his teeth, 'Get that goddam witch away from me!'

Spent and shivering she had subsided, whispering, nodding. She was beyond either of them now, beyond help or injury. A child's face shone through a child's terror, the mark of Fleischer's hand across one cheek.

She wailed, 'Why do I dream such things? What did I do wrong?'

'Look,' said Lintott to Fleischer, 'if you're waiting to drive us to the Palace don't bother. I'll walk her there, bit by bit, and try to calm her down. Right?'

The scarred man nodded, retreated to the Cadillac. As he let in the clutch he was smiling again. He was forgetting Alicia and Lintott, even as he drove away down California Street. He was dreaming of a lady called the Silver Ghost. The long revenge was done, and his part over.

'Well, that's that,' said Lintott, as though he had accomplished some humble everyday task. 'Shall we go and find your brother, miss?'

He held out his arm and she laid her hand upon it, and smiled at him quite unexpectedly. He noticed that the wind had veered, and was blowing salt and fresh into the city.

'Not too cold, I hope, my love?' cried Lintott cheerfully.

She smiled secretly to herself, not answering him.

'Do you remember me, my dear?' Lintott asked again.

She nodded, compressing her lips. Serious as the frown between her brows.

From the edge of Chinatown the tower bell of old St Mary's Church rang sweet and clear. A clock chimed. Lintott consulted the plain face of his watch, and snapped the cover shut.

'Five o'clock on the dot. She's in a good mood this morning,' he said affectionately, speaking of the city as of a capricious and well-beloved woman. 'We're going to have a lovely day. I can feel it, and smell it.'

Tranquillity on the grey hills terraced with white houses. Peace in the bay where the ships rode at anchor, lights bobbing. Cool and still, San Francisco lay in the promise of bright day. Behind the hills of Berkeley the sky turned from dark to lighter blue. As the sun rose the street-lamps faded, their night's vigil done.

'I'd rather have her than Paris,' Lintott confessed, from his faithful, from his susceptible heart. 'I shall think of her. Yes, often. As she is now. As she has been. All moods. I don't know how I like her best, really. I don't mind. Perhaps I like her best when...' he remembered the sea-fog that crept up and enfolded the city in a milk-white dream ... 'when she's most my own...'

'Listen,' Alicia whispered, lifting one hand, intent. 'Listen!'

A milkman was trying to calm his horse. Unrest was in the air.

Unrest in the great house at Belmont, in the caged spirit of Francesca Barak. Towards dawn she put aside pretence of sleep and rang for her temporary maid.

'I shall ride before breakfast,' she explained, in that honeyed drawl which was not to be disobeyed.

The girl drew back the curtains, rolled up the blinds, in silent protest.

Francesca said, 'I shall wear my English riding habit.'

The maid was new to her service, and marvelled within herself at the self-imposed ritual, as though the lady were about to attend a hunt. The heavy rope of hair braided at the base of her neck, the gleaming leather boots, the black habit and hard hat. Francesca Barak tied her stock and consulted her face in the glass. A pale and elegant stranger looked back at her. She picked up the large diamond pin bestowed by her husband, and laid it down again. She reached into a small drawer of the dressing-table and took out a scuffed leather jewellery box. This time the maid spoke, seeing the plain turquoise and pearl scarf pin.

'That's not half so fine, ma'am!' Then, blighted by the frown, 'But real pretty!' As the finished product drew on its leather gloves, 'Shouldn't I ring for a groom or somebody, ma'am?'

The delicate black eyebrows barred this suggestion also.

'I shall saddle her up myself,' said Francesca sweetly. 'In my father's house we had to be able to look to our own horses. We had to understand them, like people. I thank you for rising so early on my account.'

The handle of her crop was inlaid with mother-of-pearl. She switched up her long skirt, smiling at the sleepy maid, and walked to the stables. Something was afoot and must be pursued, or escaped. Something oppressive, though the air was cool and clear as a washed rose.

She had filled the pocket of her coat with sugar lumps, from the bowl kept ready in her room. Her perfect, her too-perfect doll's face, became warm and gentle in the presence of those she understood, who understood her. She lit lamp after lamp in unhurried succession until their combined radiance illuminated the silver-mounted harness in the tack-room, the silver miniature horse-heads on the doorpost of each stall. She moved from one restless animal to the other, remembering the failings and virtues of each as though they were her children. The dark tailored skirt of her riding habit trailed across Roman tiles. As she spoke, the horses quietened, but in her wake they reasserted their subdued terror. They tossed heads, swished tails, whinnied at the unknown, stamped and snorted at nothing.

The crystal chandelier, shipped from the palace of a Venetian doge, swung imperceptibly. The redwood and mahogany stalls creaked fear so softly that only a wild creature could hear it. Puzzled, Francesca reached the far end of the stable and embraced Orange Belle, and felt the tremble beneath the hide. So they stood together, woman and horse, soft muzzle in soft hand, nuzzling sugar: the one unable to convey the meaning of its dread, the other unable to divine it.

They would ride, that was the answer. They would ride and out-ride whatever possessed the pair of them. The union she could not attain with her husband was here in the stable, without payment or pricing. The smell of leather, the fine feel of reins, the clean sound of hooves, the splendid banners of mane and tail, were hers – and she theirs.

She fetched Belle's saddle and bridle from the harness

room. If only we could ride away for ever, she thought. But there was no road to ride that did not lead back to Bela Barak.

'I was looking for you,' said his gravelly voice behind her.

Francesca quietened Belle's start and plunge, answering at random, 'Whatever has gotten into these horses? They are scared sick!'

He was impatient of their nervousness, crying, 'I have news for you.'

She returned to her mare, unmindful of him, saying, 'Hush, honey, hush!'

Her trim back outraged him. Her caresses were for Orange Belle who gleamed sandy, silvery, in the lighted stall. The Palomino bent her arched neck and looked dark and velvet into the world of Francesca's smile.

Barak's mouth was dry. His wife's indifference wounded him as her anger could not. Out of the bruise of rejection he shouted, 'Why can I never talk to you? Why in hell can't I talk to you?'

Afraid, she said, 'Wherever are those grooms? What do we pay them for? There is a mare in foal right now. Somebody should be sitting up at night with her.'

'Where are my sons?' he shouted, and hammered the red-wood stall with his great fist.

Belle reared, whinnied, eyes rolling.

'Would you mind very much not doing that?' Francesca asked, keeping her fear and her temper under control. 'Would you very much mind not raising your voice in that fashion?'

'I know all about you!' he cried. 'I know everything about you.'

'Hush, honey, hush,' she whispered into the silver mane, afraid.

'I punished him, and I shall punish you, Francesca.'

She said clearly, turning at last to face him, 'Now I have had enough, Bel. I am going to my father's house and I shall not come back. This time no amount of money will bring me back.'

Then he brought the gun from his coat and said, 'Stand on

one side, Francesca. I am going to shoot your horse.'

The mare nudged Francesca lovingly, and turned her eyes of night on Barak. His black eyes shone, savouring his wife's pain since he could not savour her love. But she stood in front of Orange Belle, and spread out her arms steadfastly like a shield.

Lizzie wrapped her arms round the magician like a shield. Within their warm slim circle he turned and muttered in his sleep.

They had fulfilled their programme. In a nightmare of near-emptiness and silence, through which the occasional face glimmered, through which a cough or a clap sounded like thunder, they had performed with frozen aplomb. At first, the few spectators, aware of some hoax or savage joke, exaggerated their applause. The critics stood for one particularly fine illusion, and beat their hands together frenziedly. Then the sheer weight of showing appreciation began to wear them away. They faltered, they yawned, they were sorry. During the intermission they all left.

Salvador had not addressed a single word to Lizzie afterwards, except to instruct or question her on some trifling matter to do with the apparatus. She, sick at heart, was silent, knowing they could not keep up this farce night after night. Wordless, they returned to the hotel and could not eat. Restless, they dropped into a half-doze. Terribly, they dreamed. The magician dreamed he was a marionette, manipulated by a giant hand. Lizzie dreamed of Alicia, crouched in the centre of the stage, hands on either side of her face, listening.

'Listen,' Alicia whispered, lifting one hand, intent. 'Listen!' Then she said, frowning, 'Oh, how strange!'

Her tensions had vanished. She was becoming part of the vision instead of beholding it. Then Lintott was most curiously aware of something about to happen, of a sensation about to make a sound, of a sound so loud and ominous as to be a sensation, of the ominous made manifest.

'No-o-o-o,' cried Lintott, and heard the cry as though it were outside himself.

The moaning of nature in travail, the rumbling of a thousand trains, the roaring of a godlike predator over humble prey. He was caught up, taken into the mouth, held and worried; spat aside by a fury which came in from the Bay at seven thousand miles an hour, moving from East to West, tunnelling and buckling the cobbles as though they were waves of the sea. The city stumbled into dreadful dance. Bells gave iron tongue in terrifying discord. Brick and stone toppled, wood splintered, foundations shuddered, rails and pipes writhed. Then there was silence for a little space of time.

Lintott crawled to Alicia and pulled her close with an arm that shook. The earth was not at rest, only resting. He braced himself as it began again.

Grating, rending, grumbling, tearing. Toy houses tumbled, toy ships heeled over, toy people perished. On the filled sites of old swamps and riverbeds the thoughtless sprawl of wooden buildings lurched and fell. In the grip of this ancient force the beautiful and the corrupt, the wise and the inconsequent, were dying together. A pause. Another worrying. Another pause. Then idling, diminishing tremors. Then, nothing. Then, the first wail of terror.

The mare screamed in terror, as Francesca stood crucified before her, as Bela Barak levelled his gun. The stable floor was tilting, turning, this way and that. They were falling apart as it broke into a trot, into a canter, into a gallop, as it stampeded. Then heaven opened and the Apocalypse rode forth with flowing manes and flying tails. No saddles, no bridles, no sitting, no reining. Starting eyes and thundering hearts. All speed and pace, faster and faster, with a roaring in the ears. The majesty of their hooves shook the earth beneath them. Pounding, shaking, hammering, fading, dying. Silence. Like a dream, like a terrible dream.

In Lizzie's dream her father shook her violently by the

shoulder in urgent exhortation. She heard him say quite clearly, 'Stir yourself, my lass!' He was shaking the mattress, the bedstead, the floor, in his anxiety. Lizzie switched from a sleeping to a waking nightmare and rode with the room.

Confusedly, she thought, 'Oh, it's the Chinese Year of the Horse!' Then waking further, cried, 'Oh, what's the matter, whatever's the matter?' trying to hold down the bed.

The giant's hand released the marionette that was Salvador, in his dream, and smashed down on the hotel roof. Wardrobe and closet doors flew open, releasing a flight of garments, like ghosts. Drawers were jerked out and upended. Furniture collided, somersaulted, skated down the room on frantic casters. The chandelier plummeted and smashed on the sidling carpet. The glass in the windows was sucked in and out before it burst into a shower of fragments. As the giant tried to uproot the building and squeeze it to pulp, he ground his mighty teeth and groaned with effort.

They clung together and formed partners for a violent *Sir Roger de Coverley*: and forward and back, and hold a hand, and curtsey and bow and turn around, and sidle through and sidle back, and cut a caper – clash, bang, smash!

The second act pitched both Lizzie and the magician out of bed, and rolled them into a heap of rucked carpet and fallen clothes. Lizzie shrieked as she fell, but Salvador lost consciousness before his bruised mouth could form a prayer for mercy.

In the hour of emptiness, the sandwich-boards rattled on the corner of Market and Battery, in the breeze from the Bay. Their paper prayer uncurled upon the wind, bearing a message no one wanted to read. It lifted and swayed delicately, reaching out fingers of white and blue to the blind windows. The dark held portent, the air stood witness. Gas lamps sighed. Sleepers turned in their beds, muttering oaths or pleas. The quietness was swollen, like a fruit about to burst.

As that final moment was impaled upon the face of the Ferry Clock, the sandwich-boards flung themselves before a divine presence. For here in Babylon was the terror and justice of

God, as they had proclaimed. He was peeling away the walls
and casting them down into her streets. He was crumbling the
city in His hand and letting the pieces fall. Bells clamoured
His praise in cracked discord. Houses knelt before Him.
Lucifer came forth as fire. C–O–M–E ... T–O ... G–O–D ...
fluttered ... AM ... I..

In the silence after her death, dust wrapped her in a pall.

TWENTY SIX

LINTOTT WAITED, LISTENED, raised his head. It was done. In a silence which seemed as inhuman and awesome as the earthquake, he scrambled to his feet and patted his arms and legs. He was still there, all there. Bruised, shocked, alive.

Alicia lay where he had given her the little sorry comfort of his embrace. He touched her tentatively, turned her over. Her eyes stared, unafraid. They had looked upon destruction before it came and were ready for it. The only movement in her utter stillness was a trickle of blood from the corner of her mouth. Lintott felt for her pulse, laid his ear delicately to her bodice, held his pocket-mirror to her parted lips, closed her eyes. The face of infinite contemplation was before him.

He sat down beside her and wiped his hands carefully, folded and replaced his handkerchief meticulously.

'Rest my legs a bit,' he told himself, 'afore I take her home.'

He looked about him for landmarks in the choking shambles that had been a city. He found a candy bar in his pocket and ate it slowly.

'Hungry,' Lintott explained to himself.

When he considered that his strength would support the girl he turned to her again. Smoothed her fair hair and dusty dress into decent composure, lifted her. She was light enough. He started off for the Palace Hotel.

It was as though he peered into a thousand broken private lives. This lace curtain pinned by the beam of a fallen roof, that handsome mahogany bed perched perilously on the edge of a torn floor, a family living room in fearful disarray. On the ripped streets lay horses, seemingly fashioned out of marble. Drunken frame-houses froze in mid-lurch.

Silent, with his silent burden, Lintott passed silent people who stared at him incuriously. Nor was he surprised that none offered help or condolence. Each human being was, for the moment, alone with a personal catastrophe.

A man in striped pyjamas, wearing a top hat, came solemnly into view. He paused to look at the day, put up his umbrella and strode briskly down the rubbled street. A girl in a nightgown, clutching a cold roast chicken in both hands, ran past. Singly, in twos and threes, in small groups, the inmost carnival of San Francisco emerged. Women in ball dresses glittered with jewellery. Two fashionable young men in summer clothes, straw hats and kid gloves, pulled a vast mahogany table. Behind them two young women, in trim suits and patent-leather shoes, pushed the other end. All four were hilarious.

At the side of the road a young woman rocked a baby whose head dangled and tossed with every movement. Parents wheeled prams full of pictures and clocks. By their sides trotted children, faces bewildered, clutching toys. People had flung coats or quilts or blankets over their night attire. They were coping with shock, in laughter, in tears, in a walking apathy too terrible to contemplate.

Lintott saw the stars and stripes flowing proudly from the flagpole of the Palace, and began to pick his way down what had been Market Street. A girl hurried past him, wringing her hands, saying over and over to herself, 'Oh, my father is dead and my mother is dead. Oh, my father is dead and my mother is dead. Oh, my father is dead...' Men carried furniture on their backs, women dragged children by the hand. A young couple were sitting in front of a home-made stove, consisting of two bricks and a toasting grill. Her tailor-made skirt was torn, she wore a gold bracelet. They fried bacon, oblivious of those who passed by, saying nothing. Two men were slapping each other's backs, hysterical with amusement. They were both clad in pink-striped pyjamas. 'Snap!' they were shouting. 'Snap, snap, snap!' Laughing until they could scarcely draw breath. A baby fell from the torn pillow-case slung on his mother's back. She stumbled on as though the weight were still with her, unknowing. People stepped over or round the infant, since it was dead.

Dr Power, a London physician staying at the St Francis Hotel, had dressed in his black frock-coat and striped trousers and was making a clinical observation of human control under extreme pressure.

'Would you permit me, sir?' he asked Lintott, and took the Inspector's pulse rate. He cast an eye on the girl lying beside the Inspector, and lifted her hand. 'I'm afraid she's dead, you know.'

'That's why we're sitting here a bit,' said Lintott. 'She grows heavier with the distance, it seems to me, sir.'

Dr Power lifted his top hat and walked on.

Lintott's shoulders ached, his eyes smarted. Again he lifted his burden and negotiated the obstacle race which had been a broad thoroughfare.

In the lobby of the Palace Hotel the clerks ran to and fro, and the guests left in whatever state of dress they thought fitting. Lintott walked slowly in, and the same incurious stares hovered and fell. He laid Alicia's body gently on a velvet couch by the wall, and went over to the desk. He asked for Salvador's suite, and while the clerk looked through the register as though it were the Domesday Book, a number of guests in nightdresses and pyjamas returned. They had decided there was time to dress and pack. One man enquired for his bill, insisted upon paying it, and waited for the receipt, fingers tapping. The rest of his party sat around in the velvet chairs near Alicia, their glances resolutely casual. They had enough trouble of their own, without discovering whether she was sleeping or dead.

'The elevator is out of order,' said the clerk apologetically.

'I'll manage,' said Lintott sturdily, surveying the staircase with some misgiving.

Yet he surmounted even this last obstacle, and laid the girl upon another gilded chaise-longue, by a shattered vase of flowers, outside Salvador's private suite. He knocked.

'Don't bother to knock. Just break it down!' cried Lizzie's voice, high and harsh.

She was laughing and crying together. He searched for the cause of the door jamming and could find none.

'Lizzie!' he called. 'It's Father! I think you've locked it by mistake!'

She stopped laughing. Weeping quietly now, on the other side of the door, finding and turning the key. As she opened it and began to sob, he put his dusty arms round her dusty shoulders and let her have the mood out in peace.

'Whatever made me do a silly thing like that?' she kept saying. Then, 'You're safe. Oh, Father, you're safe.' She indicated the magician lying motionless upon the floor. 'He's been there, like that, since it happened.'

He righted a chair for himself and another for her, and took off his hat. His questions were entirely practical. He had survived and gained strength.

'Is Mr Salvador alive? Good enough. Miss Alicia's dead – outside on the sofa. And that's good, too, because I think she was a bit strange up here, in the end!' Touching his forehead with great reverence and delicacy, to indicate that he did not blame her for that aberration. 'Have you had breakfast? Then I'll get some for us. Of course there'll be some breakfast! They've still got kitchens in this here place, haven't they? I'll cook it myself if I have to. Where are that old couple?' Though they were no older than the Inspector in years he referred to them as if they had been his parents. 'Then fetch them, Lizzie. We shall have to get out of here and we must be together.'

'Where shall we go, Father?'

He might have been organising cities after major earthquakes all his life. He began to tick off the probabilities.

'I should think that the gas and water mains have gone. The roads'll be blocked. Lucky if they've got any telegraphic services going, and if they have they'll lose 'em. Why? Because this city's going to burn, my girl, that's why. Because she runs the risk of cholera and riot and looting and Lord knows what else. There'll be no transport for a bit, and what there is will fetch small fortunes – which we haven't got. We'll be hungry and thirsty and have nowhere to sleep but the ground. So I've got to get moving and see us right, as far as I can. Have to find a stretcher for Mr Salvador. You and me'll carry him.'

'What about Alicia, Father?'

'The dead don't matter, my girl, and that's the truth. We shall have enough trouble with the living. Everything's gone, you see. Everything people rely on and take for granted. Hospitals, food supplies, medical supplies. There'll be hundreds and thousands buried alive, wounded, shocked, needing to be looked after. Well, well. Breakfast first. I'll be back!' With his old humour he added, 'Don't lock the door on me, Lizzie!'

TWENTY SEVEN

Wednesday, 18 *April – Saturday,* 21 *April* 1906

FIRE! FIRE! FIRE! Little fires, soon smothered. Bigger fires
that you can't swat out. Four fires north of Market, around
Sansome and Washington, but these buildings are made of
brick and pretty fire-proof anyway. A dozen fires south of the
Slot, and this is worrying, those frame-houses burn fast. But
no panic, because the city has the best fire-fighting service in
the West, and the greatest Fire Chief we ever served under ...
you didn't hear about what happened to Dennis Sullivan? He
was hurt bad. They took him into hospital only fifteen minutes
after the 'quake struck. So who will take his place? Old Fire
Chief Dougherty? He must be one hundred years old! Still he
is a game old guy and we have the best fire alarm system in ...
you didn't hear about the alarm system? That alarm system is
on the floor right now in a million pieces! Aw! firemen don't
need telling. We know when we're wanted. Look at that, will
you? Horses rounded up and calmed down and hitched on
to the old pumping engine, the boys aboard, the whip cracking, and ... jump her lively!

South of Market don't look so good. Alice's lodging house on
Steuart has sparked off the ship's chandler's next door, and
they are blazing like a pair of torches. Quick with the hose,
find the hydrant, turn the valve and stand ready! No water?
Just a trickle. What do you mean, just a trickle? We need
a lot of water. Look at those frame-houses going like they were

matchwood, which they are! Try the hydrant on Mission. No water? Try the one on ... Jesus! The water mains are busted, and now there are fifty fires in fifty different places. So what do you do? You open the sewers and drain them dry. And you in those houses that we can't get to – do you have casks of wine, casks of vinegar, casks of anything in your cellars? Did you fill a bath-tub after the 'quake, maybe? Some pails, kettles, basins? Well, you just throw all the liquid you can find on to those fires. If there is wet sand on a builder's site, use it for smothering. Squirt that siphon of soda water, you won't be needing it any more. Because Dennis Sullivan is dying in the Southern Pacific Hospital, and the alarm system's gone and the water mains are busted, and San Francisco is burning, burning, burning...

Fire! Fire! Fire! Roll up, roll up, for the greatest show on earth, folks. And bring your momma and your poppa and your Aunt Mamie, too, to watch a city burn. We been here since 5.30 this morning, folks, and we're holding her, and we ain't ate no breakfast yet! But there is a lady cooking breakfast in a two-storey frame building, just a couple of doors west of Gough on Hayes, and she will make history of Ham-and-Eggs. On account of her chimney flue is cracked, and the wall sparks up. So it is just a wall, and the boys are fighting everybody else's fire? So she is trying to put it out, but this is a very ambitious fire with plans of its own, and it crosses Gough to the west – though they hold it on Golden Gate Avenue and Octavia, after a while. And it crosses Franklin to the east, and really makes a break to the south, finally crossing Market at Ninth, touching Twelfth before midnight, and meeting up with another talented joker – which has eaten the frames south of Market – and they both start in on Mission.

This is democracy, folks, we all burn! Wood and brick and stone and steel. Tenements and skyscrapers, apartments and mansions. Here we are down in Market where all the fun is, watching a spunky building hold out. Will she, won't she? The flames are licking those stone walls, and the windows are exploding, and the dome at the top shines like a full moon, and – these red and orange streamers are spouting, and the dome is smoke ... Hey, did you see that flag wave? Did you see those stars and stripes blowing? That's the Palace and she's still standing, because they are fighting with their own water supply and keeping that great roof wet. Folks say that if the Palace burns then 'Frisco goes too. Everything else is going on Market, including a bundle of newspaper buildings: the *Call*, the *Examiner*, the *Chronicle*, the *Evening Bulletin*. Say, does anybody know what's happened? Sure, the whole world knows. James Hopper of the *Call* was out and about soon after 5.30 a.m. Ed Gleeson of the *Daily News* says how do you reduce Hell to a single paragraph? Willie Wasson, the *News* editor, fixed a monkey wrench and flywheel to a press, and printed the scoop of all time by foot and hand! They're selling copies in the lobby of the Palace for a dollar apiece. The chief operator of the Postal Telegraph office tapped out a message for posterity at 6 a.m. and stayed on duty until 2.20 p.m. Maybe his greatest statement was *We are on the job and we are going to try and stick!*

Arnold Genthe is taking the pictures of a death-time with a 3A Kodak Special. Eugene Schmitz is busy trying to win a medal instead of an indictment. General Funston has decided to be the hero of the hour. They could quarrel over this, but they do not. Great events bring strange alliances, and San Francisco is burning.

You think it is this simple, that we fight flames? Listen, we are beating them out with our coats and the hose-pipes are charred. The temperature up there at the top of those skyscrapers is 2000°F and creates its own draught. Our faces and hands are blistered and our clothes are scorched. The gas is exploding in the sewers and vomiting dirt and cobblestones twenty feet into the air. On top of this we have dynamite squads, and right now they are fighting trouble with more trouble. Some are killed and some are injured, on account of misfiring and bad judgement, and every time they use dynamite the fire spreads. They are doing no good and they will not quit, and the noise don't quit, neither!

Martial law? No, sir, General Funston just brought in around seventeen hundred troops, with more coming from Monterey and Vancouver Barracks and Alcatraz Island, and they are patrolling the streets with fixed bayonets. That is all. Sure, they have orders to shoot at sight, by proclamation of the Mayor, but that is only if you are caught looting or committing some crime. They are not trigger-happy, and they are setting up hospitals in military tents in the Presidio grounds, and when the dead start to stink and have to be buried they will volunteer you for diggers. They will also volunteer your transport. And, like I said, they are doing a great job with the dynamite. I forgot to say, they sent for the Marines also.

The Palace flag finally struck when those 130,000 gallons of water gave out. That was when we left Market to burn.

'It's me, sir, Inspector Lintott,' said Lintott, bending over the man on the home-made stretcher. 'We're about to take you out of here. I'm afraid your sister died in the earthquake, sir. I brought her back.' He spoke frankly, briefly, knowing that the magician wanted the truth. 'Now shout out if we hurt you at all. We'll do our best. Here's Fredo and Esmerelda, right as ninepence, and we've all had a good breakfast or lunch or whatever it was. All set, sir?'

Salvador whispered, 'What will you do with Alicia?'

Lintott said heartily, 'We'd already thought of that, sir. Had a little conference, the four of us, while you were asleep. We don't fancy taking her out there, there'll be all sorts of rough and ready buryings. Communal graves and that. So we're leaving her here. Esmerelda and Lizzie have laid her out. She looks a proper picture, sir. Nobody's going to search the rooms, too busy saving their skins. This here place'll be alight in an hour or so.'

Salvador whispered, 'That is good. That is fitting for her.'

Lizzie asked gently, 'Did you want to see her?'

He moved his head in negation, whispering, 'No need. I see her always.'

'Have you got everything ready then, Lizzie?' Lintott said

briskly. 'Have you filled those bottles with water? Here, put this brandy under the blankets on the stretcher – they're giving it away downstairs, in the bar, to the last to leave! We seem to have got lucky. Ready? Right, off we go!'

Columns of smoke, columns of flames, one mile, two miles into the sky. So that if you are not too busy, owing to the fact that the earthquake hit an awful lot of places, you can see it from way off. Like a hundred miles away you can see San Francisco burning. We are the greatest firework display on earth at night, only we are in trouble again, owing to the weather. Right now we are having the coldest anybody can remember this time of year, and the wind isn't helping any!

We seem to have lost an audience some place! Did anybody see an audience anywheres? Well, I saw folks on the hills, and folks in Golden Gate Park, and folks in the grounds of the Presidio. They didn't look like no audience. They looked like those lines of refugees you hear about. Right now they are being moved out of the fire centre by the troops, and moved from A to B and B to C if they are sick, and all of them are also moving around voluntarily owing to the cold, and no camp fires allowed, and a shortage of blankets.

So we have to run the show all by ourselves, and since this is a full-time entertainment we are busy right now making a stand on Powell. The troops are hauling dynamite up Powell. You should try that some time for exercise! But we are not magicians, and we can't stop those embers flying in the wind and heat, and one of them flew to a wooden church near Bush Street, like it was a special messenger. And the message carried on to Pine and turned up Mason to California and the palaces of the Big Four are going, going, folks – marble burning like coal, windows melting. A sneaky red ribbon curving round the Fairmont from Sacramento, and goodbye to Mark Hopkins, to Stanford and Huntington and Crocker. Back, boys, back. The Powell Street stand is over, but you aren't out of business. No, sir. Mission is blazing and the Ham-and-Eggs is frying and Chinatown has done a vanishing trick and Russian Hill is next on the programme. Say, they sure have class on Russian Hill. Humphrey's Castle actually survived, owing to the fact that they sprayed the woodwork with quarts and magnums of Krug's private cuvée of champagne.

'I'd best see if I can get some more water, Lizzie,' said Lintott, 'and there might be a bakery open, you never know. I'll be back when I can.'

They had erected some sort of tent over Salvador which Lizzie watched anxiously, since a fine rain of hot cinders stung flesh and scorched clothing. All five of them wore damp handkerchiefs which covered the lower part of their faces. They were one small group in the estimated thirty thousand people camping out in the Presidio and had reached there in a journey longer and more terrible than they cared to remember. Around them were refugees in various states of health, shock, fear and grief. Nobody was entirely sane though, like drunkards, their intoxication took many forms. Some wept, some laughed, some were silent, some hysterical. All had suffered great losses. Their possessions littered the debris-laden streets of the city, as they had abandoned pianos, sewing machines, bird cages full of silverware, trunks, tables, chairs, mattresses. Their families had been decimated. They were mourning for the dead, seeking the missing.

As Lintott picked his way compassionately across the huddle of humanity he saw a tall woman dressed plainly in a black blouse and long skirt. She was moving from group to group, enquiring, giving information. As he approached she looked up and smiled.

'We have found blankets,' she said, 'and they will be distributed during the day. Mothers and children and the sick will have priority. The garrison cookhouse is baking bread and brewing coffee. If you have anyone seriously sick we can find room in the Letterman Hospital.'

'Thankee, ma'am,' said Lintott, taking off his hat.

General Funston's wife inclined her head gracefully, and moved on.

They say there is help arriving from all over the U.S. of A. They say that President Roosevelt has put the American Red Cross in the front line to receive donations. There are medical supplies and food supplies being packed right now in freight cars, from New Jersey and Texas and Colorado, and Chicago and New York and Oregon and ... There are schoolkids collecting piles of tinned stuff in the playgrounds. There are steamers full of doctors and nurses sailing here. There are tin boxes in every shop and house collecting for San Francisco. There are folks all over the world emptying their pockets for us right now.

Right now we are taking a stand on Van Ness, which we know is the last stand, along of the fires being one fire and if it ain't stopped here it will stop nowhere. So the troops are lining up their field-artillery pieces and they aim to blast those houses opposite, and we are ready to fight alongside with what we been using so far, which is mostly hope and guts.

But don't you think San Francisco is all fire news! No, sir. Life goes right on here. They are collecting the mail today, whether you have postage or not. Babies have been born under trees and inside tents and on lawns. A couple even got married this morning.

Sure seems a pity to have all the fun to ourselves. Bangs and flashes, and that goddam dynamite backfiring. Thirty-six hours we fought so far, did you know that? Then the flames took hold of the western side of Van Ness. I turned to look at the guy next to me and there was tears rolling down his face like they was rolling down mine. Then we held it again. We held most of it, that is. It took a half dozen blocks before we got it under control again. You should've been here, watching. You missed all the fun, all the goddam fun.

'Where do you think you're going, bud?' said the blue uniform, said the rifle, said the bayonet.

'I was wondering whether there was a bureau set up yet, anywhere,' Lintott replied. 'I had some good friends here as I wanted to enquire after, officer.'

'Look, bud, we all have good friends, but we can enquire afterwards. Right? We have two pretty tough jobs on right now. We have an awful lot of bodies that need burying, and we have a fire out there that needs fighting. Maybe you'd noticed? You can take your pick.'

'I'll help,' said Lintott honestly, 'if you could just tell me whether there is a place I could enquire...'

'You see this gun? Well, I think it is aimed at your right eye. Now I want to have a little talk with you. Come closer. This is martial law. You may not like it and I may not like it, but it goes. Is that understood?'

Lintott reached for the spade which had fallen from the boy's hand.

'Yeah, he is plumb tuckered out. He's been here as long as I have, which is twelve hours. Get digging.'

In Natoma Street the prostitute dressed in a pink silk négligée, wearing scuffed pink satin slippers, walked between the rows of refugees with a bucket of water and a dipper.

'Drink and be happy,' she said, smiling. 'Water tastes better than beer.'

The woman wandering half-naked through the labyrinth of blackened ruins laid her hand on the arm of anybody who was passing, and spoke to them earnestly.

'Jesus of Nazareth is watching over us,' she said.

By the side of the road a man polished a grand piano rhythmically, evenly, as a stable-boy would groom a race-horse.

A priest moved between fire-fighters and soldiers, black skirts brushing the tumbled stones. One of the men pointed to a shapeless bundle a few feet away. The priest bent over the disfigured face, making the sign of a cross, giving absolution. 'And here, Father,' said one fireman. 'We took out seventy-five, but most of them are dead.'

The arm waved once, twice, from the bricks. 'We can't get

277

him out,' they told the policeman. He shot and missed. He shot again. The arm jerked and fell.

'Stay right where you are!' the soldier ordered. The two men put their hands on their heads. The jewels they had taken from the corpse quivered, brilliant in the night flames of emerald, of sapphire, of ruby, of gold. 'You not gonna shoot us, are you?' asked one man. 'No, sir, we aim to hang you high. As an example, you understand? Nothing personal.' They swung gently, on the blackened beam. The soldier said to his colleagues, 'May as well put these in our pockets – for safety, you understand?'

The roar in the ears was a constant factor. The heat drove them to a safe distance. The rain of hot ash smouldered and stung. The smell in the nostrils and the smoke in the lungs hurt. No one slept and no one was sane, because San Francisco burned, and burned, and burned.

I guess they must've been tired, but those goddam dynamiters set off a charge in the Viavi Building on Van Ness, and the embers fired the north side of the street. So Friday, 20 April 1906 will be another day. We have help, did I tell you? First we had an audience, then we didn't have anybody, now we have help. All those sleeping beauties done woke up, and they are using pots and pans of water and soaking their shirts and swatting out the little fires. Buckets and brooms and homely weapons, you understand? Not like the great equipment we got. Not like charred hosepipes and no sleep and no water.

Will she, won't she? Every time we think we have made it she throws up another surprise. Lady, do you *want* to burn down? I mean, I am asking you nicely. I mean, I am saying I will go home – except that I have no home – if you just want to burn right down!

'This street is going to be dynamited,' said the young cavalry lieutenant, and his horse shifted nervously on the rough ground. 'Will you inform the people around here? Thank you!'

He touched his cap at the sentry's salute, and picked his way carefully over the debris.

Making a megaphone of his dusty hands, the sentry bawled, 'We're gonna dynamite this street. If you want anything in the grocery stores go to it!'

He watched the usual mêlée of bewildered human beings, trying to decide what to take and what to leave. Under the spell of his levelled rifle they calmed down, formed into a line outside the store. He saw that flour and bacon and hams and coffee and sugar were reasonably distributed. One little girl, about four years old, fulfilled the dream of a childhood. Unchecked, she reached carefully between the jagged edges of broken glass and lifted out a whole jar of candy. Nobody stopped her. Most felt a smile rising, even though they were too weary to let it reach their lips. She carried the giant glass jar away with difficulty, but with such dedication that they knew it would survive everything but her appetite.

The price of an old automobile has gone up to two thousand dollars. You can pay three dollars fifty for a can of sardines and a loaf of bread. Water is short, so folks catch it in a bucket from the gutter. The only way you can wash is to take a dip in the Bay, if you can get to the Bay, otherwise you don't wash. Everybody is doing their best. Father Hannigan is feeding two thousand a day at St Mary's Cathedral on Van Ness, right in the thick of the trouble. The ferrymen are making a fortune. Little kids caught stealing, and maybe they are hungry and maybe they don't know it is stealing, but just the same they have a placard hung around their necks. It reads, *I am a thief.* Anybody else caught thieving is shot dead or hanged, which is swift and simple justice. They placard the bodies, too, and run them through with bayonets.

You know they say folks make things up in a major crisis, like the lady who saw leopards slinking through the ruins. But we saw something this morning that nobody made up. We saw rats in the ruins gnawing a body, and chased them off. They were real big sassy rats and they will be back. Tens of thousands, pouring out of the sewers and the walls and the roofs and under the floors. They carry a different message from fire and its name is pestilence.

The Mare Island team on Van Ness knew their job when it came to explosives. We tasted victory along Van Ness – until the gale blew in on Friday evening and the fire decided to make a final banquet of the wharves, but this time we had the US warships pumping water from the Bay. The Mayor was with us all night as we blew up factories and sheds and warehouses, and played hosepipes and tore down buildings with ropes and axes. And the heat was so great that they had to soak the decks to stop them from joining the waterfront.

You talk about the burning fiery furnace, well this one was a ringer for the original Bible story. We hung on to those hoses and played them until we dropped. This was lumber district, which didn't help any. But by the morning of Saturday we had done two good things. We saved the waterfront, and we stopped one of the biggest fires in history.

The man in the scorched remnants of a uniform, whose face was as hardworn and black as his once-bright helmet, weaved to and fro among the tents in the grounds of the Presidio. He could barely frame the words he so urgently needed to communicate.

'You seen my wife?' Too tired to give her name.

Outside a makeshift shelter he staggered and finally fell. Lizzie, coming hurriedly forward, took the blanket from her shoulders and spread it over him. He turned his face towards her: the mark of the nozzle burned in his palms.

'It's out, Nell,' he said briefly, trustfully.

FAREWELL!

*Remember the last! the last!! and
only opportunity of seeing the
Palace of Pleasure and Delight!*

Barnardo Eagle, The Royal Illusionist

TWENTY EIGHT

May 1906

LINTOTT SAW A MAN and a dog in a ruined doorway. The placard in front of them read *Scotty and Patch say Hello to all their Friends!* Lintott gave a great shout of joy. Scotty was laughing, blue eyes mocking, brown face keen. Patch leaped and barked round the Inspector's legs.

'Well, well, well,' said Scotty. 'You still hanging around that lady they call San Francisco?'

'Just helping to clean up a bit, afore I go.'

Scotty nodded and smiled.

'She's like a pretty woman after a long illness, right now. But she'll be back again, prettier than ever and twice as chipper. Say, one nice thing, friend – apart from the pleasure of seeing you again – everybody now has one blanket and little else. Like us. I had a guy along this morning that told me he never felt so free in all his life. I guess he will change his mind when his insurance dough comes through, but for a while he got lucky!'

'I've been trying to find out whether you were dead or alive,' Lintott confessed. 'You and a few others.'

'You could use some information, friend? No, no,' as the Inspector reached for his wallet. 'Today I am as rich as everybody else, so I do not need money. Isn't that a great way to be, friend?

'The Mayor, Eugene Schmitz, is now a hero, but this will

not prevent the Grand Jury from charging him with police graft, franchise graft and rate graft. Which is an awful lot of graft! His little friend Abe Ruef was apparently wondering whether some of that nine million dollars in Relief Funds could not be diverted into his ever-ready pocket. But no, I guess not. He is now trying to save his own skin, and so is the Mayor. I am telling you that those two gentlemen will bring each other down. Oh, and a very important millionaire was found trampled to death in his once-splendid stables over at Belmont. His widow was found walking around in a daze looking for her Palomino and carrying a silver-mounted saddle and harness over one lovely arm. They say she will recover, particularly since they found the mare soon afterwards without a mark on her golden hide. I hear the lady will not be penniless, and she should look great in her widow's weeds, ordered from Mr Worth of Paris. We do things in style here, friend – even the mourning!

'Likewise, what was left of a ruby Cadillac and driver was also discovered not far from this city.'

'Had he been burned to death?' Lintott asked, remembering Alicia's prophecy.

'How did you know? Sure, he died hard.'

'Ah!' said Lintott. So savage justice had been done. 'Well, thankee. And what happened to you two, then?'

Scotty shrugged, and offered Patch a biscuit.

'This lady woke me around five o'clock on a certain fine morning, and indicated it was time for us to leave. Never argue with a woman's intuition! I packed our multiple possessions, closed the door of our French-styled château, and followed her. She seemed to know where to go. Like everybody we have been cold and scared and hungry and thirsty, but we are alive – and the sun will shine, and the city will rise again, friend.'

Lintott held out his hand.

'You are telling me goodbye,' said Scotty, shaking it warmly, 'and I am sorry. For this and for other things, but I guess you understand that I had to stop talking, friend, and pass you on to somebody who might help you another way. You looked great in those sandwich-boards – Inspector Lintott!'

Lintott jumped slightly, frowned, smiled, laughed.

'My grapevine is both long and sneaky,' said Scotty, grinning, 'and all I do is sit right by the side of it, and listen to the wind talking through the leaves.'

Lintott threw the green rubber ball into the air, and Patch caught it in her mouth. Then he marched away for the last time, to the strains of the harmonica. Scotty was playing, in fun, in fellowship, in admiration, in understanding.

Joshua lead the battle of Jericho, and the walls come tumbling down...

'Bavaria?' Lintott cried. 'However are you going to get them all there, Lizzie? And how are you going to get back by yourself afterwards – that is,' sarcastically, 'if you're proposing to come back, of course!'

Esmerelda was stirring soup in the iron pot over their camp fire. She waved the ladle emphatically at the Inspector.

'Circus take us home. Salvador gets well in circus.'

'We can well afford the fares, Father,' said Lizzie significantly.

'Look!' Esmerelda commanded, leaving her culinary operations, taking care no strangers observed her.

She stood very close to Lintott, so that he could see the fine dark down on her upper lip. She lifted her black skirt, and showed him the contents of her flannel petticoat. Alicia's jewels had been sewn patiently into pads and pockets.

'She confided this little treasure-trove to me yesterday,' said Lizzie, amused and exasperated. 'I was at my wits' end wondering how we should manage. She said she had decided she could trust us! If that isn't the limit, Father, after all you and I have done for the lot of them!'

He smiled to himself, observing that the groups had changed once more. She would be coming back home, as soon as she decently could.

'Well, well, my lass. She don't speak much English, and

we're only a couple of strangers. She was right to look after her own folks afore she trusted others. Very good!' he shouted to Esmerelda, as though she were deaf. 'Very good, ma'am! Here, Lizzie, don't you try selling them until you're across the Atlantic. If you attempted anything of the sort round here you'd be strung up afore you could say how-de-do!'

'Look!' Esmerelda commanded, enjoying herself. She smiled, nodded, thrust something into Lintott's reluctant hand and closed his fingers over it. 'For you. Good man. Salvador pays well. For you.'

'I can't take this, ma'am,' Lintott protested, peering surreptitiously at a large ruby drop on a gold chain. 'Whatever would I do with it?'

'You could always give it to Mother,' said Lizzie acidly. 'She'd keep it for best, and never wear it!'

'That's enough sauce from you, Lizzie.'

'Keep. Sell. Good man.'

'It's all you're ever likely to get for risking yourself halfway across the world,' Lizzie advised drily. 'She seems to be the private financier in this little circus, so I should do as she says, father. I dare say *I* shall end up penniless, wearing a diamond tiara!'

He said absently, 'Mrs Esmerelda'll have to take it back until we're all safe ashore. How would I get past the Customs?' He said keenly, 'So you're taking him to the circus, then, to recover? How long will you be there?'

'For as long as he needs me, Father. He's picking up again nicely. I'm a good assistant, you see, and he's used to me. I'll get him on his feet again, and find a substitute, and then I'll be back.'

He surveyed her with his old irony and affection, with his new respect.

'And what about yourself, my love? What about you?'

Her hair was untidy. She wore a man's jacket over her blouse and skirt. Yet she seemed more at ease, more contented, than he had ever seen her. Her eyes now held some of the serenity he saw in Scotty. Humour was not far from the surface of her talk. Her gestures were few and confident. She had been brought upon the rock of herself, and found that it stayed fast.

'Oh, I'll think about that when I have time,' said Lizzie briskly. 'Come and have a word with Salvador now you're back.'

The magician was sitting cross-legged before his golden crucible. A blanket draped his shoulders, and he gave it the air of a king's mantle. As they entered the tent he looked up and smiled.

'I have thought of a new illusion,' he cried, with something of his former panache, 'but I am very humbled, my friend, when I look around me.'

'Ah! Ain't we all?' Lintott murmured, shaking his head.

'No, no. I speak of the magnificence of this cosmic performance. Now I understand what is meant by *The Creation*, my friend. How can my paltry talent contend with the majesty of this event? And yet, being an artist – I must attempt! It will take a great deal of electricity,' he added. 'It would be necessary to wire the auditorium, too...'

Outside, Esmerelda ladled soup into enamel mugs. Fredo was walking on his hands to amuse a group of children.

Salvador gestured, alight with enthusiasm. Lintott thought of Bessie, alive and well again, and the tales he would tell her – skilfully edited – under the summer trees at Richmond. Lizzie, alone among them, had nothing in particular to dream of – and yet there seemed to be more waiting for her than for anyone else. In the wasteland that had been San Francisco a shop-keeper was painting letters roughly, on a rough board. He wanted to say that they had nearly died, that they had survived, that life would go on. He had written *Yesterday we were closed. Today we are open. Tomorrow we start building*.

He brought out his wife and children to look at it. Neighbours commented. Strangers read it, smiling, and passed by. He read it again, forming the words silently with his lips. He saw that it was good, and went into the house for supper.